# An American Summer

# By Frank Deford

### FICTION
Cut 'n' Run
The Owner
Everybody's All-American
The Spy in the Deuce Court
Casey on the Loose
Love and Infamy
The Other Adonis


### NONFICTION
Five Strides on the Banked Track
There She Is
Big Bill Tilden: The Triumphs and the Tragedy
Alex: The Life of a Child
The World's Tallest Midget
The Best of Frank Deford

# An American Summer

a novel

# FRANK DEFORD

SOURCEBOOKS LANDMARK™
AN IMPRINT OF SOURCEBOOKS, INC.®
NAPERVILLE, ILLINOIS

Published by Sourcebooks, Inc.
P.O. Box 4410, Naperville, Illinois 60567-4410
(630) 961-3900
FAX: (630) 961-2168
www.sourcebooks.com

Library of Congress Cataloging-in-Publication Data

Deford, Frank.
  An American summer : a novel / by Frank Deford.
    p. cm.
  ISBN 1-57071-992-6 (Hardcover)
  1. Poliomyelitis—Patients—Fiction. 2. Baltimore (Md.)—Fiction. 3.
Teenage boys—Fiction. 4. Young women—Fiction. 5.
Friendship—Fiction. I. Title.
  PS3554.E37 A83 2002
  813'.54—dc21

                                                      2002003401

    Printed and bound in the United States of America
        QW  10  9  8  7  6  5  4  3  2  1

For Juliet McAdams Carey

# Acknowledgments

In his enthusiasm for this book, Hillel Black played a far larger role than just editor. His support guided *An American Summer* into being, and I am especially indebted. So, too, my warmest thanks to my agent, Sterling Lord, who has shepherded all fourteen of my books into print, but who has never been more devoted and determined than he was with this work.

Doctors Beryl Rosenstein and the late Neil Lebhar were kind enough to advise me in matters medical. Were it not for the manifest great spirit of Anneen Dunn and the generosity of her family, which I remember yet, so vividly, after all these years, I could never have conjured up much of the core of *An American Summer*. And, of course, I am glad to be able to use this story to recall the wondrous contribution of Jonas Salk, that meant so much to the health and well-being of us all.

—F.D.

# An American Summer

*For the memory of Kathryn Slade*

*And for Kathryn Slade Bannister-White,
so that now you will know
your namesake*

# 1 *April 13th, 1955*

The news from Michigan was so stunning that, at school, it was broadcast over the P.A. into all our classrooms: Dr. Salk's vaccine worked.

It worked. We were safe again. At our desks, we cheered as if the Orioles or the Colts had won a big game.

Outside, we could hear car horns honking and church bells chiming in celebration. We had conquered polio. That was always the way it was phrased: *we*, first person plural, and *conquered*—just as sure as hell as we were going to do to the communists next. Polio was now Exhibit A that we could not lose at anything, not for forever and a day.

There weren't many of us in any classroom who didn't know somebody who'd had polio, and most of us even knew somebody who'd taken the worst of it—paralysis or death. Anyway, you couldn't avoid polio then. The fight against polio was ongoing. It was marshaled by the March of Dimes, which had peppered little coin-slot containers in almost every corner of commerce. At amusement parks, they would actually park some poor polio patient in an iron lung right there on the arcade amidst the thrill rides and the games with the March of Dimes cannister next to it. We all gave, and we all thought: there but for the grace of God....

The March of Dimes was run by, significantly, the National Foundation. That was all: the National...could there be any other foundation in our nation? Was there any other disease? Polio was different—even from what AIDS is now. After all, polio struck down children. *Infantile* paralysis. And it appeared capriciously, at random. Remember this, too: at that time we could go about, as we pleased, everywhere. Night or day, in the United States of America, we were safe. Doors were unlocked. Children didn't shoot one another. They didn't take drugs. They didn't even know drugs. Oh sure, there were the communists. But even as we climbed under our desks for Civil Defense drills, nobody ever seriously considered the possibility that the commies might dare actually drop an atom bomb on us. Come on, get real.

Only polio was the something else again. If we actually didn't any longer still have a president with polio, we did always have a beautiful poster child to remind us that nobody—not even the prettiest—was home free. This year, there were national poster child twins wearing gingham dresses above their braces. Polio Pointers for Parents were sent home from school, and regularly, there was the Mothers March on Polio. Fathers worked, mothers marched. Every summer, when the epidemic surged again, the newspapers would dutifully publish a daily tally of infections and deaths, just as they toted up a "holiday death toll" for automobile fatalities on the Fourth of July and Labor Day and such.

Of course, even if official reminders of the menace were everywhere, there was nothing like the personal drumroll our mothers kept up on the subject. For God's sake, Christy, don't ever go there, you might catch polio. Watch it—they just mowed the lawn there. So? Because why? Because polio. Don't you dare drink out of a water fountain. Are you crazy, Christy? You did what? Do you *want* to get polio?

Of course, I knew Mom was being ridiculous. That was because I was still a kid, and therefore, not unlike the United States, I was invincible and eternal. Only everybody else was a prime candidate for polio. But Mom, being a foolish grown-up, was unaware of this truth. Mom never missed a Mothers March on Polio. One year, when we still lived back in Terre Haute, she was even our neighborhood's chief Mother for the March.

Yet as blithe as I may have been about polio *vis-à-vis* me, I was certainly never unsympathetic about other people's polio. On this glorious day of deliverance, as soon as I got home from school, I ran to my bike and pedaled furiously over to Kathryn Slade's house so we could celebrate the good news together. I knew Dr. Salk's vaccine couldn't help her. I knew it was too late. But I couldn't imagine that here we had immunization, we had Dr. Salk's magic elixir—we had conquered!—and it couldn't do anything for Kathryn. At all. I had to believe the cure would come next. Soon, surely.

But however happy Kathryn was for the rest of us, she would not let me get too excited for her chances. She just shook her head ruefully. It was still one of the few things Kathryn could do as well as the rest of us: shake her head ruefully. And then, as quickly as she could, she changed the subject. "Just six more weeks, Christy," she said happily. "Memorial Day. My father still calls it Decoration Day. Anyway, Decoration Day or Memorial Day—just six more weeks 'til the Grand Opening."

That was when Kathryn's pool would be back in business.

## 2 *Early that Summer Before: 1954*

The decision was made: I would join Pop in Baltimore as soon as school let out. I didn't want to go. Sue and Hughie were going to stay with Mom in Terre Haute until we could sell the house there. Actually, Mom had wanted Sue to be the one to go live with Pop. That certainly made more sense, inasmuch as Sue was a girl and therefore she knew how to cook and make beds and sew some, so she could help take care of Pop. Sue was seventeen, too, which meant she could drive, so she could even go to the market for Pop.

At that time, however, Sue was terribly in love with Danny Daugherty (and he with her). It was a romance of such long-standing that Pop even referred to Danny as "His Nibs"—although, of course, only out of Sue's hearing. But both Mom and Pop felt guilty about making Sue leave Terre Haute because she only had one more year left in high school, so he said, "Well, Cecelia, let Christy come. It'll be good for a father and son to camp out together. We'll go to ball games." The Orioles had just come to Baltimore that year from St. Louis. My father explained, "It's a big-league city now—and just when the Bannisters are going there."

"That's an omen," Mom replied. "Big league."

So Pop sat me down and explained what the plan was. "You will have four years before you even go off to college," he told me. "You will have all your best years in Baltimore. You'll make so many friends. Hell, soon you'll even forget Terre Haute."

That irritated the loyalist in me. "I will not either, Pop. I'll never forget Terre Haute."

"Hey, kiddo, I'm sorry. I didn't mean it like that. You'll always be a Hoosier, Christy. But it will fade. Things fade in life. Eventually, even Danny will fade from your sister's life. But it *is* unfair that Sue won't have her senior year here. Why, I think she could even be prom queen. I think Sue's got prom queen written all over her."

"Yes, sir." As much as I hated to admit it myself, I had to begrudge Sue that. She was "pretty as a picture," according to all my parents' contemporaries, and she had "a great pair of jugs," according to my own contemporaries. Whatever, Danny Daugherty was one lucky guy, undeserving of her, I believed, even if His Nibs was the best player on the high school basketball team. Even now, when I think of my first appreciation of beauty—coming of age, sex division—I think first of my sister Sue and how perfectly glamorous she looked in 1954, the year we left for Baltimore.

Of course, at the time, you can be damn sure I never told her that.

The reason we were moving was because my father was going to become the president of a company. That was very exciting. In the abstract. My father, the president. But then, the honor meant we had to pick up and leave where I'd lived all my life, where we had our roots. Me, I would've preferred staying in Terre Haute and just telling everybody my father had had an *offer* to be a president. He had *qualified* to be president, but he had *turned down* the opportunity. I thought you could be just as impressed about my father that way without us all going somewhere else where he would actually *be* a president.

Mom never said it, but I'm sure she didn't want to go either. She was strictly midwestern and suspicious of the East. She was convinced it was overrun by communists back there. And she was just so settled. As Pop told me, "A man has his work, Christy. You could put me down in the middle of Bora-Bora, but as long as I had the plant to go to every day, I could still be happy. But it's different with a woman. Terre Haute's been your mother's home for almost twenty years and Indiana all her life. This is one big move for her."

Besides, it killed Mom that Sue couldn't be prom queen. Mom even asked Pop if Mr. Gardner, whose family owned the company in Baltimore—Gardco, it was called—couldn't just hold the job for a year. But Pop explained, "That isn't the way business works,

Cecelia," and that was the end of that. In our family, my father wore the pants.

So Pop met me at the Mount Royal train station downtown in Baltimore on June 27, 1954, and drove us out to our brand new house, which was over the line into the county, the suburbs. I didn't say anything, but it struck me immediately as a very funny-looking house—not because the house was itself anyway ugly, but because of where it stood. It was all alone, all by itself, standing there on a new street that went in a semicircle. First house, first street, in a new development called Nottingham Valley Estates. This was because, as I would learn, every development everywhere always chooses a British name to suggest class, and in Baltimore, the best addresses were always valleys, so it was practical to shoehorn a valley into every title too.

It didn't matter, though. Everybody in their prewar houses just sneered and called where we lived "the subdivision." A development was new to this fancy lay of the land. It smelled of *noveau riche*. It took away pleasant, open space. Altogether, it was just plain jarring, upsetting to the natural order of things in what was a very placid and structured neck of the woods.

Enough that I had one strike against me just for where I lived. The second strike was just as devastating, even if it was altogether unintentional. I mean, my father meant well. He just didn't know how stupid he was being when he said to me, "Great news! I've got a job for you as a paperboy."

"Oh," I replied.

"I was a paperboy when I was your age," he explained, and then he detailed all the glories and advantages of the position. He added his favorite personal paperboy anecdotes. Then he concluded, "This is the perfect way for you to meet friends."

"Chucking papers up on a porch?"

"Don't be facetious, Christy. *If* you pause on your route when you see boys your age. It's the perfect way of striking up a conversation."

"Yes, sir." Even when Pop was boring and bubbleheaded as he was now, I still didn't cross him. I had no reason to. He was loving and trusting, exactly as fathers were supposed to be. It always intrigued me when I read about coaches who could get players to run through a brick wall for them. Why would you do that for a coach? That's what you were supposed to do for your father.

Pop pulled out a piece of paper, an advertisement in the Baltimore *News-Post* soliciting paperboys. "Wouldn't you know, the route right around here is available. Stroke of luck. So I told the fellow in charge"—he pointed to a name—"uh, here, a Mr., uh, D'Ionfrio, that you'd be calling him in a couple of days, once you get the lay of the land. And he promised me he'd hold the route 'til he talked to you. How 'bout that?"

"That's great," I replied, lying through my teeth. Besides, if only I had known, if only Pop had known. The reason that the route in this area was open now was because it was always open. It was open in perpetuity. Nobody in this part of Baltimore *ever* read the *News-Post*. Instead, everybody read the *Sun*, morning, evening, and Sunday. The *News-Post* was the Hearst paper, strictly *de classe*, read almost exclusively by what we still called the colored people and by the poor whites—what we generally lumped as the hillbillies and the Dagos and the Polacks—which is what we called them, impolitely, in polite conversation. They were the ones who worked in the plants. Baltimore was a manufacturing town with lots of plants. Gardco, my father's new company, manufactured porcelain enamelling for things like refrigerators and bathtubs. When he was at work, we always knew Pop to be "down at the plant."

It was at the plant where he saw all the workers taking out their *News-Posts* with their thermoses and lunch buckets and therefore, where he decided, reasonably enough, that everybody must be devouring *News-Posts* all over greater Baltimore. In fact, though, in many sections of town—most especially in the very section where I had been designated *News-Post* route boy—I might just as well have been trying to peddle the *South China Post* or the Manchester *Guardian*. Two days later, knocking on doors, I found this out very quickly.

"Hello, would you be interested in home delivery of the Baltimore *News-Post* with the *News-American* on Sunday for only—"

"I'm sorry, we already get the *Sun*."

Or, "Hello, ma'am, for only pennies a day, I will personally deliver the *News-Post* to—"

"No, thank you, son, we've been reading the *Sunpapers* all our lives."

This went on with only slight variations for eighteen houses. It did not help, either, that it was ninety-three degrees, not counting the humidity, which was soaking me through. Now this is not to say that folks were rude to me. They couldn't have been nicer, my new Baltimore neighbors. Three of them observed that it was so hot you could fry an egg on the pavement, and several more explained that it was not the heat, but the humidity. Two even offered me lemonade, which I hastily accepted. But one of them told me that she didn't even know "a single soul in all the world" who had ever read the *News-Post*. Ever. It was becoming crystal clear to me that nobody in these fashionable environs was interested in home delivery of the Baltimore *News-Post*. I couldn't have given it away.

I did, however, grow ever more entranced by my surroundings, as I had moved on from mere high-end territory into a neighborhood sublime. These houses, I knew, must be estates. Long, boulevard-like driveways cushioned by great box bushes on either side wound up to great be-chimneyed brick mansions that were set amidst lush green lawns that were invariably being tended to by talented black gardeners. Dogs barked at me, but more out of friendly curiosity than vigilance, for these were safely sequestered manors that robbers wouldn't dare invade. At that time, a certain civility was expected of the common criminal.

Anyway, after yet another rejection, I found my way back down the long driveway, and dismounting there from my Schwinn, I paused, ready to pack it in and to tell Pop that I just had to get into a new line. But I could hear him explaining to me about how a winner never quits and a quitter never....

So I decided to try a few more houses, and I wheeled out of the driveway onto what passed as the main road in these parts—Old Florist Avenue. Almost as soon as I did, though, a little white fluffy dog came strolling toward me down the street with no apparent concern whatsoever. Even though two cars had to swerve from clipping him, he simply popped over into the other lane and, tail up, kept ambling blithely on.

Just then, from opposite directions, I spied a panel truck topping the hill and a royal blue Chrysler Imperial honking its horn with a woman screaming out the window. Unfortunately, this diverted the truck driver at precisely the wrong moment. He took his eyes off the road ahead to check out the Imperial, and I could see the panel truck was surely going to hit the little dog.

Instinctively then—or more, perhaps, as I mused over time, guided by the hand of fate—I let my Schwinn fall to the side of the road. Glancing both ways to make sure that I really did have time, I dashed out in the road, scooped up the puppy, and, following my momentum, ran off the other way in front of the truck.

Actually, it looked closer than it really was. Distraught as I may have been about my failure at business, I was not prepared to throw it all away on a strange puppy dog. But if I made it safely across the road with plenty to spare, the lady driving the Imperial saw from her vantage a much more dramatic rescue. Beside herself, she jammed on the brakes, jumped out even faster than did the old gray black man who was accompanying her, and rushed to my side, calling thanks to me the whole time. It was embarrassing. I thrust the dog on her mostly so that it might divert her, and although she did pause to coo at the little thing, she promptly got back to thanking me. "What you have done, young man, is the single most wonderful thing I have ever witnessed in all my life."

"Gee," was all I managed to say. As effusive as my mother could sometimes be in her unstinting praise of me, I had never experienced anything quite like this before.

And then even though the dog was squirming every which way in her grasp—ready, momentarily, I was sure, to bound back onto Old Florist Avenue—the lady released her right hand and thrust it out to me. "Young man," she announced, "I am Aurelia Slade, and it is my great pleasure to meet you."

"How do you do, ma'am. I'm Christy Bannister."

"You are an extraordinary human being, Mr. Bannister, and you must come home with me straightaway."

"Ma'am?" God knows my father had instructed me carefully enough not ever to get into a stranger's car, so instinctively, I lifted a wary eyebrow.

"Why, you must receive a proper reward for saving Cromwell's life at the very risk of your own."

Uh-oh. This is how childnappers always did it, leading the gullible kid astray with promises and lures. But I would be too clever. "Aw, I don't deserve any award. I was just—"

"My gracious. We not only find a hero, but one who is modest and unassuming as well. Cut from the same bolt of cloth as Lucky Lindy himself. Come along now." She tugged at my sleeve.

"But my bike."

She barely halted to look over her shoulder. "Herbert, you bring Mr. Bannister's bicycle back to the house," she called out to the black fellow.

"Yes, ma'am," was all I managed to say as I got into the car. There Mrs. Slade dumped the dog into my lap. Some kidnap avoidee I was. Not only had I been pirated away, but I had given up my vehicle without a fight.

Mrs. Slade swung the Imperial around, headed back the other way, then turned into the next long driveway. She patted the dog on my lap. "This is Oliver Cromwell," she explained. "A Sealyham from Wales."

I didn't understand this meant the breed originated there. Rather, I took this to mean that the dog was newly arrived from Wales, just as I from Terre Haute.

"Don't they have cars in Wales?" I asked. "He's not one bit scared of cars."

Mrs. Slade smiled, if just a little bit, and wryly. "Oh, we can't blame Cromwell. As much as anyone in the world, you'd think that Kathryn and I would know how vulnerable pretty young things can be."

"Yes, ma'am," I answered, not having the foggiest.

# 3

I'd seen some of the fanciest houses in Terre Haute, thank you, and marveled at many I'd been to today unsuccessfully peddling the *News-Post,* but even in the face of that opulence, I'm sure I couldn't help but display the hick's wide-eyed admiration as Mrs. Slade drove me down the driveway toward her mansion.

As we approached the front door, Mrs. Slade said, "Well now tell me, Christy, whereas it is my own biased view that you were surely delivered to us from heaven this morning, where can we actually say you came from?"

"I'm from Terre Haute. Indiana. I'm a Hoosier, ma'am."

"I see. But how did you happen to get to Old Florist Avenue from the state of Indiana?"

"Oh, that. We just moved. I live on Dogwood Circle now." That drew a blank. So, hastily, I added, "In Nottingham Valley Estates."

"Ah," she exclaimed, wrinkling her nose, "you're the house in the subdivision."

It was the only thing Mrs. Slade had said that I didn't like, but I was catching on that disapproval of where I lived was universal. So I merely replied, "Yes, ma'am," and then I hurried before her up the steps to open the screen door. It felt a little odd, holding the door for Mrs. Slade to her own mansion, but I was altogether assured by now that this was not a kidnapping caper, and my father had reminded me often enough about holding doors for ladies. "Christy," he would say, "you have not been raised in a rabbit hutch."

"Why, thank you," Mrs. Slade beamed as she stepped inside. It's safe to say that I certainly was hitting on all cylinders with her.

A black maid in some sort of lacey get-up rushed to greet us. Mrs. Slade dumped Cromwell with her. "Maizie, tell Kathryn that her pride and joy was heroically rescued by a young Lochinvar from Indiana," Mrs. Slade announced.

"Yes'm," replied the maid, although I didn't think that she got that message verbatim.

"And bring us some cold drinks into the library, if you would please."

"Yes'm."

It actually was a library, too. It held far more books than I had ever seen in a house in my life, lined in paneled shelves that reached all the way to the ceiling. This grand array of magnificent volumes was broken only by dark and stately library-type portraits of noble ancestors so that it reminded me very much of *Clue*. Aha, Miss Scarlet did it right here with a candlestick.

Nevertheless, no matter how clear it was to me that the Slades were people of unlimited substance, Mrs. Slade confused the issue. She was not at all like the snooty, rich society women in the movies and the funny papers who wore tiaras and evening gowns and held lorgnettes all the time they were being shocked by the dreadful behavior of good, normal folk like me. The fact is, I had taken to Mrs. Slade and liked her immensely, and so I didn't quite know what to do when she promptly went over to her desk, pulled out a large checkbook, and asked me, "Would fifty dollars be enough?"

Fifty dollars? Fifty dollars was not only *enough* for a kid in 1954, but it was so much that nobody could even believe a kid could get that. I blanched. "I can't take that, Mrs. Slade. That's—"

"Well, all right, Mr. Bannister, what would you take?"

Good grief—I hoped she didn't think I was holding out for more than fifty dollars. Quickly then, inspired, I pulled out my little order pad. "Ma'am, what I would like is for you to buy home delivery for the *News-Post*."

"You mean...the newspaper?" It was obvious from that tone that a commitment to the *News-Post* had never previously been a serious subject of discussion in the Slade household.

13

"Yes, ma'am. I have a summer special I'm offering for home delivery for the *News-Post*, plus—*plus*—the *News-American* on Sundays."

Mrs. Slade snapped, "Well, I'm not the least bit interested in a summer special." I dropped my head. Here was the proof of my worst instincts, that this lady would actually rather *give* me fifty bucks outright than *get* the *News-Post* for a whole lot less. But Mrs. Slade wasn't finished. "However, I would like to purchase a full year's home delivery."

"Yes, ma'am!" I shouted, thrusting the order pad toward her.

"So," she asked, filling in her name, "and how is the newspaper business going today?"

"Well, to be honest with you, not very good. The dog-catching business is going better."

Mrs. Slade chuckled, and without further ado, she picked up the phone and started making a call. There was no answer there, so she made another. Although Maizie, the maid, came in then with the cold drinks on a silver tray, Mrs. Slade didn't even put the phone down. She stayed right on the case, only beckoning me to do the honors. So I opened two RCs (with the first silver church key I'd ever seen) and listened as Mrs. Slade sold *News-Post* home delivery to her neighbors.

She would start, "Eleanor, I have the most attractive young man here, and he is selling the *News-Post*, and—"

Invariably, each time she would pause at this point because, obviously, her friend had interrupted her by saying, "The *News-Post*?"

But then Mrs. Slade would go on. "Yes, the *News-Post*. But I want you to do this for me." Hand cupped over the phone, "How long is the summer special, Christy?"

"Ten weeks," I whispered. There really wasn't a summer special; I had just dreamed that up. Ten weeks would take me through the summer and back to school, so, well, it was special to me. After that, I figured Mr. William Randolph Hearst would have to handle the sales of the Baltimore *News-Post* on his own.

Certainly, though, my new sales partner, Aurelia Slade, was

cooking with gas. Only once, in fact, did we have to get into the hard sell. That was when a Mrs. Ewing kept asking Mrs Slade why in hell she should buy the *News-Post* when she had gotten along without it very nicely all her life. Mrs. Slade finally just shook her head and handed the phone to me. "You try," she said.

"Hi! Christopher Bannister, your neighborhood *News-Post* home delivery salesman."

"Well, Christopher, we already get the *Sunpapers*, morning, evening, and Sunday," Mrs. Ewing said, "and my husband also gets the *New York Herald-Tribune* and the *Kiplinger Letter* in the mail. Why in the world should we also get the *News-Post?*"

Mr. D'Ionfrio had explained to me what to say in this instance in order to close the deal. "The *News-Post* has the best Oriole coverage in Baltimore," I declared proudly.

Unfortunately, it did not appear that Mrs. Ewing was much of a baseball fan. "The best what-all?"

"You know, ma'am, the Orioles—"

But I didn't get any further because Mrs. Slade put down her glass of RC, yanked the phone out of my hand, and screamed into the receiver, "Dammit, Edna, you are the cheapest person I ever met in my life. Stop arguing with me. When is Ludlow's birthday? When is it? November 17th—all right. You tell Ludlow I am giving him an early birthday present now myself so he can read all about the Orioles. It's a summer special, Edna Ewing, so stop being so cheap." And she slammed the phone back down and started writing the Ewings' name onto my order pad. "Don't worry, Christy, I shamed her, so she'll pay for it herself. I know Edna like the back of my hand."

We totaled up. Mrs. Slade had gotten me fourteen summer specials and two year-long subscriptions—hers and one of her sons'—plus five more sales she guaranteed me as soon as she could pin the pigeons down. I polished off the last of my RC and rose to leave. "Mrs. Slade, I really, *really* appreciate your help," I said.

"And I appreciate yours. And Christy..."

"Yes, ma'am?"

"I wasn't just whistlin' Dixie when I was building you up in all those phone calls. You are a fine young man."

I paused. I didn't know whether I was supposed to say a thing like this, whether it might be out of order. But I blurted it out anyhow. "And you're a real nice lady."

She smiled. "Why, thank you, Christy. I'd kiss you for that, but you're of an age when that would only make you blush." She shook her head, and in reverie, "God, if we could only keep men awkward like that for all their lives."

I nodded in assent, figuring that was the polite thing to do, but as I turned to leave, that was when I heard something approaching—on wheels, it sounded like. Then I heard another woman's voice that said, "Well, Mother, weren't you going to introduce me to the handsome stranger?"

I looked up—not quite appreciating that I was the object in question—and there, up the three steps that led into the living room, was my first glance of Kathryn. She was laid out on her gurney, her portable respirator 'round her, with a large black lady behind her providing the locomotion. A little basket attached to Kathryn's chaise held Oliver Cromwell.

Mrs. Slade cracked, "Ah, are you cutting in on me again, Kathryn?" Then she reached for my hand and, rather formally, led me up the steps. First, she introduced me to the heavy-set lady, whose name was Lavinia. Then, "And Christy, this is my daughter, Kathryn Slade. Kathryn, Christy is your knight in shining armor, who saved our noble Cromwell." For emphasis, she swept the little dog up in her arms and nuzzled him.

"Hello," Kathryn said. "And my deepest thanks." She had a wonderful smile, and I know I would have been struck by that even if there were much more that she had.

"I'm glad I could do it," I said.

"I'm sorry it took me so long to come down to see you," Kathryn went on, "but Lavinia had to get me out of my regular iron lung and into this portable respirator. This one works on batteries."

"Oh," I said. Although I didn't know it at the time, I was favorably impressing Kathryn because I neither averted my eyes from her, nor did I stare. When she talked about her respirator, I looked at her respirator; when she stopped talking about it, I looked at her. My parents had always told me to look at whom you were speaking to, so I was just following orders. But as Kathryn would explain to me later, most people who met her couldn't act naturally. Some people would address her mother or Lavinia, or they would look away as they spoke. Others had a tendency to speak very loudly to her as if she must also be hard of hearing. Somehow, I had got it right.

"I can't breathe on my own," Kathryn explained. "I need this damn respirator just to make my lungs work. I had polio six years ago. I only had it for about a week. So this isn't polio. This is what's left after polio." I found it odd the way she said that to me—not whining at all, not even being cynical. Just simply, matter-of-fact.

I moved a little closer and continued the conversation. "I'm sorry. We had a really bad polio epidemic two summers ago in Terre Haute. I'm from Terre Haute—"

"Indiana," Mrs. Slade broke in.

"I know where Terre Haute is, Mother," Kathryn said, grousing. "It means 'high ground' in French."

"It does," I said.

Kathryn winked at me. "Didn't think I'd know that?"

"Not many people do."

"You'd be surprised at the crap I know."

"Kathryn reads a great deal," Mrs. Slade explained.

"'Deed she does," Lavinia chuckled.

"Anyway," I went on, "I had a pretty good friend down the next street. His name was Harold Wyatt, and he got polio, and—"

"Did he get it worse than me?" Kathryn asked.

"Well..." I paused for a moment. Oh well, in for a penny, in for a pound. "Harold died," I said flat out.

Mrs. Slade winced, but Kathryn didn't. Instead, she said, "You didn't answer me, Christy. What I asked was did Harold have it worse than me?"

I glanced over at Mrs. Slade, but she only hunched her shoulders a little bit as if to say you're on your own, kid. So I just looked straight down at Kathryn, and I said, "Well, with most people like you stuck like this, I'd say Harold had it better dying. But with you, I'd say Harold had it worse."

Softly, Mrs. Slade said, "Thank you, Christy."

"Yeah," Kathryn said, "that's an awful nice compliment."

"It was supposed to be," I said.

"Well, it's been very nice meeting you," Kathryn said. "Would you shake my hand?" I reached down and took hers in mine, but of course, it just flopped there in my palm. Just as Kathryn couldn't breathe by herself, neither could she move any part of her body except her head. So for a moment, I hesitated. "Don't worry, Christy, you can't break it. I'm pretty unbreakable." So I smiled and grasped it every bit as firmly as I would anyone's, looking her directly in the face.

It was a very pretty face, and it was ringed with auburn hair, but of a shade I've never really seen on anyone else. I came to think that was probably because her hair meant more to her after she lost her body. It grew more beautiful to compensate for the things that had also been beautiful, but that no one could see anymore. Kathryn always made sure that her hair was perfectly in place. Lavinia, the old black lady who took care of her, combed it all the time. So did her mother. And I found out Kathryn was very exacting about one other thing; any lipstick she wore had to play off her hair. That was her one great concession to vanity.

I shook her hand up and down just as I would anyone's. "I've been very pleased to meet you, Kathryn," I said.

"Good. And you'll be here at the pool tomorrow morning?"

"What?"

Kathryn looked over at her mother. "You didn't invite him?"

"Well, quite frankly, Kathryn, Mr. Bannister and I have been involved in some intricate business transactions, and we haven't had time for—"

"Okay, will you, Christy? Will you come use my pool?"

"Gosh, sure. I mean, I have to ask my father. My mother's still back in Terre Haute."

"Oh, don't worry. Just tell your father you won't catch polio here."

"Kathryn—for God's sake," Mrs. Slade cried out.

"Oh, stop it, Mother. That's all the parents care about, and you know it."

I broke in. "I'll be here. I don't swim very well, but I'd love to come here. Thanks."

"I'll teach you," Kathryn said. "I was a helluva swimmer."

"She was," Mrs. Slade said—and so proudly. "I want you to know that Kathryn was terrific in just about everything she tried."

"More's the pity," Kathryn said, but only with irony.

I realized then that I was still holding onto Kathryn's limp hand. Of course, she couldn't feel anything, so I made a point of reaching down with my left hand, too, so I could hold hers in both of mine. Kathryn's eyes followed my action, and when I could see for sure that she was looking, I squeezed her hand. Then when I looked back up at her, she winked. Let me tell you, Kathryn Slade could wink with the best of them. So, what the hell, I winked back.

Kathryn certainly wasn't anywhere near my age, and of course, she was also a girl, but still I could tell: she was my friend. She was my first friend in a new city, and it felt good to have one friend.

# 4

"It's their pool? At their house?" My father wanted to make sure he had that straight when I told him that night. In 1954, private pools were rare possessions indeed, reflecting the most extraordinary affluence.

"Yeah. It must be Olympic size."

Pop whistled. "Well, all right," he said. "If you're absolutely sure that this lady actually invited you to use the pool—"

"I am. I promise. She said—"

"Okay, Christy, but you are not to breathe a word of this to your mother when she calls."

"Come on, Pop, I'm not going to catch polio at a *private* pool."

"You just told me the daughter *had* polio."

"But I told you: she caught it away from the pool."

"All right, I said you could go. Maybe you can meet some friends there." But then, one more time, "Still, we will not tell your mother."

"Yes, sir."

"I don't mean *lie,* Christy. We will just not bring the subject up."

Satisfied, he opened a beer, and then we started to barbecue some hamburgers. Barbecue was something of a new attraction that summer, one of the more visible early signs of the burgeoning suburban vogue. Charcoal, however, was not easy to light in those days before supermarket briquettes came coated with the devil's own formula of brimstone, so it took Pop quite a while before he got the fire going. But those charcoaled hamburgers tasted really good. We took them inside and started to watch some television. There wasn't much furniture in the house. Just a little that we had to add new to the bulk of what would come when Mom and Sue and Hughie arrived.

For a TV, Pop had splurged on a little Philco with rabbit ears that made for some pretty fuzzy reception. It didn't much matter, though. What was on that summer was mostly reruns and variety shows. Variety was still respectable in America in the fifties. Variety was yet the spice of life. It was before everything was niches.

Anyway, on this particular evening, even if there had been something on one of the three channels that we were dying to watch, it was obvious to me that Pop wasn't of a mind to. He was extremely distracted and jumped like hell when the phone rang (it was only some guy calling about the landscaping). Then, shortly after that, he told me he had to go out and get some cigarettes, which was just an excuse, I knew, because I'd seen a whole carton of Pall Malls up in his room. But I didn't say anything. He must have been really worried about something or other. When he finally got back, I was in my room listening to Chuck Thompson broadcast the Orioles game on my radio, but Pop just stuck his head into my room on his way to bed.

I'd never seen my father like this before, but then my father had never been a president before, so what did I know? The next morning, he had already gone to the plant by the time I got up, so I just put on some shorts over my bathing suit, got on my bike, and went over to the Slades'.

Mrs. Slade came to the door when Maizie called. "Oh, Christy, I'm so glad you're here," she said, proudly showing me three more of my summer special *News-Post* deliveries that she'd signed up. Let me tell you, Mrs. Slade was really into it. "I've still got the Andersons and the Taylors to get to when they come back from the shore."

"Hey, that's great, Mrs. Slade. I called up this Mr. D'Ionfrio, who's the route manager, last night, and he was so impressed he's going to put me in for *News-Post* Paperboy of the Month."

"Gracious, that's the most exciting thing I've ever heard," Mrs. Slade cooed. Then she threw an arm around my shoulder and steered me outside around the side of the house. "Now, Christy," she began, "I shouldn't tell you this, but I know you can honor confidences."

"Yes, ma'am."

"Well, I just want you to know that my dearest friend in all the world is Grace Gardner." I nodded even if the name didn't mean anything to me. "And when I mentioned to her about this guardian angel of Cromwell's transported to Old Florist Avenue from Terre Haute, Indiana, she interrupted me and said, 'Why, Aurelia, that must be Bob Bannister's boy.' And I thought to myself, of course, Frank—Mr. Gardner—had hired a new president for Gardco, and I remembered the man came from Indiana, and here that knowledge had gone, phffft, right out of this rapidly senile mind of mine."

Now I had the drift. "I promise, Mrs. Slade, I won't tell anyone."

We had come to a small gate. She laughed. "No, no, Christy. The secret isn't that I'm going senile. I'm afraid everybody knows that. I haven't come to the secret yet."

"Yes, ma'am."

"No, what I wanted to tell you was that Grace told me that Frank thinks your father is the most...the most brilliant business-man he ever met." I beamed. "Yes, Frank Gardner thinks your father hung the moon. And, of course, Grace said, 'Aurelia, you are not to repeat one word of this.' But, at the risk of my seeming terribly untrustworthy, dammit, I think a boy should know what a top-notch father he's got."

"I am pretty proud of Pop."

"Well, you should be, Christy. And I don't mind telling you that I told Grace, 'Well, if that's the way Mr. Bannister is, then you should know that his boy is a chip off the old block.'"

I blushed. "Thank you, Mrs. Slade."

"Well, I meant every word of it. But you are not to breathe any of this. Frank Gardner would skin me alive if your father knew he had Frank wrapped around his little finger." She held up her little finger for emphasis.

So I crossed my heart for emphasis. "Cross my heart and hope to die if I tell."

"All right, let's go get that swim now." She pushed through the gate and I followed. "We don't have many rules at Kathryn's pool, but I expect them all to be followed to a *T*."

"Yes, ma'am."

"First is, you children can only come in the mornings during the week. The afternoons and weekends are for the grown-ups, you understand. But you are never to go into the pool unless there is some adult here. Now, when is it your mother's arriving from Indiana?"

"About a month. Around the first of August. We haven't sold our house back there yet, and Pop says you can sell a house better if it's still lived in."

"I see," Mrs. Slade replied. We were cutting through the most wonderful vegetable garden, which was special, I thought, even though there was hardly a vegetable on God's green Earth that I cared for. But all the rows were so perfectly neat, all hoed, each identified with empty seed packets set on sticks in the ground. There was spinach, I could see, lima beans, lettuce, tomatoes, radishes, and corn which was already waist high. Mrs. Slade plucked a little tomato and tossed it into her mouth. "Do you like cherry tomatoes?" she asked, although I was completely thrown off because she pronounced it *tomahtoes*, which was the first time I had imagined—let alone actually heard—a real American pronounce it that way.

"Not right now, thank you, I just had my breakfast," was what I managed to say in reply.

"This started out as a Victory Garden during the war," Mrs. Slade explained, "but the judge enjoyed gardening so much that when he came back from the marines, we kept it. Of course, Herbert does most of the work now, but we allow the judge to take the credit." I nodded, feeling good about being taken back into Mrs. Slade's confidence again. We were moving now between the rows of corn. "Good Maryland sweet corn," she told me. "Not that awful horse corn so many places grow. I'll make sure your mother gets some when it's ready." I nodded again. "And when she gets here, you can tell her I want her to come over and meet me. Then some mornings she can stay and watch you and the other children swim. The mothers sort of take turns playing lifeguard." She paused then as we came to the end of the rows of vegetables and entered the most magnificent flower garden. "You know, Christy, I didn't even ask you if you had any siblings."

"Any what?" I'd never heard that word before, and my first thought was that it must be something like allergies.

"Siblings. Brothers or sisters."

"Oh yes, ma'am. Sue is seventeen and Hughie was just eight."

"Well, it goes without saying that they're invited to come over to Kathryn's pool, too. But, hmmm...seventeen?" I nodded. "We usually find that once a child turns sixteen and gets a driver's license, he doesn't want to swim with the younger ones anymore. So your sister probably won't have much interest. But at least we'll have you two summers before you start driving."

I smiled. In all a person's life, nothing takes longer for time to pass than the last couple years leading up to a driver's license. "Anything else?" I asked.

"How do you mean?"

"You know, any other rules?"

"Oh, let's see. Weekday mornings only. No swimming unless an adult's here. Hmm." We stopped again because we had come to the gate on the other side of the flower garden, and as I put my hand on it to draw it open, Mrs. Slade laid hers on mine. "Well, there is one other thing, Christy, and although I make a point of telling all the children, I really don't believe I need to tell you. Nevertheless...." I cocked my head. "We built this pool for Kathryn after she got"—a sigh—"her polio. At the time, we thought perhaps it would be good therapy for her, that we could take her into the pool and that would help her. We were inspired by memories of President Roosevelt. Do you remember him, Christy?"

"Well, not really, but I know he had polio."

"And he swam a lot for exercise."

"No, ma'am, I didn't know that part." I was only four when he died.

"Well, Mr. Roosevelt did. But he was only paralyzed below the waist. It's much worse with Kathryn. We couldn't get her in the pool at all. She couldn't go in the water with a respirator, and she always needs a respirator."

I nodded sorrowfully.

"So here it is, Kathryn's pool, but Kathryn can't go in it. But by God, it is still Kathryn's pool, and unless it's too hot, she likes to come down and have Lavinia push her into the shade so she can lie there and talk to the people who come. So, the pool turned out to be good therapy for Kathryn after all, didn't it?"

"Yes, ma'am."

"All I ask anyone is that if Kathryn does come down, they should go over and say hello to her and chat with her if that is her pleasure. All right?"

Well, I was affronted. Very stoutly I replied, "Mrs. Slade, I wasn't raised in a rabbit hutch."

She tilted her head when she heard that. That must have been a Terre Haute expression that had never before surfaced in these more cosmopolitan environs. But then she broke into a smile and laughed, hugging me with one arm. "No, Christy, I can tell very well that you were not."

Just then, we came round the box hedge and there, laid out before me picture-perfect, was Kathryn's pool. It reminded me of some pond in a glade in a fairy tale book. The pool itself sparkled in the sun with Herbert's whole brilliant flower garden circling it at a distance of lawn. Beyond the flowers came more huge box bushes, all neatly trimmed, with some leafy maples all but concealing the Slades' house. In fact, only from Kathryn's own room was the view of her pool unobstructed.

Mrs. Slade was used to seeing how taken people were with the sight when they first came upon it. She let it all soak in. "God's tear," she finally said softly.

"Please?"

"I've always believed that it was here God shed His tear for Kathryn."

"Yes, ma'am," I said. The pool was God's tear. I understood that. And even 'til now, I've never seen so pretty a place on this Earth that nature and man brought together in conjunction than Kathryn's pool.

In fact, so overwhelming was the whole vision that the sheer magnitude of the pool itself was lost on me at first. It really must have been Olympic-sized, too, even if I wasn't quite sure what those dimensions consisted of. Anyway, it was absolutely gigantic for a private house. Kathryn's pool spoiled me for all time, all pools.

"Be careful now, no diving in the shallow end," Mrs. Slade cautioned me, and although I nodded, I really didn't take the full measure of her admonition because I didn't appreciate how large the shallow end was. It extended out for many yards, never more than two or three feet deep because the original idea had been to carry Kathryn into the water after the fashion of President Roosevelt.

"Now, you can change in there," Mrs. Slade went on, pointing past the shallow end, back into the garden where Herbert was toiling, to a pool house that you could barely make out under the vines that climbed all over it.

"Oh, that's okay, I've got my suit on under—" I started to say, but just then I heard this incredible whistle and:

"Hey, Christy, over here."

Of course the voice belonged to Kathryn, but I had to peer to see where she was way back on the other side, deep in the shade, amidst some mothers who were chatting there with her, smoking cigarettes and knitting. So, she whistled again.

And God, could Kathryn Slade whistle. She could whistle much better than those really good whistlers who put their two fingers in their mouths and let a blast go that way. I honestly believe still that Kathryn could out-whistle any man. Kept a feminine touch, too, even if I'm sure you'd doubt that.

Immediately, all the kids stopped what they were doing and even the smallest of them scrambled out of the pool, hurrying over to her. "Oh yes, one thing I forgot," Mrs. Slade said. "There is this one other rule. If Kathryn whistles, everybody has to hustle right over to her."

"Come on, Christy, on your horse," Kathryn hollered, and I ran over. Already, all the other kids were lined up by her. There were perhaps a dozen of them, all ages, starting with some who were still almost babies in water wings. It extended up from there through some of about Hughie's age and on to two girls who were close enough to my age that I made sure to completely avert my eyes from them. Then over to the side were three boys, roughly my contemporaries.

"How old are you, Christy?" Kathryn asked for openers.

"Fourteen," I replied nervously, knowing that everybody still took me for twelve—except maybe for thirteen on a very good day.

"Well, that's just right," she said. Wrong. Promptly, I noticed that two of the boys grimaced that Kathryn would dare to so glibly associate me with them. The third—a big, chubby kid named Buddy something who still had girl-type tits instead of muscles for a chest—instantly declared, "I'm fifteen," as if that instantly let him off the hook from any association with me. In fact, he ran back to the pool even before I finished shaking hands with the other two boys, whom Kathryn identified as Timmy and Jake.

The whole time Kathryn kept talking to them about how fortunate they were to have a terrific new pal, both of them kept one eye on Buddy in the pool, trying to gauge whether he thought they should have anything to do with me. Evidently, Buddy did not bestow his blessing. Anyway, whatever chance I had for at least a tacit acceptance vanished when Kathryn bade me to strip down to my bathing suit, for there it was revealed upon my dirt-brown trunks, a little round Red Cross Junior Lifesaving patch.

I had proudly earned that honor the summer before at a YMCA camp my mother had shipped me off to at the Lieber State Recreation Area over in Putnam County, which she had deemed, in its rusticality, a safer haven from polio than Terre Haute might be. How was I to know (until Kathryn eventually clued me in) that the absolute twerpiest thing a boy could wear in urbane teen territory like this was a Red Cross Junior Lifesaving patch?

But what did I know now? So, quickly enough, Timmy escaped from me and my patch back to Buddy and the pool. Jake would have rushed off with him, too, except that Kathryn fixed her eyes on him, freezing him to that spot. "Christy just moved to Baltimore, Jake," she declared.

This obliged him to ask, "Where'd ya come from?"

"Indiana."

"Oh yeah. Where dya live?"

I made myself say it. "Nottingham Valley."

I saw his expression. "The subdivision?" Incredulous, he was.

I managed to nod my head.

"Where ya goin' to school?"

"Rodgers Forge."

"Yeah? *Public* school?"

I nodded at that, too, but with puzzlement, inasmuch as I'd never heard the question before. Heretofore, I thought it was just understood that school *was* public school. This was like someone asking if you wanted to eat lunch and then saying: food?

"Oh," Jake replied. And then, surely only because he saw that Kathryn still had her head twisted around looking at him, he forced himself to say, "So you, uh, wanna go inna pool?"

"Sure."

Even then, as best he could, Jake avoided me once we got in the water. On the occasion when I got close enough to him to say something altogether innocuous like, "How long you been coming here?" he merely mumbled a response then ducked under as fast as he could. Even with that, when Jake surfaced, Buddy called out in a loud, snotty voice, "Hey, Jake, it's about your friends."

I ducked under myself then and stayed down until my breath started to give out. When I came up, Lavinia was rolling Kathryn away. I waved to her, and I could see her smile back at me even as Buddy and Timmy and Jake were snickering about me and my twerpy Red Cross Junior Lifesaving badge bathing suit.

Never mind. Almost every morning after that, I would get on my bike and ride over to go swim at Kathryn's pool.

# 5

The first time I heard Sal Carlino's name was one evening when Mrs. Patterson came over to work on business with Pop. I didn't know what exactly it was that Mrs. Patterson did for Gardco, but then I didn't know what anybody did for Gardco. I barely knew what Gardco did.

But, whatever, as I came to the door of the den where they were working, Mrs. Patterson just happened to mention Sal Carlino's name. Pop dropped his pencil right away and shook his head. "You know, Trudy," he said woefully, "I still can't understand why Frank didn't even *mention* this to me when they were courting me."

I stopped in my tracks—not really hiding, you understand, just standing there. Very quietly. They were turned the other way, working on TV tables. Mrs. Patterson said, "Because, of course, Bobby, they wanted to leave the dirty work for you."

"It's just so damned unfair," Pop said, and he threw his head back, running his hands over it, every bit as much beside himself as he'd appeared to me the few nights before when he went out for cigarettes even though there was a whole carton in the house.

"Aw, Bobby, I know," Mrs. Patterson said, but as she turned to Pop then, she saw me in the door. I stepped inside. I had come into the house to show Pop the lightning bugs I had caught and put in a jar. Baltimore was sort of the lightning bug capital of the world. Professors at Johns Hopkins University paid a penny a lightning bug for research. They were studying how they lit up or why or something of that nature. Anyway, it was easy money inasmuch as lightning bugs were a cinch to catch; they lumbered in the air—I imagine because, unlike other bugs, they had those big lights on their asses to lug around.

I had met Mrs. Patterson a little earlier when she'd followed Pop home from the office one afternoon. Now she came over with him, and they both took an immediate interest in my lightning bug collection. There was no more talk of Sal Carlino, and in fact, I forgot all about the name until two nights later when I really did eavesdrop on Pop. Now, I didn't mean to. I was supposed to be asleep, but I was listening to the Oriole game on the radio hidden under my pillow when I heard a voice other than Chuck Thompson's. Quietly, I got up and started to the door, but then I realized that the voice was coming from outside on the patio. I peeked out.

Pop was down there talking to himself. Or really, I figured out, he was working on a speech he was going to deliver to Mr. Gardner. He would stop and start, try new things out. But basically, it went like this:

"Now Frank, you brought me here to run your company. And I know it's *your* company. The Gardner family. Mr. Phil started it, and you and Walter and Evelyn. And that's fine. I'm not under any illusions. But I believe—deeply believe, Frank—that this kind of decision is one that should be left to the president."

In some versions, Pop would go on to say, "I have to be honest with you, Frank. I'm not sure I would've picked up my family and come to Gardco if I had known about this situation."

And then he would end up in this vein, "Now, don't misunderstand me. Tom is a terrific young man—and I'd be saying this even if he weren't your nephew. But I just don't believe that he's ready for that much responsibility...right now. And Sal Carlino is one of the most respected men in the porcelain enamelling industry, Frank. Anywhere in this country P.E. men get together, you only hear the very best things about Sal. He's a honey of a guy. (Long pause) I really wish you would reconsider, sir."

Or, "I have to ask you to at least put this on the back burner for now, Frank."

Or, "You wouldn't have hired me if you didn't respect my

opinion, sir..." And I heard several more variations on that theme before I finally tip-toed away from the window and went back to bed.

I waited a few days for the right moment. Then one afternoon Pop called to tell me he had to work late again that evening, so I could tell he felt a little guilty about leaving me alone. He got home even later than he'd said, too, so when we went out on the patio with a beer and an RC, I thought the time was ripe. "Pop, can I ask you something?" He nodded. Long ago, we'd had the where-do-babies-come-from seminar, so he knew that wasn't facing him. I leaned in. "The other night when Mrs. Patterson was over here—"

"What about Mrs. Patterson?"

"No, no, sir. It isn't Mrs. Patterson. It's what you two were talking about when I came inside with my lightning bug jar."

He relaxed. "Oh. What was that?"

"You were talking about Mr., uh, Sal Carlino. And you seemed pretty upset, and so I wanted to know if you could tell me about—"

There had been occasions when I had asked my father questions, and he had no difficulty telling me that he didn't want to answer me, that I was still a kid, and it was just none of my beeswax. But he didn't pull that now. He only sighed and said, "It's just business, Christy. It's just a part of business."

"You seemed so upset, Pop."

"Yeah, well, we'll work it out. You work things out in business. Part of being a good businessman is being a worker-outer."

There had, of course, been times before when Pop had been evasive with me. I could accept that because I also knew he'd never lied to me. In fact, my father was so truthful that it would make it a little difficult for me when I first started to get out in the world and found that most other people weren't so constitutionally honest. Pop always said, "Christy, being honest isn't just a matter of telling the truth when you're asked. It is living the truth when no one's watching."

"Well, sir, then who *is* Sal Carlino? Can I ask that? Or is that all part of business, too?"

He chuckled and took a swig of his beer. "No, you can ask that. In fact, I enjoy talking about Sal. Because he's a honey of a guy. A honey of a guy." That was the highest praise my father could offer. A honey of a guy was even better than a gentleman. "Sal's what you call a self-made man. He's our general manager, and he's one helluva business-man in P.E. And he never even had a college education."

"But Pop, you didn't graduate from college, either."

"True, Christy. But I *went* to college. Two years at IU. It was only the Depression that made me leave. People understand that. Even though I don't have that sheepskin up on the wall, people in the business know I'm a college man. Now don't mistake my point, Christy. You can't be a college man any longer unless you *get* that sheepskin. Don't you go to college and drop out and try to give me a lot of who-shot-John about being a college man. That doesn't fly anymore. Not since the war. Not since the GI Bill."

"Yes, sir."

"But Sal is not a college man. Hell, I don't even know if he grad-uated from high school. He just got a job at the plant and worked his way up. He had native intelligence, Christy, what we call street smarts. And during the war, when a lot of the men had to go into the service, Sal got his chance to shine. And he came through with flying colors."

"He became a businessman?"

"Yes, he did. During the war, we retooled the factory. Gardco stopped making porcelain enamelling, and they—we—we started mak-ing interiors for tank turrets, stuff like that. And Sal was the one that really took that tiger by the tail. He's a self-made man, Christy. Why, Salvadore Carlino is what this country of ours is all about."

Promptly then, Pop sat back, and with his arms folded, still clenching his beer bottle in one fist, he made me to understand that this particular conversation was concluded. In our house, we called this posture of Pop's—well, Mom called it—can't-you-see-your-father-doesn't-want-to-discuss-that-anymore?

Still, I wasn't quite ready to let this go altogether, and so, as innocuously as possible, I made a flanking action. "So, Pop," I asked, "how do you like Gardco?"

"Well, I like it fine. But I must say, Christy, I've never heard you so interested in my work. The whole time we were in Terre Haute, I don't think you ever asked me word one about business, about working at Kessler Brothers."

"That's because nobody ever asked me about your business there. I was just Christy Bannister. Everybody knew me and knew our family, so nobody ever said, hey, what's your father *do?* But ever since I got here and people don't know me, they always ask."

"Like who?" my father said. "Like who asks?"

"Well, like over at Kathryn's pool. The mothers ask."

"So, whaddya tell 'em?"

"I just say you're the president of Gardco, which makes porcelain enamelling, and usually that's good enough. Sometimes, if Mrs. Slade is around, she'll say how she and Judge Slade know Mr. and Mrs. Gardner, and—"

"Oh?"

"Yeah, they're *real* good friends." I desperately wanted to tell Pop how Mrs. Slade had told me how much Mr. Gardner was pleased with him, but she had made me swear to silence, and so I bit my tongue. I just said, "But not even Mrs. Slade knows what porcelain enamelling is."

So, Pop laughed and explained to me for a while about porcelain enamelling, which I will not bore anybody else with by repeating it. Then he told me about Gardco. "We're a real leader in the industry," he said.

"Wasn't Kessler Brothers a real leader in the industry, too?"

"Yes, it is. There are probably several companies you could say that about. But Gardco has always been a leader in P.E. Starting with Mr. Phil, the founder. But his son, Frank, has been running the company, and he's getting older. Mr. Gardner—Frank—hasn't got any boys. There's his younger brother, Walter, but"—and Pop leaned closer, conspiratorially—"just between us chickens, I'm afraid Walter's light on his feet." I nodded sagely, pleased that Pop would share such hush-hush intelligence with me. "And then there's Evelyn, the sister. Now she's never really been prominent in the business, but she has a son Tom, who's like the heir. But Tom's still wet behind the ears, so they needed someone from outside."

33

"That's you, Pop."

"You got it. So Frank Gardner kicked himself upstairs and made himself the chairman of the board, and I'm—"

"The president."

"That's right." He offered up a little smile. My father hadn't been a president so long that he didn't still enjoy hearing the title.

"And so what's Mrs. Patterson?"

"Well, she's just the office manager. But Mrs. Patterson is very qualified for a woman."

"What's her husband do?"

Pop paused for just a moment. "It's my understanding that she's a divorcée," he said very formally.

That rocked me back a bit. I knew movie stars like Mickey Rooney got divorced, and there was a fellow named Tommy Manville who was regularly in the newspapers for divorcing and marrying (I think he was up to about a dozen now), but certainly in my experience, normal, run-of-the-mill folks rarely got divorced. Especially women. And here Mrs. Patterson, a divorcée, had been in this very house (albeit briefly). But I didn't let that shocking revelation waylay me from what I really wanted to know. "And what's Sal Carlino?"

"I told you. He's the general manager. He reports directly to me."

I wasn't trying to be a nosy kid. But that piqued me further. So I pressed on. "Well, if he's so good and all, how come Mr. Gardner didn't make *him* the president?"

My father roared at that. "You ask good questions, Christy," he said, slapping me on the knee. "You oughtta be a lawyer. You wanna be a lawyer?"

"I'm not sure what I wanna be."

"Nothin' wrong with that," Pop said. "I was your age, I didn't have any idea what I'd become. I just fell into the P.E. business. After I left IU, I was sellin' plumbing fixtures on straight commission, and that's where I met the Kessler people. Dumb luck. Met your mom the same way. I used to have to come into an office where she was workin' part time as a clerk. A lot of life is dumb luck."

Pop polished off his beer as he pondered the vagaries of life, took a last drag on his cigarette, and flipped it out toward where all the lightning bugs were drifting about. It probably confused all hell out of them. They might've thought that the cigarette flicking by was the world's fastest lightning bug. "Well, Christy," Pop said, "it's all because it's time for a new generation of leadership. Not just at Gardco, you understand. In America. Sal is up past sixty, and I know you think I'm old as Methuselah, but in the business world, I'm still considered a young man."

"Yes, sir."

"My generation has been through a depression, and we've been through a world war, and if anyone has ever been tested, it's my crowd. Now it's time for us to move to the fore. That's what Mr. Gardner himself first told me when he contacted me. It's time for my generation to step front and center."

Pop stood up then, waving his hand. "But this is too damn much talk about Gardco. I've got to stop bringing the office home with me."

"Aw, I don't mind."

"Nah, kiddo, it's not fair to you," he said. It was obvious I'd hit something of a nerve asking about Sal Carlino because except possibly when Mrs. Patterson had to call him after work about some pressing problem at the plant, Pop really hadn't dealt with business anymore once he came home to spend the evening with me. "So," he went on, reaching into his pocket and brandishing a couple of tickets, "so—tomorrow night. It's time you and me saw a real big league baseball game together."

"Oh, Pop, great! And we're playing the Indians, and they're in first place."

Happily, he threw an arm around me, but just at that instant: boom! We heard this huge explosion coming from out front, and it surprised and frightened me so, that as much as it embarrassed me, I fell against Pop so that he held me to him, pulling me close with the arm he already had around me.

"What the hell?" he said. We froze. Then we heard laughter and a crash, glass tinkling, shouts, and at last, the long wail of a car horn, uninterrupted.

Still, over that, a voice came through clear, "Hey, subdivision!

35

Go fuck yourself, subdivision."

With that, Pop gently pushed me away from him. "Don't worry now. I know these kinds of gutless bastards," he muttered. He took a couple steps toward the noise around the front of the house. "You stay here, Christy," he told me, then purposefully jogged off toward the front of the house. The horn kept on blowing.

I waited for a moment, then dashed after my father, pausing at the corner of the house to watch. He was heading right toward a car that was idling in the street in front of our house. The street light there had been busted—by rocks, I guess, or a well-aimed beer bottle—but the car's lights were on. I could make out that it was a Chevy, slung low with mud guards and a fox tail on the antenna. I could also see a couple boys standing in front of it and a couple more inside, but it took me a while before I realized that the horn that was blowing didn't come from the car in the street, but from our car parked in the driveway.

One of the vandals yelled, "Look out!" when he spied Pop approaching, but the two boys in front only held their ground, laughing mockingly at Pop.

"Hey, subdivision daddio," the larger one yelled.

Pop used some discretion, pausing a fair distance of ground from the intruders. But he minced no words. "You goddamn sonsofbitches, get out of here."

"Ohhhh, listen to the subdivision daddio. He's mad," the big kid said. He was obviously the leader, but all of them were dressed the same in motorcycle chic get-up: jeans, white T-shirts (with cigarette packs in their sleeves), and long greasy duck-tail haircuts.

The horn from our car kept blaring. The leader stepped up toward Pop, and the boy on his flank followed forward, if a half-step behind.

Pop stood his ground. "Get your asses outta here, or I'm callin' the cops," he said. He was remarkably calm and forceful. He put his hands on his hips and glared at them. Me, even over in the shadows, I was scared to death.

Pop didn't see the third boy. He had been over at the mailbox, preparing to blow it up with a cherry bomb. Only at the last did I spot him circling behind Pop, sneaking up. Pop kept looking ahead, facing the two boys before him. It was hard to hear anything with our horn blowing. I started to scream a warning. But the words stuck in my throat. I started to run to Pop, but my feet stuck to the ground.

The two boys standing in front of Pop certainly saw their buddy, though. They laughed at Pop, interspersing "Daddio" and "subdivision" and a lot of "fuck yous." The third boy kneeled on all fours right behind Pop. He never saw it coming. The oldest, silliest kid trick. The two boys in front of Pop stepped right up to him, but he held his place. Although he threw up his hands at the last moment thinking they were going to swing at him, the larger boy had only to jerk out his hands, pushing Pop in the chest, sending him tumbling backward over the boy behind.

He wasn't hurt. I could tell that. But he looked so foolish. The one boy scrambled to his feet and stood there with the other two, just laughing. Then the leader said, "Go on, light it," and the third boy dashed back over to the mailbox, took out a Zippo, and lit the fuse. Then he, like the other two, ran to the car and piled in.

They were patching out, throwing the finger, and shouting more "fuck you" variations at Pop when the cherry bomb went off in the mailbox. The smoke blew out of the front, the explosion collapsing and twisting the metal. Pop turned away, covering his face, and then slowly, as he realized that the only damage had been done to the mailbox, he rose up from the ground, dusting himself off.

Only then, finally, did I run over to him. "You okay, Pop?"

"Just my pride hurt, Christy. I shoulda seen it coming. I shoulda hit that bastard first."

"There was too many of 'em, Pop."

"No, I know those creeps. Drapes. J.D.s." Drapes was the Baltimore word for J.D.s—especially J.D.s with long hair. J.D.s meant juvenile delinquents. "I've seen that type all my life. School. In the service. Down at the plant. Cowards. Bullies. Hit one, all the others would've turned tail. I'm just sorry the goddamn drapes made me look like a jackass in front of my boy."

"They didn't, Pop. You were really brave."

He smiled at that and rapped me on the bicep. "Yeah, 'til I got knocked on my keister. Come on, let's get the horn."

We walked over to our car—it was a maroon DeSoto—threw open the front door, and yanked out the supple green branch that had been fit over and under the steering wheel so that it held the horn down—"sticking it" in the vernacular of the Baltimore J.D.s.

"You gonna call the police?" I asked.

"No. I didn't get their license number. And they're outta here by now. Anyway, they won't be back."

"They won't?"

"Oh, no, I told you, Christy. I know this kind. They got their kicks, picking on us just because we're new and moved in here. Judas Priest, you'd think people around here would be happy to see new houses going up. That's progress, Christy. That's good old American progress."

"They kinda like things the way they've always been around here," I said.

"Well, whatever, we've seen the last of these drapes. They'll find somebody else to torment now." He took out a cigarette and lit it, surveying the scene. "But don't you mention this to your mother."

"Oh no, sir."

"It'll only upset her. Now we're not gonna lie to her. We're just not gonna mention it. Okay?"

"Yes, sir. I promise. Just like I haven't said anything about Kathryn's pool, either."

"Right. Bannister word of honor. We'll just keep this to our-selves."

We locked the door to the car then, and the next day, Pop ordered a new mailbox—but a different model, the kind that goes up on the porch, flush against the wall, right by the front door, where it wouldn't make a target. Just in case.

# 6

What Buddy liked to do was dunk me and hold me under. He enjoyed doing that to just about everybody, but once the fresh meat from the subdivision arrived, he concentrated all his bullying in my direction. Buddy was cleverly evil; he'd make sure Kathryn or the mother(s) in charge were looking the other way. Then he'd grab me and hold me under just a millisecond short of my expiring. Buddy had an absolutely uncanny knowledge of gauging precisely how much every swimmer at Kathryn's pool could endure under water.

Then, no matter what you might say in protest, he would smirk and reply, "That's what she said." It was an expression he'd picked up from some real shoe older guy. You were supposed to say it— suavely, knowingly—when somebody said something that could be twisted to mean something any typical female and/or run-of-the-mill nymphomaniac might say in a sexual context. For example, if somebody said, "Put it in," because you had something to go into the car, a real cool guy would say, "That's what she said." Or, if you told a friend who was playing a record you liked, "Don't stop it," he would say, "That's what she said."

But Buddy didn't understand either A) sex, or B) double entendre, so he would offer that clever rejoinder to virtually all statements. Like after he dunked me, I would gasp, "Hey, cut it out, Buddy."

"That's what she said," Buddy replied, smirking, swimming away.

If I talked to Kathryn at all, he would dunk me as soon as I got back in the pool. He called her "the gimp." Honest to God, I hated that worse than the dunking, even though the two invariably came in tandem. "Hey Bannister, talking to the gimp again?" Dunk.

"Come on, Buddy, you almost drowned me."

"That's what she said. Heh-heh."

But then, mercifully, the next Monday, Buddy wasn't at the pool. It wasn't just that he had missed this one morning, either. Hallelujah—he'd gone off with his family to the beach in Delaware for a whole month's vacation. They said "shore" in Baltimore instead of beach—"Buddy's gone down th' shore." But however it was articulated, Buddy had departed Kathryn's pool, and I—we— were freed from torment.

Instantly, too, with Buddy away, both Jake and Timmy became friendlier to me. On my most confident days, I even decided that Jake actually liked me more than he did Timmy, only they were classmates and I understood the protocol. Jake couldn't *act* that friendly to the strange new boy from the subdivision.

That Friday, we were playing our favorite game, which consisted of jumping off the diving board, catching a rubber ball one of the other players threw, and then trying to throw the ball into an inner tube floating in the pool before you hit the water. Kathryn whistled, and immediately, we all scrambled out of the water and ran to her. But as it happened, she had whistled just as my last toss landed square in the inner tube, putting me a point ahead in the competition. Immediately, Timmy announced, "That didn't count because Kathryn whistled."

"Yeah," I protested, "but I was already in the air. Jake had already thrown the ball. You get to finish the play. Like if the quarterback throws a pass just before the game ends, you can still catch it even after the clock runs out."

"Look, this isn't the Colts. This is Kathryn's pool."

I was furious. I felt absolutely cheated. So I put it on the line. I turned to Jake for his opinion. He ducked his head and hemmed and hawed, but finally, he delivered himself of an absolutely rational decision. "It counts, Timmy," he declared. "The play had already started."

Timmy stuck out his chin and pouted. "Hey, whose side are you on?" he asked.

Jake said, "Look, I'm just trying to be fair."

Myself, I didn't respond in any way because I appreciated how tough it had been for Jake to come out openly in favor of me over his old pal, Timmy. I just ran over to where all the kids were gathering around Kathryn. She whistled again for a couple of stragglers, and as soon as they got there, she nodded her head to Lavinia. She started handing out envelopes.

When I saw that the others were ripping them open, I tore into mine and examined the card there. It was very fancy, inscribed, some sort of invitation:

*5th Annual*
*MARINES DAY*
*Kathryn's Pool*
*Noon Sharp,*
*Sunday, September 5, 1954*
*RSVP: TUxedo 5288*

Kathryn twisted her head and saw my puzzlement. "You'll be here, won't you, Christy? Your whole family. They'll all be in Baltimore by then."

"Well, yeah, but what is it...exactly?"

"You never heard?" Timmy asked. "You never heard about Marines Day?"

"It's a family party. Always the Sunday of Labor Day weekend," Kathryn explained. "The last time the pool is open in the summer."

"It's really neat, Christy," Jake said, and all the other kids murmured their approval, too. "All of us do the cooking and everything. To thank the Slades. And there's games and stuff for everybody."

Kathryn went on to explain further. Her older brother, Patrick, had christened the party its first year because he noted that the impromptu competitions just happened to be on land, sea, and air, just as it was in the marines. Patrick's father, Judge Slade, had been a big marine in the war. So after that, it officially became Marines Day—an instant tradition.

"Like what sort of games?" I asked.

"Well," Kathryn said, "the land part is egg toss and three-legged sack races—mothers and little children."

"My mommy and I won the race last year," a little girl named Millie popped up. It was easy to tell how excited everybody was just thinking about Marines Day.

"And the air is diving," Jake went on. "The best is biggest cannonball—that's mostly the fathers."

"The fattest ones always win," a little boy named Ernest giggled.

"The best jacknife is for anybody," Timmy said.

"I'm the judge," Kathryn declared. "I'm the only judge for each and every event."

"And so what's the sea?" I asked.

"Races in the pool," she replied. "The feature attraction is a terrific race just for you older boys—a medley."

"What's a melody race?" I stupidly inquired. I thought maybe it was some sort of trick event where you had to sing something while you swam. Everybody snickered. Thank God Buddy wasn't here.

"Not melody," Timmy sneered. "*Medley.*"

"A medley is a combination race," Kathryn explained. "You have to swim four different ways: freestyle and backstroke and breaststroke and underwater. You'll be in that, Christy. It's called the Great Medley."

Everybody looked at me. "I don't know," I said.

"You have to do *something*," Timmy snapped. "Everybody who comes to Marines Day has to go into *some*thing."

"He's right," Kathryn said. "And you're too old for stuff like the egg toss, and you're too small to do a good cannonball. Can you jacknife?"

She knew I could barely dive in from the side of the pool. I shook my head. Timmy snorted.

"Then you'll be in the medley," Kathryn pronounced. "Okay now, everybody, get those invitations to your parents and mark down September 5th."

All the kids rushed away back to the pool, the mothers returned to the shade and their cigarettes. I started off, too, but Kathryn called after me. I turned back to her. "Don't worry about this," she said. "It's mostly just fun. You should see my father do the cannonball."

"The judge? His Honor does cannonballs?"

Kathryn smiled and nodded. "It's fun. You'll be just fine."

"Yeah, but still, I'm such a slow swimmer."

"Well, Buddy won the Great Medley the last couple years, so you're no worse than Jake or Timmy." That was meant to be comforting, and I suppose it was in a perverse sort of way, suggesting that I was just another loser. But then Kathryn added, "You know, Christy, you could beat Buddy."

"No way."

"Yeah, you could,"

"I can't even beat Jake. Or Timmy."

"No, I've watched you. It's just that nobody's ever taught you how to swim. I don't even know how in the world you got that Red Cross Junior Lifesaving certificate." Boy, that was the truth. "But, Christy—"

"Yeah?"

"I could teach you."

"You?"

"You don't need arms and legs to *teach* somebody."

I looked her straight in the eyes. "I know that."

"Christy, you and me can beat Buddy. Come on, he's such a pain."

I smiled. So she knew. "Tell me about it," I said.

"Come on, Christy. I'd like to race again. I'd like to win again."

I wanted to say yes right then, but I was scared. I was afraid of trying and failing, of looking like a fool before lots of people, my father included. So I put her off. "Lemme think about it. Don't rush me." I started away.

"Christy..." When I turned back, she had this huge grin on her face. And then she yanked her head for me to come closer. As soon as I did, she whispered, "That's what she said." Then she winked. I just shook my head at her. Damn that Kathryn. She knew everything.

I went back over to the pool and jumped in. Jake swam toward me. "Hey, whaddya talk to her about?" he asked.

"Oh, I dunno. We just...talk."

"You talk to Kathryn more than anybody. I mean, you even talk to her more than the mothers do sometimes."

"She's just good to talk to. Anyway, for a girl."

"It's hard for me to talk to her," Jake went on. "Maybe it's because I remember Kathryn when she wasn't crippled."

"You do?"

"Sure. You know, my parents and her parents are real good friends. Hey, we live right over there." He nodded toward the Brothers's house, which was catty-cornered through Herbert's garden. "We used to all go up to Squam Lake together—you know, before Kathryn got her polio."

"Where's that?"

"New Hampshire. The summer she got it it was right before we were supposed to go up there with the Slades. And my parents were so scared because it was that summer my brother started taking Kathryn out."

"Your brother?"

"My real big brother. Doug. Then there's Eddie, and then me. Everybody always says we're the Brothers brothers, which I hate."

"Yeah."

"So Doug was takin' her out that summer. I mean, Kathryn was all around our house and everything. And he was kissing her. And feelin' her up, too, I think."

"Oh," I said, trying to visualize that. It wasn't easy. I'd never quite thought of Kathryn having breasts before, and now here I was suddenly being asked to not only conjure up the image of them, but also of Jake's brother's hands swarming all over them.

"But Doug didn't get polio from her," Jake went on. "Nobody else did." And suddenly then, he dove under the water. He was obviously very uncomfortable talking about Kathryn, and he swam away, only coming up for air way down in the deep end. But I wouldn't let Jake get off the hook that easily. I was fascinated. I swam after him as fast as I could and confronted him under the diving board while he was still catching his breath.

"What was she like? Really?"

"You mean...before...?"

"Yeah."

"Why ya wanna know all this?"

"I just do." I swallowed hard. "All right, because I like Kathryn, that's why."

Jake considered that. He swam over to the side of the pool and hung there. My forthrightness must have impressed him. When I got over next to him, he said, "All right. She was really pretty."

"She's still pretty."

That took me over the line, and Jake wrinkled his nose. "Come on. In that *thing*? I can hardly look at her. Just her head sticking out."

"Well, that's what I mean. Kathryn's got a pretty head. You know, a pretty face."

"Yeah, well, I still don't like to look at her now. But"—he paused for a moment—"you shoulda seen her, Christy. I mean, Kathryn was *really* somethin.' For a girl. She could dive really good, and she could beat a lot of boys at tennis. She couldn't beat Doug, but she could beat Eddie. He was only a couple years younger than Kathryn, but she beat him even if he was a boy. It really P.O.'d Eddie. One year, too, Kathryn caught the biggest fish of anybody on the lake that whole summer."

"No shit," I said.

"No shit. All the old men tried to catch the biggest fish because they put your name up in the dining room on a big board in gold letters. And here comes this kid—this *girl*—and she catches this gigantic bass."

"They put her name up in gold letters?"

"You bet they did."

"No shit."

"No shit. And you know what else Kathryn could do?" I shook my head. "She could really dance. Up at Squam Lake everybody wanted to dance with Kathryn. She was one great jitterbug. You shoulda seen her shag." Jake stopped dead. "Hey, you wanna *see* her?" he asked me.

"See her what?"

"See her before she had polio."

I didn't get it. "Like whaddya mean?"

"Like we got home movies my father took. You wanna see Kathryn in the home movies?"

"Yeah, all right, I guess," I said, trying to be cool, trying not to let on that that possibility absolutely enthralled me: seeing Kathryn when she had a whole body like everybody else.

# 7

We waited until after Timmy's mother came to pick him up, and then I slipped my pants on over my dirt-brown bathing suit, put on my T-shirt, and followed Jake. Even though the Brothers's house was on a different street facing away from Old Florist Avenue, I was surprised how really close it was if you took the back way Jake showed me through Herbert's garden.

Jake's mother was out, but the maid fixed us a peanut-butter-and-bacon sandwich while Jake rooted all around in the basement for the projector and the screen and the film. It was quite a production, threading the film up this way and behind this gizmo and everything, and however you were supposed to do it, Jake couldn't get it straight. So we broke for the sandwiches, wolfing them down with milk and then cookies afterward in the pantry.

Just as we were finishing up, the screen door flew open and a big, good-looking guy came bursting in. He had on work boots and overalls, and he was streaked with sweat and dirt, so I naturally assumed that, us being around here, it must be the gardener. It wasn't, though. It was Jake's brother, Eddie, who was going into his sophomore year at Yale this coming fall. He held up his hands, though, when Jake introduced us. "Don't touch me, Christy," he said. "I'm filthy, and I gotta go right back on the job."

Eddie had gotten construction work for the summer and had just come home on lunch break to pick something up. "Where d'ya live, Christy?" he asked, drinking some milk right out of the bottle.

"Nottingham Valley Estates," I replied, bracing for the usual slighting reply.

But Eddie only answered, "Hey, we might do some work over in the subdivision next month." That was the single most non-judgmental response to revelations of my residence that I had received all summer. I therefore liked Eddie immediately, all the more that he agreed to set the film correctly into the projector. It took him about fifteen seconds.

"What're you guys watching?" he asked.

Jake said, "Christy just met Kathryn this summer, and he wanted to know what she looked like—"

"—before she got polio," Eddie said, finishing the sentence. "Well, I'll tell you, Christy, not bad. Not bad at all. Nice ass and great—I mean great—bazooms." He cupped his hands up by his chest. "Doug was the authority on that subject, though. Doug—" He stopped. "You know Doug?" I shook my head. "Doug's our older brother. And he was going out with Kathryn right before.... I'll tell you, too, old Dougie was some crazy about Kathryn. I mean ca-razy, with a capital K. He'd known Kathryn all his life, you see—she's almost next door, went to Squam Lake with us, everything, but he was two, three years older, and so she'd always been like a kid to him.

"But that spring, Doug goes to a deb party, and there is Kathryn Slade because she's coming out that year—and he doesn't even recognize her. It's like: where has this been all my life? He was going with some dame from Briarcliff, he's been hot and heavy, dating her the whole year. He's all worked up because he finally thinks he's gonna get in the Briarcliff babe's drawers, but bingo, just like that, he sees Kathryn and to hell with the guaranteed poon-tang. It was Kathryn Slade from that moment on. You remember that, Jakey?"

Jake nodded. Me, I was enthralled. I'd had a lot of first-hand experience dealing with older guys because they'd always been sniffing around Sue, but Eddie Brothers put them all to shame. He spoke cool, he acted cool, he looked cool. Why did I get stuck with a damn pain for an older sister, when here was Jake with a fabulous older brother? Eddie slapped me on the shoulder. "Well, I gotta get back to work, Christy, or my ass'll be grass," he said. "Maybe I'll see you over at the subdivision." And boom, just like that, he was gone out the door. It was as if a warm, benign summer storm had blown through the house. Eddie Brothers was so neat.

"God, he's so neat," I told Jake.

"He's okay," Jake replied, which we both understood constituted in code high praise indeed from a younger brother.

"Where's Doug now?"

"He's still around." This didn't mean Jake was being evasive; it meant he just didn't much care. So I approached it from the only angle that mattered to me anyway.

"Well, I mean like what happened to him with Kathryn after...?"

Jake shrugged. "You know, he just went back to college that fall. To Amherst. There wasn't anything else Doug could do...for her."

"No."

"Doug's married now. He married Pam. They've even got a little kid. A lot of people don't know it, but I'm an uncle."

"No shit."

Pleased at how impressed I was, Jake instructed me to close the blinds, and then he turned on the projector. There was a lot of fluttering noise, some very bright light, and then, incredibly, there was an expanse of pine trees and water, which I took (correctly) to be Squam Lake. "Good," said Jake, settling back. "I picked out the right reel. This was the first one, right after Daddy bought the camera."

Uh-oh. Mr. Brothers had obviously never seen his handiwork on the screen before he took these shots, and so the camera darted all around, rushing about so quickly that it was hard to make out much of anything except the pine trees. Even worse, the pioneer home movie technology required bright sunshine, so there would be long, pitch-black stretches when you couldn't see anything at all except maybe for the tips of everybody's lighted cigarettes.

But there were some serviceable patches in sunlight. "That's Grandpa," Jake exclaimed as a portly gentleman in a fedora set out grandly in a rowboat in search of unsuspecting bass.

"Was this the year Kathryn caught the biggest fish in the whole lake?"

"Naw, I think that was the next summer," Jake replied. "But don't worry, I got that on another film." So on we went. There was a cocktail party out on the veranda in which Jake made his first appearance. "There I am now," he informed me—all dolled up in a sailor suit, on display for some guests. And then more pine trees, another dark stretch, and shooting directly into the sun, what appeared to be a very posh gathering. "There!" Jake cried out.

"There what?"

"There was Kathryn. In the white dress. Oh, she's gone now. Didn't you see her?"

"Yeah, I think I caught a glimpse," I replied—although, of course, I hadn't. "Run it back, Jake. Run it back."

"Unh-uh, I better not try that. I'm not really good at this."

So on we plunged with Mr. Brothers's first stab at cinema. Laughing, Grandpa held up a minnow he'd snared. Pine trees. Clouds. A trek up a mountain. "There's me again!" Jake cried out. It was. I guess. A vista, apparently looking down to the lake from the mountain. Pine trees. And then, unmistakably this time, there was Kathryn.

I saw her right away. It was easy. We'd been suddenly jerked to a tennis court. Incredibly, the segment actually started out quite professionally, moving in on a close-up at the net: a young boy who made faces standing next to a girl with a forced smile that was framed by that glorious auburn hair that I knew so well. "There, you see," Jake announced proudly. "There. That's Kathryn and Eddie."

"I know," I said softly.

But Mr. Brothers didn't give us much time to linger, and quickly, the nice close-up was gone. Kathryn and Eddie were playing singles. It was difficult to tell who might have held the upper hand, though, because an inordinate amount of the footage was devoted to watching one or the other of the players from the rear as they headed away into the distance to fetch errant balls.

But then there was a pause, and then Kathryn appeared, a portrait, full and lovely, as she prepared to serve. She wore a shirt and shorts—after Alice Marble, I believe it was—tossing the ball up, reaching for it, then striding, gliding on the clay, stretching out full to hit a wide forehand back to Eddie. I caught my breath. There was Kathryn Slade. There she was, moving. And she was perfectly beautiful, you know?

Oh yes, coltish still with angled parts that didn't quite seem to fit because they needed curves to join them just so. The grace was already there, though, all the moves and the manner.

But then the camera shifted to Eddie—after all, he was the cameraman's flesh and blood—and quickly enough, the tennis sequence was over. There were more pine trees and then some grown-ups standing around, not knowing what to do with their hands and pretending to chat "for the camera." For some reason, this segment was exquisitely photographed in perfect light and went on and on.

"How old was she then?" I asked Jake.

"Let's see. It was right after the war when Daddy got the camera. Nineteen forty-six. So I was, uh, six. So it's been eight years. How old is Kathryn now?"

"Twenty-three, I think."

"So, she was...fifteen," Jake calculated, and while I don't know whether it also occurred to him, that meant that the Kathryn in the film was just about our age right now. It was as if Kathryn could be my girlfriend. If I would ever have the nerve to talk to a girl. If she would deign to have me as a boyfriend. But I certainly didn't point that out to Jake. Instead, I played the discerning connoisseur. "She hasn't got such big bazooms," I declared.

On the film, somebody showed up in a new Packard and there was much fussing over the shiny automobile. There were some new faces, too. And a cocker spaniel. Jake waited to see if he was in the scene, and when he was not, he replied, "That was later Kathryn got the big bazooms. Eddie wasn't kidding, okay? I'll show 'em to you in the film from the next summer."

The Packard drove off and there was one more stretch when all you could make out were the cigarette tips. Then, just as quickly, it was dazzling sunshine and there was Eddie diving into the lake. A race from the float to the dock followed. Much splashing. When the kids climbed out, Eddie came first claiming victory, and then

Kathryn followed, shaking her head as she hoisted herself up the ladder and onto the deck. She was wearing a cream panel bathing suit with scarlet trim. I couldn't take my eyes from her—every line, every swell, every nuance.

After Eddie confronted his father's camera, making faces, Kathryn stepped forward too, mugging for a moment. But then, instantly, the kid disappeared and the pretty girl took her place. She relaxed and smiled softly—she *posed*—drawing her wet hair back from her face, staring long and sweetly at the camera, looking into it, and looking at a boy named Christy whom she didn't know would be gazing at her come 1954 when he had almost caught up with her in age.

But, enough of that. Right away, there were more hijinks on the dock, the boys trying to toss the girls into the lake. Jake appeared in an orange life preserver—"There I am again!"—and Doug hoisted him up on his shoulders and jumped into the water with him, paddling over to where Grandpa was floating about in a king-sized inner tube, puffing on a cigar. The camera zoomed, zig-zag, up to a high platform where suddenly Doug materialized anew, diving off.

Then, there: Kathryn again, poised on that platform. This time, Mr. Brothers kept his camera on her, addressing her whole body from her long legs up the slim, tanned figure in the neat panel suit, the summer sun throwing even more red off her auburn hair, and her staring dead ahead the whole time, concentrating, waiting for the diver's inner spirit to propel her forward. Now. I saw it now. A bit of a proud, sly smile as she started, taking the one small step and then the three longer ones exactly to the edge of the platform. She sprang. Just after Kathryn catapulted herself up into the blue sky, opening her arms full wide in a perfectly executed swan dive, the film ran out, and it all went bright, searing white.

Jake couldn't figure out how to get another reel threaded, but honestly, I wasn't even sure I wanted to see the older Kathryn with the more spectacular bazooms. I liked having only the one active vision of her when she was my age, my own dream girl.

And so I left the Brothers's house and retraced the shortcut through the back to the Slades,' where I could pick up my bicycle and start off delivering my *News-Posts* for the day. Suddenly, though, as I passed by Kathryn's pool, empty now of swimmers, I heard Lavinia call out, "Mr. Christy! Mr. Christy!" I peered all around, finally spying her up in Kathryn's window on the second story of the house.

The window had been cut especially low and large in the wall, affording Kathryn a wider, unobstructed view of that world of hers by the pool. Her face appeared now as Lavinia wheeled her flush to the window. "Hey, handsome, where ya goin'?" she cried out.

"I was just over at Jake's...having lunch." I certainly couldn't tell her that I'd been watching old movies of her. As I looked up at her, though, I couldn't help but visualize that image of her on the high dive, as if suddenly she was going to spread her arms and dive out the window to me. "But, Kathryn—"

"Yeah?"

"I've thought about it like I said I would, and yeah, I'd like you to help me swim better. You know, for the Great Medley."

"Well, awayyy we go," she shouted like Jackie Gleason on TV. "Be ready to start working tomorrow."

So, that's how Kathryn became my coach.

# 8

Mom would call long distance every few nights and put Sue and Hughie on. But first she'd always ask me if I was making any friends. It was just too complicated to tell her that I did have a friend, only she was twenty-three, a girl, and she was a quadriplegic. So I just told her Jake was my friend, and maybe he really was—only he was going off to summer camp soon for a whole month, so he really wasn't any good to me as a friend.

Actually, Pop and I became real good friends. When he came home from work, we'd chuck a baseball around together, or he'd let me try and drive the DeSoto stick-shift around Dogwood Circle because, of course, there weren't any other cars. Once we went out to a drive-in movie theater, and another time we went back to see the Orioles play. In the third inning, Pop speared a foul ball that Clint Courtney hit. It was a nifty catch. In fact, when Pop's hand shot up and snared that ball, the spectators all around us cheered and screamed, "Sign him up." Boy, was I proud. I think Pop was pretty pleased with himself, too. Although I certainly never brought it up, he might've still been smarting some that I'd seen him knocked on his keister by the drapes.

I placed the ball prominently on a shelf in my room, carefully inscribing it: "FOUL BALL/caught by Pop/July 23, 1954." My father kept suggesting that I go down to Memorial Stadium and hang around, and maybe I could get Clint Courtney to autograph the ball himself. He was as popular a player as the poor Orioles could boast that summer, always called "grizzled" and known as Ol' Scrap Iron (even though he wasn't but about twenty-six or –seven). But I just told Pop, no, I didn't want to bother. "You're too shy, Christy," he replied.

The real reason, though, was that I didn't think of that ball as the one Ol' Scrap Iron hit. I thought of it as the one my father caught.

Then one evening, a few days after Pop caught the foul ball, he called me from the plant just before he was supposed to come home and told me he was sorry, but something important had just come up and he was going to be late. This was really okay with me because it meant I could have a TV dinner and then go up to my room and hear Chuck Thompson broadcast the Orioles game against the Philadelphia A's. That was the one team we could expect to beat, and Bob Turley, our best pitcher, was on the mound. "Go to war, Miss Agnes," Chuck Thompson said when Ol' Scrap Iron hit a three-run homer. "Ain't the beer cold?"

That was when I heard the explosion. Right away, I knew what it must be. Pop had been wrong. The drapes had come back after all. We were such easy pickin's, I guess. I didn't know what to do. Sure, I was scared, but I wasn't petrified. After all, this was before the Manson family, before mass murderers ran amok. J.D.s were just delinquent; they weren't violent. I don't even remember much talk about "violence" then. So, I went to my window and peeked out.

There were three of them out by the streetlight, tossing stuff up, trying to break it again. Apparently, they were emboldened. Since there was no car in the driveway, they'd obviously assumed no one was home. They'd gone right up on the front porch, blown up the new mailbox, and still hadn't heard a peep from inside.

Okay, I would take advantage of this. I remembered Pop talking about how he hadn't spotted their license number last time. So, I'd sneak out and get it now while they were still preoccupied with trying to break the streetlamp. I crept downstairs and made my way out the back door, coming 'round the side of the house. The drapes weren't even looking toward the house, so intent were they on breaking the streetlamp. But their aim was no match for their bravado.

I ducked over, out of our property, coming toward the street by way of the next lot. I was protected fairly well by some trees and shrubbery. I could peek out, see the drapes by the streetlight, then duck from one tree to another. Like I'd seen the commandos in movies. And suddenly, the low-slung Chevy with the mudguards and foxtail loomed ahead. Only it was parked sideways to me. I'd have to circle behind it to see the license plate.

I waited to make my final dash from behind the last bush and took off. I was in midflight when I heard it. Crash. Tinkle. One of the vandals had finally hit the light. In an instant, it was pitch dark. Then—wouldn't you know it?—the half-moon came out from behind a cloud just as the drapes turned back toward their car, and there I was, caught dead in their sights.

All three of them saw me at once, all cried out, and all took after me in an instant. I turned back toward the lot, hoping I might find some hiding place, but even though I tried to fool them by running away from the house, it was hopeless. In the moonlight, I never got out of their sight. The fastest one of them tackled me, and they dragged me back toward the street.

"Where'd you come from?" the one asked. I recognized him as the ringleader, the guy who had pushed Pop over.

"It's my house," I said with as much bluster as I could manage.

"You fucking subdivision," the drape who had tackled me said.

"What do you care?" I asked.

"We don't need all you new people coming in," he said, and the other drapes nodded. It was obvious they didn't really give a hoot about the subdivision. They were just typical J.D.s looking for mischief, and we were fresh meat and a terrific target, off the beaten track, all alone.

"Lemme go, then." I struggled for effect, and for effect, the two guys holding me tightened their grasp.

The leader pondered his next move. The other two awaited his decision. "Tell you what, we'll take him for a little ride. Cholly, open the trunk." He reached into his pocket and handed his accomplice the car keys.

That's when I lost it. Put me in the trunk! I've always been terribly claustrophobic. I'd've rather they punched me, kicked me, left me for dead by the side of the road. At least I'd've been by the side of the road. "Aw, no, c'mon, not inna trunk," I cried out. The terror in my voice must have been obvious. That only delighted them more.

"Yeah," the leader said. "A little ride in the trunk will be just right."

Panicky, I began to resist with all my might, digging in my heels, swinging my shoulders, trying to get loose even if I knew it was hopeless. At least it delayed Cholly from going ahead to open the trunk. He had to stay back to help restrain me. "Please, no," I cried out. "Please don't do that." In another instant I was going to cry.

That's when the headlights hit me, coming round the bend in Dogwood Circle. Oh, thank God—Pop had come home to save me in the nick of time.

"Get him outta the way," the leader said, and they all yanked me over to the side of the road and ducked down. But it was too late. Pop had seen me. His car pulled up alongside the Chevy, keeping us square in his high beams. The door opened. Pop got out.

Only, even with the light shining in my eyes, I could tell right away it wasn't Pop. The man was much smaller, and when he spoke it was no Hoosier talking, but someone obviously born and bred in these environs. The dialect was unmistakably the ugly local nasal twang known simply as "the Balamer accent."

"What's goin' on?" the voice said.

"It's our business," the leader replied. "Just go on your way, mister."

Luckily, the drapes hadn't thought to muzzle me. "Help," I managed to cry out, "help me—" before Cholly placed his hand over my mouth.

But it was enough. "You fellas, let him go," the man said.

"You stay outta this, daddio," the leader called back. "We don't wanna hurt you."

But the little man wasn't intimidated. "Don't give me that 'daddio' jive bullshit," he said, louder now. "I'm tellin' you now, let him go, now."

"Make us, cocksucker," snapped the leader.

The little man didn't respond. I only saw him open his back door, reach in, and pull something out. He held it up. It was some sort of pipe.

"Oh, you wanna fight, daddio?" the leader said.

"No, you drapes ain't worth my time fightin.' But this car o' yours—it's worth fightin.' Now, let that young man go, or me and your car are gonna tussle."

I could feel the two guys holding me loosen their grip as they tried to ponder what the hell the little man was talking about. They looked to their leader, but he was just as confounded.

"I'm tellin' ya," the little man called out, "for the last time, fellas, let him go."

But they didn't know how to respond. They just stood there holding on to me, waiting. What we saw then was the little man lift up his pipe and bring it down hard onto the hood. The noise was resounding. Even from our distance, we knew there had to be some damage.

"Hey, that's my car!" the leader cried out.

"I know that," said the man—cool as a cucumber. "That's why I hit it. Now hand the kid over."

This time, the drapes were just frozen in amazement. They only stared at the little vigilante, incapable of really comprehending what he was doing—and certainly unable to react. The man waited. But this time when they didn't respond, he gave them no more ultimatums. He simply stepped forward, raised the pipe, and brought it down flush upon the right headlight. It shattered magnificently.

"Now ya got a padiddle," the little man said, his nasal tone actually cut with a bit of humor. A padiddle was what we called a car that had only one light shining. If you were with a girl and you passed a padiddle, you could kiss her if you screamed out "padiddle" before she did—not that I had ever personally participated in this romantic caper, you understand. "And if you don't let him go, your car is goin' to be missin' a windshield, too."

Finally, the leader was able to regain his faculties—just as the little man raised his pipe again. "Stop!" the leader screamed. The man held his position, the pipe poised over the windshield. "Let the kid go," the leader said, beaten.

As soon as I felt their grip had relaxed, I tore away, running toward my savior. "Get inna car," he whispered to me, holding his menacing position, pipe on high. "Don't you come after us now, or I'll get the *police* after you," he shouted at the drapes. Then as soon as he saw me get into the front seat, he ducked back in himself behind the steering wheel, closed the door, and gunned the car away past the three drapes, who still just stood there, jaws agape, looking stupidly after us. In fact, they looked even more foolish than Pop had when they'd knocked him over. That gave me a special satisfaction.

The little man drove the car around to where Dogwood Circle came out on the main road, Charles Street. "You're probably Christy, aren't you?"

"Yes, sir. Thank you."

He turned and smiled at me at the stop sign there. "Well, son, my name's Sal Carlino. I work down your father's plant."

"Oh yeah, Mr. Carlino. I can't thank you enough," I said. And then, just as he moved the car on, I lost it. The tears began to pour out of me—great wracking sobs. Mr. Carlino pulled the car over, handed me his handkerchief, and let me cry it out.

"I don't blame you, Christy," he said. "There's no shame in cryin' after a thing like that." I nodded, sniffling now. "Come on now, I'll get you a soda, and then I'll take you back home. Don't worry, those drapes won't bother you none again."

He drove me over to the York Road where there was a Toddle House, and we sat down at the counter. In the lights of the diner, I could finally really see Mr. Carlino. He was little, too—way smaller than any of the drapes. He had a pencil mustache and very slick hair. He was wearing a short-sleeved shirt with a maroon tie, and he had lots of pens and pencils in his breast pocket. Also, I had never seen anyone with as big a key chain as he had at his belt. He wore it with the buckle over to the side.

After he ordered me an RC and himself a coffee, he said, "I was gonna apologize to your father for coming by to bother him at home. I knew it was outta place, but I've got somethin' on my mind, Christy, and I wanted to talk to him away from the plant, wheres we could have some peace and quiet."

"I'm awful glad you came by, sir. You really saved me."

"So where is your dad?"

"He's still workin' down at the plant."

Mr. Carlino blew on his coffee. He mulled that over, puzzled. "Oh? I was down there myself, and I didn't see him in his office. That's when I come out to your home."

"He musta been in someone else's office."

"Yeah. Musta," Mr. Carlino said, and then he stood up and went to the phone that was on the wall behind us. "Before it leaves my mind," he explained, popping in a nickel and dialing.

"Joey," he said, "it's Sal. Sorry to bother you late, but I got a number to run by you. Six-one-seven-three-one-one. It's onna Chevy, forty-eight or nine, I think. Just call me tomorrow whenever you get a chance."

He plopped back next to me. "Don't worry, we'll take care of them guys. That's my buddy down at the DMV. He's gonna let me know who that car is registered to, and then I'll be makin' a little phone call. After that drape or his parents hear from me, you can be sure they won't be giving you no more trouble."

"I really can't thank you enough, Mr. Carlino."

"Well, son, I'm some pissed off—pardon my French—at how Balamer is treatin' you folks." I assured him that apart from the drapes, everybody in my new hometown couldn't be nicer, and that pleased him. "Your father is the best thing ever happened to Gardco, and I don't want nobody upsettin' that apple cart."

"Well, Mr. Carlino, Pop thinks you're a honey of a guy," I said. I didn't think that was out of line to repeat that—especially since Sal Carlino had saved me from being put in a car trunk, which was pretty much, for me, a fate worse than death.

I was already back in bed listening to the last inning of the Orioles-A's game when Pop came in. I could hear him tip-toeing up the stairs, but when he heard the radio on, he peeked into my room. "Sorry I was so late," he said. "See you tomorrow."

It was funny how quick he was with me. Usually, he'd come in and we'd talk a while, and he'd kiss me good-night. But this time, he almost had the door closed before I called after him. He came back in, and I told him about all the things that had happened.

"Oh my God, Christy," he said, reaching down and pulling me up to him, holding me tight, rocking me in his arms. "You coulda been killed."

"Nah, I don't think so, Pop."

But even when he let me go then, he remained distraught, holding his head in his hands, and just saying, "Oh my God, oh my God, what did I do?" over and over. Finally, he sat up and looked at me. "I'll never forgive myself, Christy," he said.

"Pop, you couldn't help it that you had to work late."

He stood up. "Yeah, I could, Christy. Yeah, I could."

"But it's business, Pop."

He nodded, but only vacantly. He was looking away from me. "I gotta call Sal," he said suddenly, making for the door.

"Pop?"

"Yeah?"

"Mr. Carlino's okay, isn't he?"

"Whaddya mean okay?"

I wasn't supposed to know that Mr. Gardner wanted to fire Sal Carlino, but after tonight, I had to ask that even if that meant my father could figure out that I was eavesdropping. "I mean, he's got a good job and everything down at Gardco, doesn't he?"

Pop paused at the door. "Christy, Sal Carlino will have a good job at Gardco for as long as he wants it—as long as I am president." He started to close the door, then turned back and pointed a finger at me. "It's the principle of the thing, and you know what I've told you about principles."

"They don't change."

"Absolutely. And so help me God, I promise you: your old man will quit Gardco before any mother's son makes me do anything wrong to *Mr.* Sal Carlino. And you can take that to the bank."

# 9

The next morning, as soon as I came down for breakfast, Pop hugged me. Then, holding me at arm's length by my shoulders, he said, "Hey kiddo, whaddya say you come down to the ocean with your old man this weekend?"

"Really?" Coming from the heartland, I'd never been near an ocean, so that was the best news I'd heard in a month of Sundays. I arranged with Mr. D'Ionfrio to deliver my paper while I was away (which he was delighted to do—Mrs. Slade had browbeaten so many of her friends into purchasing my summer specials that now I was even up for *News-Post* Paperboy of the Summer), and we headed off to Ocean City that Friday.

Pop's plant was on the way to the ferry that took us across the Chesapeake Bay to the shore, so what we did was, I went with him to work that morning so he didn't have to double back to pick me up. I brought some stuff to read, but as I was walking down the hall with Pop to his office, Sal Carlino popped out of his. "Well, son," he said, "you don't look any worse for wear, do you now?"

"No, sir, I'm fine—thanks to you."

"Aw, c'mon," he said, slapping me on the back. "I'll show you 'round the plant." And he took me everywhere, into every Gardco nook and cranny, introducing me to virtually the entire work force, even right on the assembly line. Mr. Carlino never failed to say a nice word about Pop, too. Then, almost every time, he would add, "And lemme tell you, with Christy, the apple don't fall far from the tree." Inasmuch as Mr. Carlino had only seen me in distress and then in tears, I knew he was gilding the lily for my benefit, but it did feel nice, enjoying Pop's reflected glory.

After the tour, Pop still had a little work to finish up, so Mr. Carlino sent out for RC's and two orders of the local delicacy, French fries in gravy. We sat outside on a little bench and devoured them. "Them drapes that come after you," he said after a hefty bite or two. "You don't have to worry none. I got aholt of the one on the phone, and I scared the bejesus outta him. I also talked to a friend o' mine in the *police* department, and told him he's gotta patrol your street now. Just because it's a new subdivision don't mean you ain't a part of the precink like ever'body else. The trouble with Balamer is it's a neighborhood town, which is great, but if you, like, ain't *in* the neighborhood, then you're nowheres. But the subdivision's in the patrol route now."

Mr. Carlino was getting to be like our guardian angel. He also wanted to know all about me, especially what sort of grades I was getting in school. "You keep it up, Christy. I know your father's a college man, but I can't emphasize enough how much an education means for a boy." He pronounced it like the thing in the water, a *buoy*, which threw me off for a moment.

"Yes, sir."

"Don't think I come to work in a shirt and tie from day one."

"No, sir."

"I was just another dumb dago—sixteen when I dropped outta school at Patterson Park, and I was thirty more years workin' in plants. I wouldn'ta never got into the office if it wasn't for the war. So many college men went aways." He polished off the last of his French fries and gravy and lit up a pipe.

"I got two buoys myself," he said, "me and the missus. Salvatore Junior—the oldest—and Vinny, the baby."

"How old is Vinny?"

"Well, he's not a baby anymore. That's just a figger of speech, like. He's our youngest, so we call him the baby. There was the three girls between Junior and Vinny. He's out at Loyola now."

"Oh," I said. I hadn't been in Baltimore long enough to know Loyola was a college.

"I could kill that Junior. He's working down the Point—"

"The Point?"

"Sparrows Point. That's Bethlehem Steel, the biggest plant in Balamer."

"Oh yeah."

"And he gets Vinny a job down there this summer. Good money, Christy. And that's all Vinny can see now. Money in his pocket, get hisself a car, some new clothes, what have you. He's talkin' now about not goin' back to Loyola, stayin' down the Point. I keep tryin' to impress him about the value of a college education, workin' in a shirt and tie, but all he sees is that pay envelope Fridays." Mr. Carlino shook his head. "I b'lieve I could kill Junior for gettin' Vinny that G.D. job."

"Do you think Vinny'll go back to Loyola?"

"Oh yeah, I know he will. If he don't, he gets drafted, right? And as long as I'm payin' his tuition out there, he'll go back. He's a good buoy, Christy. He's got a head on his shoulders. But he's like so many buoys. Alls they can see is a little walkin' around money and a big pair o' tits to spend it on—you know what I mean? I'm not outta line sayin' that to you?"

"Oh, no, sir. I mean, I kinda like big tits, too. Already."

"Yeah, it's natural enough," Mr. Carlino concluded. "But here's the thing, long as I'm payin', Vinny'll finish out Loyola, and then when he goes inna service he can be an officer. A college man and an officer. Won't that be somethin' for an old *paisan* to have in his fambly?"

"Yeah, that's really great, sir."

"Well, alls I need is three more years here at the plant, Christy. I told Mr. Frank that when I hit sixty-five last April. Just gimme them three more years, Mr. Frank, I pay that tuition out Loyola, and that'll keep Vinny's ass outta them plants. Forever." He sighed.

"I'm sure Vinny'll stay, Mr. Carlino," I said. "I'm sure he'll be a college man." I could say that with authority, of course, because Pop had told me that Sal's job was safe for as long as he needed it.

Pop and I left the plant right after lunch and, down in Ocean City, found a little apartment just off the boardwalk. That evening, we tried to eat soft-shell crabs, an experience altogether daunting for erstwhile denizens of Terre Haute. Neither did we handle the surf with any more skill the next day.

"Boy, these waves are pretty intimidating, aren't they?" Pop asked me as we examined them from a safe remove. I nodded, taking another step back prudently. What a couple of midwestern rubes we were; up and down the beach, the body surfers were all bitching about how mild the surf was this day.

"What I'd like to do is come back down here later this summer," I said.

"Yeah, bring the whole family down."

That wasn't my point. "I'll be a better swimmer then. I'm kinda taking swimming lessons now."

"You are?"

"Yeah. Kathryn's teaching me."

"The cripple girl?"

"Pop," I said stoutly, "you don't have to have arms and legs to be able to *teach* something." He hung his head, shamefaced, so I told him all about Marines Day, how he was expected to compete then, too. "You have to do either a jacknife or a cannonball," I advised him. Immediately, he opted for the cannonball. Pop really wasn't much of a marine creature, a fact which was certified momentarily when he did venture out into the surf and was promptly knocked ass-over-teakettle by the first wave of any substance. That sent us both scurrying in retreat to our rented umbrella.

Pop lit a Pall Mall and nursed both his pride and his wounds. Presently, he began an altogether different conversation. "So tell me the truth, Christy, do you think the Bannisters are going to be all right in Baltimore?"

"Well, I don't think we're going to have any more trouble with the drapes, if that's what you mean."

"No, no, I know that. Thanks to Sal. Knock on wood." He rapped the umbrella pole. "But how 'bout your brother and sister?"

"Well, it's going to be hardest for Sue, missing her last year and maybe prom queen and all."

"I *know* that, Christy. We have exhausted that subject."

"Yes, sir." How pleased I was to hear that conclusion.

"Sue will get over it. She'll forget His Nibs fast enough. And she'll find a new boyfriend here. She's awful pretty, you know." I nodded my head (although that was certainly another subject I wished we could exhaust). "It's different with Sue and you. You've got to find friends, Christy. Yourself. That's never been your strong suit, *finding* friends. Now Sue, friends will find her. Fast. And then she'll just love Baltimore."

"Yes, sir."

"And then she'll thank me for making her come to Baltimore."

"Yes, sir."

"And then she'll marry some nice Baltimore boy and settle down and raise kids and Terre Haute will disappear from her mind. Disappear."

"Yes, sir." Life certainly was simple if you had a nice pair of jugs.

That evening after crabcakes and sweet corn, Pop and I did the boardwalk—bumper cars and the Ferris wheel, salt water taffy and cotton candy, even pinball machines and claw machines in an arcade. That's where I beat Pop at Skee-Ball, the first time I ever beat him at anything that he didn't let me win on purpose. Skee-Ball is the game where you roll a little wooden ball down a short bowling alley type-thing to where it comes to a hump and bumps up into a target area full of holes. If you do it exactly right, the ball will pop into the tiny hole in the middle, which is worth fifty points. I hit that bull's-eye several times to whip Pop two out of three. I could tell he was really and truly trying to beat me, even if he was happy when I did win.

It was something of a life-defining moment, me beating Pop at Skee-Ball.

Back out on the boardwalk, he cut over to the sea side, looking out over the beach to where the moon shone down on the water. Ever since, I've always thought the best thing the moon does is shine across water, making a stripe of glimmer. "You know," Pop began with that reminiscing tone of voice older people always affect at moments like these, "the last time I was at the beach—"

"They call it the shore," I interrupted. "Around here, they call the beach the shore."

"Well, they called it the beach where I was. We did. We called it the beach."

"I never knew you went to the beach before."

"It was right before I got shipped over to England, the summer of '43. We were sailing out of New York, and we had a few days, and it was hot as all get-out, so me and some buddies took the train down to Atlantic City. We had enough for one room. That's all. Four of us in one room. But what did we care? We were used to that kind of treatment. From the Depression. And I can remember going out that first night we were there onto the boardwalk. And we looked out over the ocean—just like now, Christy—and somebody said, 'You know, the Krauts'—we called the Germans Krauts then— 'the Krauts could have a U-boat out there right now.'"

"Really?"

"Oh sure, coulda been. The U-boats got one of our ships right off the coast every now and then. But that was the first time I really felt it. Felt scared. Always before, even in training, it was like the war was out there, *somewhere*. But here, when Herbie said that—Herbie Miller it was, and he was one of the ones who'd be killed over there in France, Herbie—when Herbie said that about the Krauts, it suddenly made it seem so much more, uh, vivid."

I not only listened intently, but really, quite respectfully. Pop seldom talked about his war experiences, so I was rapt when he did. It wasn't just the war, either. I was envious of just about everything my mother and father had lived through—good or bad. It was all so much more jam-packed, more historical than my humdrum era. Now my cohorts, the Depression Babies, we just skipped through, falling between the cracks that separated all the major events. We were the 'tweeners of the twentieth century, always too young or too old for the important things. Boy, did we tiptoe through. In fact, I've spent my whole life wondering if I could've managed the times that confronted Pop.

Imagine fighting in a war. Imagine having a buddy, a Herbie Miller, who got killed. Shot, dead. I wanted to ask how it happened, but I could tell Pop had something else he wanted to get at. Sure enough, after he gobbled into his cotton candy, which meant he had to use his hands, too, to jam it all into his mouth, and then licked the sticky stuff off, he went on. "Well, when I looked out there where the U-boats might be, I thought to myself, Bobby, if you get through this war, if Lieutenant Bannister is lucky enough to return home to America, God bless it, first thing he is going to bring his wife to the ocean. You know, your mother—an Indiana girl—she never saw an ocean before either. And I promised myself to bring her to Atlantic City. That was the first thing I was going to do if I got back from the war."

"Well, didja Pop, did you and Mom—"

He leaned on the railing. "Nah."

"Oh."

"Remember, we had Hughie right after the war. And then I just threw myself into Kessler, into the business. I mean, Christy, you had to get into it then. After the war, there was lightning to catch in a bottle. We were the only country in the world that was really cookin' with gas, and it was just incredible. We were working every day, all day. Business was booming, and Hughie was born, and one thing after another, I don't think Atlantic City ever even crossed my mind again...'til right now."

He lit another cigarette, and then, all of a sudden, out loud he said, "All right."

"All right what?" I asked.

"All right, I think you're old enough to know this." So I leaned in closer because whenever I heard anybody say they thought my age qualified me for certain information, I could be pretty certain that it was going to be something dirty. That's the first thing *adult* meant to a kid: dirty. And sure enough, Pop went on. "The fact of the matter is that after we left the boardwalk, we were all going to a whorehouse. One of the guys knew there was a whorehouse on Tennessee Avenue. You know what a whorehouse is?"

"I think so, yeah."

"Well, it's where you pay for a bad woman. That's not a very nice thing, is it Christy?" I dutifully shook my head, although in fact, I was too titillated to have any moral nerves touched. "But sometimes men do these kind of things. Even *married* men. Even when it is clearly against the Ten Commandments. Even married men will go to a whorehouse when they're lonely." He took a long drag. "It's the loneliness that pushes men over the line, Christy."

"So that's why you went to the whorehouse?"

"*Was* going, Christy. Now, I'm not proud of some of the things I've done in my life. I'm not proud that I left you alone at home the other night when the drapes came by."

"But you had to work late, Pop."

"Well, anyway, nobody can be perfect, and all's well that ends well."

"I think you're a pretty good guy, Pop."

"Thanks, kiddo," he said, and he wrapped an arm around me, drawing me closer to him. I think he even might have cried if he weren't a man. "Yeah, I think when Bob Bannister stands before St. Peter, he'll say, well, let him in because there's not a whole lot of flies on him. Some. But not a whole lot. I think he'll say that." I nodded, wholeheartedly endorsing that conclusion. "And don't worry, Christy. The whole point of what I was starting to say is that because I did think of your mother when I looked out and saw where the U-boats might be, because of that, I couldn't go to the whorehouse with Herbie Miller and the other fellows."

"So you *didn't* go?" I'm sure my tone revealed my relief. As much as I reveled in being included in the adult community, I was still a little skitterish about hearing my father talk so frankly. Winning at Skee-Ball had only cracked the door to grown-upville.

"No, Christy. The guys teased me, but I couldn't bring myself. I stayed faithful to your mother."

"Always?"

"I never once went to a whorehouse."

"Never?"

"Never. Anywhere."

Of course, if I had been listening closely, I would've recognized the fine line Pop was drawing with the Bannister word of honor. But I just beamed, thrilled at this benign ending to these raw, real men's confidences. "Well, you ought to feel real good about yourself, Pop."

"Sometimes I do, kiddo. Sometimes I do. Like I sure feel good about bringing you down here with me." He slapped me on the back. "And I promise you, as soon as your mother gets to Baltimore and gets settled, I'm finally gonna keep that promise to myself and bring her down to the beach."

"To the shore," I said.

"Yeah," Pop said. "To the shore."

# 10

Back home, my summer took on a pattern. The days I filled with Kathryn. Timmy had gone off on vacation, too, so I was the only big boy left at the pool. I devised ways to handicap the inner tube game so that I could play fairly with the younger boys. Sometimes, too, Linda and Aggie played. They were the older girls. Occasionally, if I absolutely couldn't avoid it, I even spoke briefly to them.

Any port in a storm.

Besides, Aggie was not bad as a swimmer, and although she threw like a girl, she did have some success chucking the tennis ball into the inner tube. Linda, on the other hand, actually had little breasts. She knew she had them, too, and was obviously disappointed that I was all she had to show them off to now that Buddy and Timmy and Jake had all gone. But for Linda, too:

Any port in a storm.

More and more, though, I would be with Kathryn. God, but she was fun. We'd clown around together in the mornings when the pool was crowded, and then afternoons after I delivered my papers, I'd sneak back. Alone at the pool, Kathryn would coach me in swimming. Since her regular companion, Lavinia, the big heavy-set woman she adored, was away on vacation, Kathryn had a fill-in named Emma. Kathryn didn't take much to her, though, so more and more she got me to push her about.

Any port in a storm.

One morning, she whistled for me to bring her closer to the pool, and after I got her set, right there in front of the mothers, she said, "Hey, I need some lipstick on."

"You mean me? Me put it on?"

"You catch on quick, Dick Tracy."

I was mortified. To be seen putting lipstick on a girl. "I don't know how to," I said, my voice getting all edgy.

"You mean you never had chapped lips in Indiana? They don't have chapped lips in Indiana? You've never put any LipAde on?"

"That's *chapped* lips, Kathryn. That's not lip*stick*." My voice was going all over the place; in cases like this, my mother would always say, Christy Bannister, will you stop your whining this instant?

"It's all the same, Christy."

"No, it isn't. I've seen girls put lipstick on, and they go all like this." And I mimicked that part where women kind of roll their lips inside out.

"Hey, not bad," Kathryn said. "I can't do that as good myself."

"Yeah. That's rich."

"Look, Christy. Just reach into my basket and pull out my lipstick. You are being monumentally foolish. There aren't male lips and female lips, you know. I'm not asking you to put a bra on me."

"God, Kathryn, will you keep it down?"

But she knew how to get at me, and she loved it. "Or put on my Kotex."

"Aw, come on, Kathryn, now cut...it...out."

"All right, all right. Just do my lipstick now, and I'll never ask you again."

I looked all around to make sure no one was watching and then quickly slapped on her lipstick. Of course, Kathryn made a huge to-do about rolling her lips, but still, I don't think anybody saw.

But never again did she ask me to put on her lipstick. She knew I had drawn a line in the sand.

It was especially hot that July, there was potential for eggs frying everywhere on sidewalks, and so even in the shade, Kathryn would start to perspire terribly. Emma would mop her brow, but on many days, it was so unbearably hot that she would have to retreat to her bedroom. It was air conditioned, which was quite a luxury then. Movie theaters didn't advertise movies so much as they did air-conditioning. All the marquees said:

*It's COOOOOOOL inside!*

So, since Kathryn's room was so comfortable, I had a selfish reason for taking her up there. But still, I wanted to go with her. I liked her so. And I was fascinated by her. I simply could not understand how she could tolerate her condition. I had as much curiosity for Kathryn as I had admiration.

One morning was particularly sticky, so it wasn't long at all before she whistled for me. The Slades had built an elevator for Kathryn because although there was room enough in the mansion to provide her with downstairs quarters, they wanted her to keep her own bedroom to maintain as much of her old life as she possibly could.

Kathryn had changed her room around a lot, though. It wasn't as if she'd kept it as a teenager's room, the way it was when she was seventeen and could still move. Rather, artifacts from throughout her life surrounded her—photos of her school classes, some trophies, a few stuffed animals, her diploma from grade school, the yellow-and-black Maryland flag, and her father's Marine dress cap. There was also one picture of herself and Doug. It wasn't very good, but it was the only one she had—the two of them in a group picture at a debutante party. She was standing next to Doug in the back row, and they were barely visible behind all the other boys and girls in their tuxedos and gowns. But, altogether, it was a good room. Kathryn's room felt a lot like Kathryn.

This morning, though, even before we got up there, she started teasing me on the elevator. "I saw you with Linda again," she began.

"Well, yeah, with Linda *and* Aggie."

"You like her, Christy? I think she likes you a whole lot."

"Come on."

"No, really. Remember, I was a girl once. I can tell these things. Besides, you're kind of mysterious, Christy. Nobody knows who you really are. You're like the gunslinger who comes to town in the movies." I liked this part. It wasn't embarrassing, so I didn't interrupt. "You don't have any brothers or sisters here. You don't even have a mother. You just materialize every day on your bike. Girls like that."

"They do?"

"A little mystery is good, Christy." She paused then and spoke with some kind of weird accent: "For love." Then she laughed as I rolled her off the elevator down toward her room. "Linda's got nice little titties, too," she exclaimed rather gaily.

I stopped pushing. "Come on, Kathryn. If you don't stop that, I'm just going to leave you right here and go get Emma."

"Well, don't tell me you didn't notice." I started pushing again.

"Hey, okay, maybe a little."

"So, maybe you're gonna be an ass man, Christy." She giggled. I stopped pushing again and walked around to the front where I could look at her sternly. It didn't bother her, though; once she started tormenting me about girls and I took the bait, there was just no stopping Kathryn. "So what's the big deal? A lot of men get turned on by asses instead of—"

"Dammit, Kathryn." I even put my hands on my hips. "Are you gonna stop? Or what?"

"Aw, don't get your balls in an uproar," she groused, infuriating me all the more by dragging *my* male private parts into the fray. But while I was seething, she added, "Whaddya want? You want me to think you're a fairy?"

And that trumped me. Completely. I made some kind of grumpy noise and resumed pushing her into her room. "Thanks," she said. "That's sweet of you, Christy." She looked out the window down on her pool. Then she turned back to me, but when she spoke, her voice had lost its buoyancy, and she'd turned wistful. "Don't worry, Christy. A girl likes it. A girl likes it when a nice boy looks her up and down." She raised her eyebrows. "Well, hell, sometimes a girl likes it when it's not even a nice boy who looks her up and down. Sit here."

I pulled up a chair, right by her.

"You know, when I first got polio, I used to dream a whole lot, and I was always walking and running. Sometimes I was even swimming. I was riding a horse. I was still all normal in my dreams. And then even that stopped."

"You stopped dreaming?"

"No, I've never stopped dreaming. But all of a sudden, I wasn't running anymore. All of a sudden, I had polio in my dreams, too. I couldn't get away from it. Except. You know what?" I shook my head. "I don't have my respirator on, Christy. I still have polio. I still can't move. But I don't have my damn respirator on. At least people can see me. They can see I'm a woman. They can tell I'm a woman. You know? I'm not just a head attached to a respirator."

I tried to just keep looking at her as if I were having a normal conversation. But I didn't know what to say. I knew I must be wise, for Kathryn did not want me to be compassionate. That blurred too much with pity. But I wasn't wise. After all, I was only fourteen years old. She understood. She changed the subject somewhat. "Have you ever met Doug? Over at Jake's."

"No, I was only there a couple times before Jake went to camp."

"Of course. And Doug doesn't live there anymore. He's married now. He has his own house in Ruxton." I just nodded. I certainly didn't tell her how Jake had told me so much about Doug and her. I certainly didn't tell her about the home movies. I mostly played dumb. And she went on. "Doug was my beau when I got polio. It was only puppy love, Christy. It wouldn't have lasted. I know that. You never marry the boy you love when you're seventeen. And I'd known Doug all my life, too, just about."

"Oh."

"See, I'd always had a crush on Doug. The older man. And it was just that summer he saw I was grown up. That was the summer season when I came out." She saw the puzzlement in my face. "I was a debutante, Christy. It was called coming out. Like, into public. It all happened very fast. I grew up, came out, fell in love, and got paralyzed—all just like that. But at least I had a few weeks with Doug." She beamed at the memory. "And I was absolutely...enthralled."

"I'll bet," I said.

Kathryn cocked her head. "You don't mind me telling you this, do you, Christy?"

In fact, I didn't mind at all. But I did feel a little guilty, a little deceitful. I already knew a lot about this, hearing it from Jake and Eddie. I even knew Doug had felt up Kathryn's bazooms. But I knew enough to keep my counsel, and I just answered Kathryn's question. "No, I don't mind," I said. "I like hearing about it." That was true, too. "I want to know about you, Kathryn. I do."

"Thank you, Christy. Sometimes I just need someone that I can tell these things to. You see, nobody ever asks me about me."

"So," I said, leaving that alone, "whatever happened to Doug?"

"Oh, he couldn't handle it. That's all. He came to see me at the Home for Incurables. That's where they put me right away. Great name, isn't it? The Home for Incurables. Made me feel like a million bucks: oh, Kathryn, we're putting you in the Home for Incurables. But I understood. It's the pity. It helps them raise money easier. For the poor incurable cripples."

But then she shook her head. No, she wasn't going to get into that now. Doug was the subject now. "Doug brought me flowers. Of course, I'm sure his mother suggested it. I can just hear Mrs. Brothers saying, 'Now Doug, for goodness sake, take the poor girl some flowers.' And it was sweet, but he could barely stand to look at me there in the iron lung. It was so painful for us both that I finally just said, 'Look Doug, you don't have to come back.' And of course he said, 'Oh, no, no, no, don't worry.' But he never did again. Never.

"I do still see his parents. They have dinner with Mom and Dad. Come to the pool sometimes. Mrs. Brothers always avoids talking about Doug, though. God, they could have at least have invited me to the wedding. I wouldn't have gone, Christy, and been a nuisance. Didn't he know me well enough to know that? But they could have invited me. Or he could come by every now and then and say hi and tell me about his wife. I've seen pictures. She's very pretty."

She paused then, and honest to God, I knew just what Kathryn was thinking, so what the hell, I said it, "Pretty as you?"

Boy, she positively lit up. "Nah, between you and me and the lamppost, I was prettier."

"*Are* prettier," I answered. It just came out.

"Hey, help me, Emma. There's a masher in my room," she cried out, and we laughed together. But then Kathryn wiped the smile off her face and went back to where she'd been. "Jesus, you'd think Doug's wife would come by the pool. They have a little girl. You'd think she'd bring her over. I'd love to meet her. The wife. Pam. I'd love to chat with her and coo to the baby. Come on, I can take it. I took polio, didn't I? You think I couldn't take meeting Doug's wife? For Chrissake, I'm not a fool. I know he had to get on with things. He had to fall in love with someone else and marry her."

"I don't think they're worrying about whether you can take it, Kathryn," I said. "I think they're just afraid they can't take it."

She whistled softly. "Yeah, you're a smart kid, Christy. I wish you'd been Doug. You could have handled it."

I doubted that, but all I said was, "Thanks," softly. Kathryn had almost made me cry, but I held it back.

"Anyway, I kept dreaming about Doug. When I was still dreaming that I could walk and run, I also dreamed that he would take me in his arms and smother me passionately in his kisses. But I don't think I ever dreamed that he would actually...make love to me. We never did, Christy. We were still so young and so terribly proper, you see. I'm still a virgin." Her eyes arched up and she made a clicking noise with her tongue. "Dammitall."

I said, "I'm a virgin, too." It was reflex. It was also, indisputably, the stupidest thing I ever uttered my whole life.

But Kathryn was gentle with me. She managed to suppress a grin and merely replied, "I thought perhaps you were." Then, while I was still seeking some retreat from my mortification, she added, "Well, that gives us something more in common, Christy. We're just a couple of old virgins, aren't we?"

I couldn't do anything but smile foolishly. This was not only my first personal conversation about virginity, but also, bar none, it was the raciest dialogue I had ever shared with a certified member of the opposite sex. Of course, Kathryn enjoyed embarrassing me, but this time she just liked using me to reminisce.

"So what I dream is very prim, really. I imagine that even my subconscious won't let me think about Doug sweeping me off like Rhett taking Miss Scarlett up to the bedroom. But sometimes, when I look out the window here, look down at the pool, I do imagine myself lying down there getting a glorious tan. I can see that, Christy. In my mind's eye. And Doug comes by, and he takes my hand, and we go into the water. I can just feel the cool water. And we stand there in the shallow end and kiss."

"Did you? Did you ever really do that...with Doug in the pool?"

"No. Remember? I never had a pool when I had Doug."

"Oh yeah. I'm sorry."

"That's okay." Then she turned her head to look out the window to imagine the scene again down by the pool. "It's okay for me, isn't it?"

"What?"

"To think like I do. I mean, if I can't dream on my own, it's okay to make myself daydream, isn't it? Don't I owe myself that?"

"Sure. But I still think it's terrible that Doug stopped coming by to see you."

"You're sweet, Christy," she sighed. "But how can I stay mad at him? A lot of people stopped coming to see me. A lot of my best old friends. One by one. I remind them."

I was puzzled. "Of the past?"

"Oh no. I remind them of what could happen to them. Or their children. I remind them of the worst." Quickly then, she made a face. "But I'll tell you what, Bannister"—and I knew the subject had to be changing because she only called me by my last name when she was in a coaching mode—"I damn sight am going to get mad at *you* if you don't beat Buddy on Marines Day."

"I'll come back and practice this afternoon."

"Be on time, Bannister," she snapped.

Emma came into the room just then. "Come on, Miss Kathryn," she said, "we've got to get you into your regular respirator now. Say good-bye to your visitor."

"No, Emma, my visitor will lift me onto my bed. If you wouldn't mind, Christy."

"No, I—"

"You're a very strong young man, and I'm sure you can manage me." And then she twisted her head around to Emma, and all with a straight face, "Mr. Bannister is my current beau, Emma. He's just developing an interest in titties and so I won't have him long, but for this summer of '54, he is my best beau."

Emma looked altogether baffled, and of course, the risque language made me blush for the moment. But Kathryn was getting me into the spirit, so I reached down and squeezed her hand. "Precious heart," I cooed as my mother did sometimes with my father.

"Lift me gently now," Kathryn said, affecting a southern accent. "It's been so long since a new gentleman caller swept me up into his powerful arms."

So after Emma unbuckled the portable respirator, I reached under to where Kathryn lay on the gurney and took a hold of her. She was wearing some sort of cotton gown, and when I raised her up, it was as nothing, only a feather or two in my skinny arms. Softly, I turned and laid her down in her bed, into her iron lung there. Emma snapped the chest cast around her, and that took up the breathing that the portable had just let off. Kathryn couldn't breathe for even a moment on her own. Emma began to place the pillows all around her, so I waved and left Kathryn's room to go back down to the pool.

Linda and Aggie were still there, and when Linda wasn't looking, I ogled her terribly. Once, I even cupped my hands at my eyes like binoculars and pretended, very dramatically, to eye her that way. But that was just for Kathryn's benefit. I couldn't see her behind the closed window up in her air-conditioned bedroom, but I'd've bet she was looking down at me, and I wanted to give her a good laugh.

Of course, it also gave me a good chance to check Linda out, and later on, when she happened to walk over near me, I actually struck up a *bona fide* conversation with her because now I had Kathryn's word that I was alluring and mysterious.

# 11

The next Saturday, Mr. Frank Gardner himself appeared at our house. It was the first time I'd ever laid eyes on the person who'd changed my life so, but I must say that he fulfilled my expectations. He was a preposessing man, dynamic in the way he moved down the path, rolling his shoulders as he walked with a kinetic strength that belied his age. He was wonderfully tanned, with blue marble eyes; he was also one of those rare white people who somehow looked the better for being bald.

In fact, Mr. Gardner arrived angry, but he revealed none of that to me. "Why, you must be young Christy," was all he said, flashing those baby blues. When I acknowledged that I was, he stuck out his big paw and bellowed, "Well, son, I'm Frank Gardner, and I'm glad to meetcha because your old man has told me so much about you."

I said, "He's told me all about you, too, sir."

And Mr. Gardner roared at that. "I'll bet he has! I'll just bet!"

Pop had heard the commotion by now, so he came 'round the side of the house, where he was planting some shrubs. It was a boiling hot day, and the dirt he was mucking around was pasted onto him from his hair, to his face, to his bare chest, down to his old cut-off army khakis that he always worked in. Mr. Gardner responded to this vision by holding his nose and saying, "Jesus, Bob, you look dirtier than any old fieldhand."

Pop laughed. "I thought you were still on vacation, Frank," he said.

"Yeah, the cat's away, huh?"

Pop offered iced tea and promised to wash up in the kitchen, so I held the screen door as they went in. "I have a rule," Mr. Gardner went on. "It was my father's rule, and he started the company and did pretty damn well by it, so I try to follow his rules. And the rule is when you go on vacation, stay one hundred percent the hell away from the plant. If the other bastards can't run the damn thing for a month without you, it ain't gonna work anyhow. But I came up from the shore for a member-guest at Green Spring Valley, so I thought I'd drop by and see you."

"Glad you came, Frank," Pop said. As things went along, I noticed he went back and forth between calling Mr. Gardner "Frank" and "sir" depending on the immediate level of congeniality evidenced by Mr. Gardner and by my father's confidence.

As for me, I made a big to-do about going back to the den where the TV set was. We had good reception now because Pop had had a roof antenna installed, but in fact, as soon as I turned the television on, I snuck out of the room the other way and came round some bushes beyond the patio. Soon the two men emerged outside with their cigarettes and iced tea, and I leaned in closer. I was getting to be a devious little kid. But then, that was the style when I was growing up. The idea then wasn't to clash head on; rather, children were taught to test the world by bending the rules rather than to defy it by breaking them. We were the generation of the incremental, the oblique, and what we lacked in candor, we gained in civility.

Anyway, as I lay low and listened, Mr. Gardner started in with compliments right away—Pop for the wonderful job he was doing and he for being so damn smart as to have hired Pop. Of course, from the lips of Mrs. Slade, I already was privy to this information, but I was pleased that Pop heard it from the horse's mouth. He was properly modest in his response, and Mr. Gardner moved on. "So, Bob, how do you find everybody down at the plant?"

"It's a good team, Frank," and he cited a couple of standouts.

"And Mrs. Patterson?"

"Sure," Pop said, "she's been especially helpful."

"A very reliable dame," Mr. Gardner said, and from where I was tucked behind a bush, I could see Pop nod in agreement. But he didn't say anything else, even though Mr. Gardner waited for him to. So he added, "Yeah, Bob, sometimes I think Trudy knows more about Gardco than I do. And I know one damn thing for sure, she knows where all the bodies are buried."

"I can believe that," Pop said, getting up to pour them more iced tea from the pitcher.

"All right, so what about Sal?" Mr. Gardner asked then, but this time the tone of his voice was more ominous than it was conspiratorial.

Pop stopped where he stood, holding the pitcher above Mr. Gardner's glass. "I'm glad you came to that, sir. I wanted to talk to you about Sal."

"No, Bob. We have already *talked* about him. I came because I know you still haven't *done* anything about him."

"I'd like you to reconsider, sir."

"What the hell is this, Bob? I told you: this isn't your choice."

Pop poured the drink without a word. He walked away then, putting the pitcher down. I held my breath. Finally, Pop turned back. "All right, sir, at least can you delay the decision?"

"The decision has been made."

"Sal Carlino has one of the finest reputations in the P.E. industry. He's a rock, and everybody knows it. Why the other night—"

I knew he was starting to tell the story about Sal and me and the drapes, but Mr. Gardner interrupted. "I know all that, Bob. But he's also an old dago, and it's time for a new generation to take over Gardco. Tom is ready. He needs the chance now. Some people seize responsibility, but others have to have it presented to them. That's my nephew. But give him the ball, and I know he can run with it."

Pop lit a cigarette. "Look, I don't argue that. Tom is a fine young man, but Sal—"

"Fuck Sal Carlino," Mr. Gardner snapped.

That shocked me. I don't mean I was any stranger to bad language. Already I knew about all manner of fucking—physical, spiritual, and commercial. But I'd never before heard it used quite so harshly, quite so directly as Mr. Gardner did. I think Pop was taken aback a little, too. He just listened.

"It's time you put his ass out to pasture," Mr. Gardner went on. "Jesus, we'll give him a nice pension. Sal'll be in high cotton—sittin' down there in Glen Burnie, eatin' crabs and drinkin' beer on that little boat of his. That isn't a bad life for a guy like Sal. Not at all. You think he ever expected anything like this when he started at Gardco cookin' P.E. on the graveyard shift?"

Pop dropped his head. "Look, okay, sir. Just don't make me do it before Sal goes on vacation."

"When's he get back?"

"Sal takes off in a couple more weeks. He's back around Labor Day."

Mr. Gardner pondered this for a moment. He took a long pull on his cigarette, which he kept in a holder. "I think you're making it worse for yourself, dragging the sonuvabitch out."

"Maybe. Just the same, Frank..."

"All right," Mr. Gardner said, shrugging. "You're handling everything else tip-top, so I'll give you this one. But I want it done as soon as Sal gets back. No dilly-dallying then." Pop nodded, with recognition more than enthusiasm, but Mr. Gardner let that slide. Instead, he got up and came over to Pop, laying that big hand of his on his shoulder. "Okay, tell me the truth."

"Sir?"

"Are you afraid that if I pull the plug on old Sal to move Tom up, then we'll do the same thing to you down the road?"

"That thought has crossed my mind."

"Well, forget it. Blood is thicker than water and all that crap, but Bob Bannister is not Sal Carlino. As long as you run my company right and don't do anything to embarrass me in my city, the job is yours."

"That's good to hear, Frank."

"But all the same, lemme give you one piece of advice, my friend. You're a president now. Don't get too close to the help." Pop nodded. "Arm's length."

"I know that, sir."

"Make sure you do," Mr. Gardner said, and this time he jabbed Pop with his forefinger in the chest.

"I get the picture."

"All right. 'Nuff said. The *paisan* goes when he gets back from vacation." Mr. Gardner took his cigarette out of his holder then and snuffed it out, then started to walk away toward his car.

I dashed 'round the other way, back into the house, to the den, and when I could see them out by the road, I came out to be polite and say good-bye. As it has been documented, I was not raised in a rabbit hutch. Mr. Gardner pointed to me as I approached and loudly then, so I could hear, too, "This is a good boy, Bob. My spies tell me he's been a big hit over at the Slades' pool."

I blushed as Pop proudly wrapped an arm about me. "You know the Slades, sir?" I asked, playing dumb, covering for Mrs. Slade. I didn't want to let on how tight we were and that she was passing on state secrets to me.

"Why, the judge and Aurelia are about the best friends Grace and I have, son. I'll tell you, it just about broke my heart when Kathryn came down with polio. Broke my damn heart. I swear, it was almost like one of my own kids got it. Oh, you shoulda seen Kathryn."

"I saw home movies once."

"Well, you know. There wasn't any girl prettier, was there?"

"No, sir."

"So...so...vivacious. That's the word. We never had any boys ourselves, me and Mrs. Gardner. Just the two girls. But I used to tell Tom. Tom's my nephew, my sister's boy. I used to tell Tom, sit tight, son, and let the Slade girl grow up a little, and then grab her because she's the best thing you're ever gonna find. And then, just like that, one day she's fine, and the next day the fever, and the day after that she's a cripple for life. Sometimes I think it would've just been better if she'd died when they found out she couldn't move. You know?"

I pulled myself up. "No, sir," I said. "Excuse me, but I don't think so."

Mr. Gardner just stared at me. He was playing with his key chain, and he kept twirling it, but then, without warning, he took his other hand and slammed it on the car roof. "Damn," he roared. "I guess Aurelia's right. I guess you are a pisser, son." He glanced over to Pop. "Must get his balls from you, Bob."

"And his looks from his mother."

Mr. Gardner climbed into the car gingerly since the leather was so hot. When he was settled, though, he made it a point to look back at Pop. "You Bannister boys have made a fine start in this neck of the woods," he said, and then he jabbed another finger at him. "But just remember that one little thing, Bob. That one little piece of friendly advice." And off he zoomed.

My father kept staring ahead, never looking over to me. Finally, *sotto voce*, he simply declared, "That was all about Sal Carlino. He wants me to fire him."

"Yes, sir. I thought maybe so."

"But I can't fire Sal. I told you that."

"But then, what's...?"

He didn't answer; he just interrupted me by patting me on the shoulder then pointing toward Mr. Gardner's car, which was starting to disappear round the bend in Dogwood Circle. "I don't know why any man would buy a car made in another country," he declared, and I understood that our *tête-a-tête* about Sal Carlino had been officially concluded.

I certainly was fascinated with the car, too. It was a Jaguar, the first I'd ever laid eyes on. England? It might as well as come from Atlantis. The only other automobiles I'd ever seen that weren't constructed in Detroit were two VW bugs I'd spotted from a distance. "Well, it sure is pretty," I said instinctively.

"All right, it is a pretty car. And I'll tell you what, the Eiffel Tower is pretty, too. I've seen it. Hell, they make pretty watches in Switzerland, and they sing pretty opera in Italy. There's a lot of pretty everywhere. But if you want the best, Christy, it's in the United States. Nothing America can't do if it sets its mind to it. Nothin.'"

"Can we cure polio, Pop?"

He hadn't expected any specific rejoinder, and he had to think for a moment. "Well, kiddo, that's a tall order," he finally said. "But if anybody can conquer polio, it'll be America."

"Yes, sir," I said, but I understood: cars and porcelain enamelling might be one thing, but polio was another altogether. Even for us, even for America.

# 12

Nottingham Valley Estates was growing; soon we would have company on Dogwood Circle. Two new houses were well underway, and everywhere there were stakes in the ground with little red ribbons tied to them. In fact, mornings after Pop left and I had my Cheerios, I would go out and watch Progress. The house farthest along, the one just across the street, just around the bend, was already framed. And so, invigorated, envisioning neighbors—and friends—yet unseen, I would be off on my bike, pedaling over to the Slades'.

All the boys my age were gone from the pool by now, and the confidence that Kathryn had briefly installed in me (that business about me being mysterious and alluring) was waning, so I was back to taking a wide berth around Linda and Aggie. Mostly, then, I was reduced to practicing for the Great Medley—in secret. I couldn't let on what I was up to, or even more, I couldn't let on that Kathryn was the scheming mastermind. She was expected to remain neutral for the Marines Day competitions.

First, I began trying to improve my underwater prowess. The opening two laps of the Great Medley were underwater, and Buddy was especially accomplished in this discipline. It seemed to me that he could stay underwater forever. Certainly, he was able to make it the required length of the underwater portion of the Great Medley—two laps, back and forth. Kathryn suggested to me, though, that I should work on going across underwater, coming up for air on the far side, and then going back down again. "Yeah, Bannister," she explained, "it probably is faster not coming up for air. But remember, the underwater is only the first part of the race. Then we've got freestyle, backstroke, and breaststroke. It's more tiring to do the whole underwater part without coming up for air. Do it this way, and maybe you won't be so tired at the end."

So, in the mornings, unbeknownst to the mothers or the other kids that there was a method to my madness, I would practice swimming underwater—and then the other strokes, too. Occasionally then, Kathryn would call to me, and I'd get out of the pool and stroll over to her. Then casually, I'd push her away from the mothers, and she'd advise me what I was doing incorrectly. Kick straight up and down or breathe this way or that or keep your fingers cupped—all that kind of stuff. "But don't worry, Bannister, you're getting faster."

Our conspiracy remained solid. When it was time for us kids to leave the Slades' as morning drew to a close, Kathryn would never fail to wink at me and whisper, "See you back here later." That was enough for me. After all, I didn't have much else to do anyway. As soon as I got home and made my lunch, I could hardly wait 'til I could go to the corner of Charles and Old Florist, where Mr. D'Ionfrio would drop off the day's allotment of my *News-Posts*.

Since I was, evidently, so devoted to the job, Mr. D'Ionfrio took the time to show me the craft of folding newspapers. There were two basic ways. The first, the simplest and most common, was the oblong style. But there is also a great way you can fold a newspaper square, and on those days when the *News-Post* didn't boast too many advertising pages, I would incline toward that more arcane style. "Come this fall," Mr. D'Ionfrio confided in me, "you'll almost never be able to fold square."

"Really?"

"Well, maybe some Sat'days. But usually there's too many advertisements once we get back to school. That's why summertime's the best for square." He whipped off some samples for me. Mr. D'Ionfrio was a real master of the art, too; he'd started off in the profession as a delivery boy himself. So, just as I was learning swimming from Kathryn, so too was I studying newspaper folding from another aficionado. After a while, you should've seen me fold those square papers and toss 'em, too. Like a frisbee. I could chuck those babies right onto any porch. Bingo!

I plotted my route so that I would double back and end up at the Slades'. Most days, the pool was deserted of visitors by the time I returned, so that Kathryn and I would have it to ourselves. She'd be waiting for me down by the pool while Oliver Cromwell dozed and Emma did Kathryn's hair. But as soon as she saw me come through Herbert's garden, she'd whistle and shoo Emma away. I could tell how excited Kathryn was. She really wanted to win the Great Medley. She seemed convinced I could, too. Unfortunately, I did not share this faith. Mostly, I just hoped to avoid embarrassment. I knew that nobody expected me to actually beat Buddy, so I figured if I could just be competitive that would be a sufficient symbolic victory. Regrettably, one afternoon, just before we started practice, I made the mistake of offering this observation out loud.

With a flourish, Kathryn snapped her head away from me. There wasn't much that she could physically do to express herself, so that gesture was about as explicit as she could manage. Then, when I walked round to where she was looking, she immediately turned her head back the other way from me. "Aw, come on, Kathryn," I said. "I didn't say I wouldn't *try* to win. I just said I didn't think I could."

She rolled her head back toward me, this simple movement abounding with exasperation. There was some contempt in her voice, too. "You know, Bannister, trying isn't such a big deal. I can *try* to move every day, and so what? Big deal, trying. Big deal. I want you to *win*."

It was only then that I really understood what I had gotten myself into, that I was Kathryn's surrogate this Marines Day. It was very frightening because I honestly didn't think there was a chance in hell that I could beat Buddy. So I offered her the most assurance I could. "Then I promise you I will try...*hard*, Kathryn," I declared. "I'll try *very* hard." I waited for a response, but she only frowned back at me, silent. "Well," I finally said, "what can I do?"

"You can believe."

"Believe that I can beat Buddy? But Kathryn, I don't. I just don't."

"So just believe *maybe*, Christy. That's good enough. Believe maybe. I don't really believe I'll ever get out of this respirator. But I do believe maybe. And that's enough." I mulled that over. "Well," she pressed me then, "can you believe maybe you can beat Buddy?"

"I guess."

"Good. You see, Christy, the thing about believing maybe is that you don't just sit back and take believing for granted. It's like people who go to church because they say they believe. So that's all they do. They just go. But if you only believe maybe, then you have to keep working at it. Then you have to help make the believing come true." I nodded sort of. "Okay?"

"Okay. I believe maybe I can beat Buddy in the Great Medley."

Kathryn smiled. "Good," she said sweetly. Then her tone changed completely. "So then get your heinie in that pool, Bannister, and practice some freestyle. I want you to do ten laps—you hear me?"

"Yes, Coach." I dashed for the pool, dived in, and started churning as fast as I could.

Kathryn became a real taskmaster, all the worse when we moved onto the backstroke. I hated the backstroke because you can't see where you're going and you veer, so when you twist your head around to see if you're on target, you lose valuable time. I explained this to Kathryn. This is what she snapped back at me, "Whaddya think, Bannister? You think the backstrokers in the Olympics go off in all sorts of crazy directions and bang into each other like duckpins?"

"Well, no," I replied. "But they have official pools. They have lines painted on the bottom so they can follow straight." Oops. As soon as I said that, I realized how stupid that was. But, too late.

"Hey, dummy, they're on they're backs. That's why they're called backstrokers. How can they see the lines beneath their backs?"

"Well, all right, but they have ropes and stuff."

"Okay, they do. But if a swimmer runs into the ropes, he loses so much time getting tangled up and straightening out and all, he gets beat. So, you just gotta stay straight."

I slumped. "How?"

"Into the pool, Bannister," she barked, and I jumped in. Immediately, she whistled, and Emma came over from the shade and pushed her up to the very edge of the pool. I looked up, waiting for instructions. "All right," Kathryn said, and then she paused, pondering. I waited. Finally, this is all else she said, "Think left."

"What?"

"Think left."

"I thought that's what you said."

"Right. So consider this, Bannister. The reason most people go off on an angle in the backstroke and get out of their lane and all screwed up is because they're right-handed, and so they're stronger on that side, so they naturally slide right. So, just concentrate on your left-arm motion." I stared at her. I'd never heard anything so goofy as this from any coach. "Go on, try it."

So I did. And it was amazing. Immediately, without any apparent loss of velocity, I swam straighter. "Left," Kathryn called out. Like a drill sergeant. "Left...left...left..."

"Hey," I said when I came to the side of the pool after a bunch of laps. "This is great. Who taught you this?"

"Nobody. I just figured it out myself."

"Gee."

"I was a pretty good swimmer, Christy. I really was."

"I heard," I said. I left it at that. And Kathryn looked wistful—for a moment.

Then, "All right, Bannister, this is no time to chew the fat. We're practicing here. Let's work on your mechanics now. You're kicking like a baby, you know."

So once more I took my place, and she whistled, and off I went on the backstroke again. Kathryn also called to Emma while I was doing my laps and told her she could go get a smoke. Kathryn wanted to work with me alone. I could tell that. She didn't even want Oliver Cromwell around because sometimes he could be a diversion, running around the pool yipping at me as I swam. So, after a while, she made sure that Cromwell was kept inside while she was coaching me.

Kathryn would even get peeved when her mother would come

out from the house to say hello to her. One day, in fact, she even snapped at her mother when Mrs. Slade appeared with another lady. Mrs. Slade was very frosty in return. She merely said, "Actually, Kathryn, Grace is not here to see you, so you don't have to be disagreeable." And then Mrs. Slade called for me to come out of the pool, and when I did, she introduced me to the lady. She was a tiny little thing with a cigarette holder; Mrs. Slade revealed her to be none other than Mrs. Frank Gardner herself. It surprised me. Both Gardners used cigarette holders, but he was as big as she was little.

"Well, so this is young Bannister," she said, checking me out.

"Yes, ma'am."

"My, aren't you a handsome thing? Shouldn't be surprised. I understand your father is quite the ladies' man, and I'll bet all the girls are after you, too."

Naturally, I turned crimson, and Kathryn cackled some. Mrs. Slade said, "Now, Grace, don't embarrass Christy."

Kathryn said, "Christy doesn't have time for girls right now, Mrs. Gardner. He's working on his swimming."

"Your mother told me that, and I think it's wonderful that you're coaching him."

"So do I," Kathryn said, smiling. And then she added, "But keep it under your hat, Mrs. Gardner. This is on the Q.T."

Mrs. Gardner said, "Mum's the word." Our secret remained safe.

Most days, after Kathryn grudgingly admitted that practice was over, I'd go inside and Maizie would give me some drinks. Then I'd push Kathryn into the shade, and we'd chat. It's funny. I've never in my life liked straws. People just automatically assume you want to use a straw, but I can't abide them. I like to really get into a drink, whatever it is. Straws seem so prissy to me. But, of course, Kathryn had to drink her soda through a straw, so I did, too. The one time I drank with straws was when I was with Kathryn that summer.

Kathryn had a little basket next to her mouth that could hold a glass or a bottle, and I'd put an RC in there. Then she could drink through the straw herself. It was one of the few things she could do without help, and that meant a great deal to her—so it was just two

91

old buddies hanging out in the summer's shade, sipping sodas and swapping stories.

I can't tell you all the things we talked about that summer. For example, we even talked about God himself, and Jesus, and how in the world either one of them could allow a terrible thing like polio to happen to someone so neat as Kathryn. We also talked about the Orioles, *I Love Lucy*, and about our families. Kathryn was the baby in hers: her two older brothers had long since left home. We talked about President Eisenhower. I told her about submarine sandwiches, which were new, and I promised to bring her one. Aggie didn't go swimming one morning, and I sort of understood why, so that was the afternoon Kathryn just took it upon herself to explain to me about menstruation. That was a big help. My father and my buddies had helped me understand about sex, about *doing it*, but it's hard for guys to explain to other guys about menstruation.

Sometimes we told jokes, especially knock-knock jokes and sort of dirty jokes. Occasionally, if I was really on a roll, if Kathryn had said something just so, I quipped back, "That's what she said." We got a lot of mileage out of that jocularity, too.

Sometimes we even talked about me, about how shy I was around girls, how my voice might really be changing, even about my good points (modesty forbids detail here), about my family, and Terre Haute, Indiana. We spoke of communism and how nasty it was. We discussed why we agreed that RC Cola tasted better than either Coke or Pepsi and why we disagreed about white bucks and saddle shoes (I much preferred the bucks). We talked about Oliver Cromwell and other dogs. My parents had promised me that I could get a dog when "everything got settled" in Baltimore, and Kathryn and I discussed what sort of a canine might be best for me. I wanted a dalmation even though I'd never had a dalmation before but because I'd seen them riding fire engines. Kathryn tried to talk me into another Sealyham, but as much as I liked Cromwell, I was afraid it might look fruity, me having such a cute little fluffy dog. "Don't worry what people think, Christy," she said. "Like, no matter what Cromwell looks like, he's a tough little monkey. Sealyhams were bred to kill badgers."

"Oh." Unfortunately, I didn't realize how menacing badgers could be.

I liked *Captain Marvel* the best and tried to win her over. But Kathryn stuck with *Superman*. She did get me reading *Winnie Winkle* in the funny papers, and we often discussed her travails. Winnie's husband had amnesia, if I recall, and that was an issue. We didn't talk much about movies, though, because it was terribly complicated for Kathryn to arrange being brought into a theater, so she'd pretty much given up on that. We did talk a lot about Abbott and Costello, though, because she'd seen them in the movies before she got polio, and now we both could see them on TV.

It's perfectly amazing all the stuff Kathryn and I talked about.

Sometimes I would also light a cigarette for her. Old Golds. It was sort of foolish because she couldn't inhale, but she liked having one in her lips, the smoke curling up, inasmuch as that would help her feel more sophisticated. "Come with me to the Casbah, dahling," she would sigh huskily after I took the cigarette out of her lips. Of course, like most kids my age, I was already sneaking a smoke now and then, although Kathryn told me (in no uncertain terms) that I couldn't have so much as a puff until after the Great Medley.

We talked about all this, the summer of 1954. We talked about the future, too, only not too much after she told me once that she didn't think she'd "be around much longer" unless there was a miracle. So, we talked about the future more in general—although sometimes about mine in particular. "Whaddya wanna be when you grow up, Christy?" she asked me.

"A doctor, I think," I declared. Just like that. Just as if she'd asked me my name. It just came out.

"I didn't know that."

"Me neither. But I think I've decided." So far as I knew, there'd never been a doctor on either side of our family, and I'd never even considered the profession before.

"Why?"

"Well, I guess because of you, Kathryn. I've thought sometimes how much I'd like to be the doctor to cure your polio, and I know that'll be cured before I grow up, but then maybe I can cure something else. If I become a doctor."

"Oh," she exclaimed, her eyes sparkling. "That is *so* sweet of you." She just beamed. "I've had an effect on you, haven't I?" I nodded. "Gee, in all my life, I never had that before. An effect. And I never thought I would."

"You didn't believe maybe."

"No," she grinned back at me. "Touché."

I flipped the cigarette away and took her hand. "Well, it's just that I guess you're my best friend for now, and you made me think about stuff."

So Kathryn Slade was the reason I would become a doctor. Even if I never have cured a disease, I do think about her every now and then, especially those times when I operated and put someone's body right again. I do think of Kathryn, still, even now.

At that moment, though, as I squeezed her hand, she winked back at me, and then she started singing this way: "Sh-boom, sh-boom, la-da-da-da-da-da-da-da, sh-boom, sh-boom."

Immediately, I chimed in, and we did the chorus again together, "Sh-boom, sh-boom, la-da-da-da-da-da-da-da."

I'm sorry. I know you would've had to have heard this—heard "Sh-Boom"—to appreciate it. "Sh-Boom" was the big hit that summer. Monster hit. By the Crew Cuts. Even if it wasn't quite exactly rock-'n'-roll, even if it was just sort of putative rock-'n'-roll, it certainly seemed revolutionary to us. "Sh-boom, sh-boom...."

Kathryn loved "Sh-Boom" before anybody else I knew, so she'd already taught me to love it, too. This put me squarely in the "Sh-Boom" vanguard, the first time ever I'd been ahead of the cultural curve. One night, when I started singing "Sh-Boom" to my sister on the phone, Sue was blown away. "Sh-Boom" had only just now reached Terre Haute, and here I knew it. Verbatim! It was the first time ever that she had approved of me as a brother.

This afternoon at the pool, Kathryn and I really cranked it up. If I remember, there was only one verse besides all the la-da-da stuff, and we hit it together now:

Oh, life could be a dream
If I could take you up in paradise up above,
If you would tell me I'm the only one that you love
Life could be a dream, sweetheart.
Sh-boom, sh-boom.

I began whirling around, hanging onto Kathryn's hand, dancing in my bathing suit, twirling down under her hand, even then taking her hand over the top of the respirator. Sometimes Kathryn laughed so hard it was difficult for her to keep on singing "Sh-Boom." What a glorious afternoon it was—all the better that it wasn't just the sun shining on her out there between Herbert's garden and God's tear. No, this was an altogether different day for her because she was part of it. She was helping someone. She had a purpose. And Kathryn wasn't only singing, but she was singing with someone who was dancing with her. "Sh-boom, sh-boom..."

Oh, we were laughing so gaily, so...raucously. When we finally paused to take another sip of soda through our straws, I spoke very firmly, "Kathryn, I want you to know this. I really do believe maybe. I promise. I believe maybe we can win the Great Medley."

I said "we" on purpose because I thought of it in those terms. More important, though, she knew what I meant when I said that. She closed her eyes and smiled. When she opened them, she said, "Yeah, now I believe maybe too you can win, Bannister."

"You mean *you* didn't believe maybe either?"

Kathryn just winked and sang, "Oh, life could be a dream sweetheart. Sh-boom, sh-boom...."

# 13 *August 1954*

As soon as the rest of the family arrived in Baltimore at the subdivision, Mom took charge of the movers, Sue went up to her empty room, and I showed Hughie the territory. He was especially impressed with two big holes that had just been dug farther along Dogwood Circle—the foundations for the next two houses. Where we'd lived in Terre Haute, Hughie'd never been privileged to enjoy two big holes and huge piles of dirt adjacent to our property, so he was immediately more than pleased with our new residence.

Sue was sniffling. When she wasn't sulking. It had been eighteen hours since she'd been wrenched away from Danny Dougherty, whom she loved as no girl had ever loved another boy.

Occasionally, she would appear to come out of her funk (sulking can be tiring), but then one of us would say something that would somehow remind her of His Nibs and off she'd go again. It didn't take a whole lot. For example, if you happened to idly mention, say, shoes, Sue would moan, "Oh, I love Danny's Bass Weejuns soooo much," and there she went. Never before had she been quite this much of a pain.

But, even as absence makes the heart grow fonder, so did Sue sweat. She couldn't avoid it. It was something like ninety-five degrees, day after day. You could, as Kathryn told me, soft-boil an egg under your armpit. And Hughie would come back every day raving about this fabulous swimming pool. Sue was cracking under the heat, not to mention the humidity, which everybody did, because it's not the heat, it's....

Finally, after about a week of sweating, Sue emerged from her room at lunchtime to announce that as a special favor to Hughie and me, she would accompany us to Kathryn's pool the next morning. Unfortunately, just then the postman came down the walk with the day's second mail delivery, and included was the first letter from His Nibs. Sue devoured it, broke into tears, ripped it up into pieces, and dashed back up to her room.

It only took Hughie and me a few minutes to patch the letter back together. Here was the gist of it from Danny Daugherty: well, he was quick to acknowledge that, as they had agreed on their last date in Terre Haute, that they would love each other eternally. But, nevertheless, it had occurred to him that, separated as they were by hundreds of miles and (even) a time zone, it might be best for *both of them*, for their general emotional well-being, if "we started dating other people." Platonically. Just as friends. For something to do nights. To pass the time.

I wanted to go up and tell Sue that I'd never thought he was good enough for her, but I knew this just wasn't the right time for that. So, pronto, I got the hell out of that asylum, picked up my day's bundle of *News-Posts*, and wended my way back to the Slades'. "I really thought Sue was gonna come," I told Kathryn, "but now I can't even imagine how long this stupid letter from His Nibs will set her back."

"You think maybe she'd come if I personally invited her?" Kathryn asked.

"Well, maybe."

So Kathryn sent me after some stationery, and together we worked up a letter for Sue. No diplomatic message was ever more carefully crafted, with every word considered for any nuance that Sue might possibly take offense at. We could not be insensitive to her plight, but neither could we sound patronizing. Finally, as Kathryn dictated, this is what I wrote:

Dear Sue,
    Christy has told me so much about you. I understand it's been something of an adjustment, moving here, but I would

hope that you would come by with Christy tomorrow afternoon and get a nice swim when there's no one else here. Maybe we can have a nice chat, too.

Yours very truly,

Kathryn signed her name herself. She'd learned how to do that holding a ball-point pen in her mouth. First, though, we even debated that.

"You don't think my wiggly signature will scare her off, do you?" she asked me. "I mean, it won't make her think I'm retarded or anything, will it?"

"Nah, I've told her all about you. She's just being a big pain."

"Okay, put the pen in my mouth."

So, she signed it, and then, at Kathryn's suggestion I also added the *piece de resistance*:

P.S. "Sh-Boom" is my favorite song, too.

As you can see, we pulled out all the stops.

We even enlisted my father in the plot, and he was delighted when I told him about Kathryn's letter. "Give it to her at the dinner table," he suggested, and when I did, he waited 'til Sue read it then asked to see it himself. Reluctantly, she handed it over. He read it with great interest. "My, what a nice invitation," he said, passing it to me to give to Mom. "Isn't it, Cecelia?"

"Oh, Pop," Sue whined.

"Oh, Pop, nothing," he said. "This young lady has made a genuine effort to have you come to her pool, and you will go. Tomorrow."

"This is so very lovely," Mom said, putting the note down.

"Please, Pop, I just don't wanna go," Sue said, changing her tone, now playing Daddy's little girl.

But he was ready for that, and he merely stared her down. "I'm sorry, Sue, but this is not a topic for discussion. The Slades have been wonderful to Christy"—daggers from Sue to me—"and the judge and Mrs. Slade are very good friends of the Gardners, and I will simply not permit any child of mine to be rude to them."

99

Sue sized up the situation. She could see that neither her personal anguish nor her flirting helped. So she threw her napkin down onto the table and turned her fire onto me. Shoot the messenger. "I don't see why I have to go see some old cripple just 'cause she's Christy's friend. I never make him see any of my friends."

Even before she had finished, I had sprung to my feet, my chair clanging back against the radiator behind my place. Then I threw my napkin at Sue—and it was a good thing I wasn't holding a knife or fork at that moment because I was so furious I'm sure I would have hurled them. Then despite all the dirty words I knew, I screamed, instinctively, the very worst that came into my head, "You stink, Sue!" And then I just stared at her, breathing like a panther.

Mom was appalled. Hughie stopped jamming food into his mouth at the very lip. And for all the crying Sue had done, all the theatrics of the last week, she just froze, genuinely terrified of her brother gone berserk.

My father only looked at me, gently raising his hand. When he saw that I was only quavering, unsure what exactly to do next, he gave me one of those I'll-take-care-of-it looks, and after he sort of watched me back down into my chair, he turned to Sue. Measuring his words, doling them out very carefully, he said, "Sue, I don't condone the way Christy just acted—"

"At the table," Mom interjected. Whatever you did wrong in our family was magnified if it took place At the Table.

Pop ignored her. "But you had that coming, honey."

I was smart enough to suppress a smile. Sue gasped: the nerve that he wouldn't side with her! Pop went on more sympathetically now, "You know, Sue, I understand how very hard this has been for you, leaving Terre Haute, leaving Danny..."

A sniffle at that mention, but clearly only for effect. Anyway, Pop ignored it. "But you have lost a boyfriend," he went on—long pause, "while Christy's friend has lost pretty near..." short pause, "everything."

Sue ducked her head. No acting here. For real. The rest of us kept our eyes on Pop. This was the first time anybody in the family had dared to place Sue's distress into some kind of rational perspective, and it was of great relief to all of us. I even suspect it was liberating for Sue because now that it had been publicly demonstrated that there were worse things in life than a broken romance, she was, in effect, freed from carrying on so.

Contritely, she nodded at Pop. He touched her hand—no hard feelings—and then looked down the table to Mom. "Cecelia, I will leave work early, after lunch, and bring the car back here, and then I will personally deliver Sue and Christy to the Slades'."

Sue nodded. The first major difference between girls and boys, revealed, is that girls know how to cut their losses. She was even looking very somber now, in fact, the better to illustrate penance. "So, good, that's the end of that," Pop declared in his most paternal tone. "There'll be no more unpleasantness."

"At the table," Mom added.

And to punctuate the point, Pop resumed eating. So did we all, reaching for our forks, spearing food. Precisely then, when everyone had moved on, I looked back over to my sister and spouted, "And hey, Sue, she's not an old cripple. Kathryn's...*great!*"

Sue glared at me. Pop said, "I told you there would be no more unpleasan—"

"Well, she should apologize for what she called Kathryn. If I'd said something like—"

My father did not raise his voice. He merely looked at me with resignation and then said, "Leave the table, Christopher."

I didn't let on, but that was a victory of sorts. I'd just about finished eating, anyhow, and I knew we were having Brown Betty for dessert, which I could take or leave. So without a word of protest, only pausing to look smugly toward Sue to make sure she knew that I didn't give a rat's ass about leaving, I made my exit.

I had stood up nobly for my Lady Kathryn, and I felt triumphant and chivalrous.

On the way over to the Slades' the next afternoon, Sue put the sulk back on, only sullenly answering Pop just "yes" or "no." But he knew his daughter as well as he knew me, and so he let it go, refusing to acknowledge that she was irritating him. I could tell it was getting to Sue, for what's the point of sulking with your parents if they don't say stop sulking, will you? Pop knew, though. He knew that the instant Sue encountered someone from without the family circle she would be all sweetness and light, so he indulged her, dropping her off at the Slades' without comment or judgment.

And, of course, Pop was dead right. As soon as Mrs. Slade appeared at the door, Sue cooed and oozed "ma'am" every three words and complimented her on everything—even rugs. It would've made me sick to my stomach except for the fact that I was so fed up with her pouting that suffering her as a hypocritical goody-goody was a relative improvement. "I just knew Christy Bannister was going to have this sweet a sister," Mrs. Slade said while Sue looked over at me with this unbearable expression of utter smugness.

Mrs. Slade led us out to the pool then, and right away, I wish you could've seen the expression change on Sue's face. She'd been sufficiently impressed being witness to the stylish opulence of the Slades' house, but her eyes grew even wider when she saw Kathryn's pool and the great, bright gardens all around it, bees buzzing and butterflies dancing. "Wow," is what Sue whispered, echoing my stab at articulation the first time I'd taken it all in.

"See, I told you so," I whispered back.

And then: there she was. There was Kathryn. First I heard her. She was telling Lavinia, who was back from her vacation, to move her closer to the pool. And then, as the gurney came 'round the arbor from out of the shade, I turned to look at Sue's face, to watch her at the moment when she saw Kathryn come into the sunshine.

I knew how she would react because I'd seen other people when they met Kathryn for the first time. Like Sue, they had all been told what to expect. They were prepared to see a young woman paralyzed with polio lying in a chest respirator. But what they were never prepared for was Kathryn's face. Only there it was, just like anyone else's face, coming out of the respirator, out of that awful abyss. It was sweet and smiling and so very pretty—and so terribly, terribly tragic.

Oh, Kathryn's face had lost some of its definition. Maybe it was a little slack. Sure. But not so much to deny the beauty that was there, or to cloud the imagination of how much more beautiful that face had been once upon a time before it was only a face attached to a body with polio.

Sue dealt with this the best she could; she smiled bravely.

As for Kathryn, "Hi!" she said brightly. Always she spoke that way, right away when she met someone, because she knew how hard it was for them, and she wanted to put them at ease. She was the one with the polio, but she wanted to help them. It wasn't that Kathryn was just being nice, either. No, as she told me one time, it was more a matter of her doing her job. If she couldn't put visitors at ease, then it wasn't going to be any fun for her. Kathryn was very practical.

I took my sister's hand and laid it on top of Kathryn's, and then I nodded to Sue—yes, go on—and she did. She shook the hand after a fashion, and although Kathryn couldn't feel the shake, she understood the gesture and smiled. I could see Sue soften, and I knew then that she was glad she'd left her room and come here.

Mrs. Slade said, "I'm going to leave you young people alone. Come along, Vinnie, you can help me." And she and Lavinia left.

"Thank you for asking me over," Sue said to Kathryn. "Gee, this is about the loveliest place I've ever seen. Anywhere."

Kathryn asked her to sit down in the chair by her head. "Christy tells me"—Sue glanced over to me dubiously—"that you've had a little...uh, boy trouble. I'm sorry."

"I'll get over him," Sue said stoutly. Well, that certainly was a new tune.

"I had a boyfriend when this happened to me," Kathryn said. "I've told Christy about this."

"You and Christy talk about a lot of stuff, don't you?"

Kathryn glanced up at me. "We're friends, aren't we, Christy? Friends tell each other things."

"Yeah," I said. "Yeah."

"Gee, Christy never talks that much to me."

"You're a sister," I said.

Sue frowned. Kathryn looked at me crossly. "Oh, don't be a child, Christy. You've never been a child with me before. So don't start being a child just because your sister's here."

This shifted the edge to Sue, and she pounced. "Right. He's *always* childish with me."

"Me? That's a laugh. You've been a pain ever since you got to Baltimore."

"All right, all right," Kathryn snapped, rolling her head over to me. "You know, Christy, someday somebody's gonna break your heart, too."

"See?" Sue said. Well, snarled.

"It's no fun," Kathryn went on. "Apart from, you know, getting my polio, the worst thing that ever happened to me was when I knew Doug didn't love me anymore."

Instinctively, Sue reached over and touched Kathryn's arm. Kathryn liked that a lot. So few people touched her. It wasn't that they thought they could catch polio from her. Everybody knew that wasn't the way it worked. No, it was just that everybody was uncomfortable around Kathryn. It was probably even harder than looking at her head coming out of that respirator. "I'm so sorry," Sue said. "That must have been awful."

Kathryn sighed. "I was just about your age. I was looking at you now, and I was thinking it just stopped for me then. It just stopped for me when I was"—she arched her eyebrows—"you."

Sue didn't know how to respond, and even I was a little embarrassed. Things that Kathryn and I could talk about so easily seemed different when someone else was there. Even if it was my own sister; well, probably especially because it was my own sister. "I think I'll go in the pool," I said.

"Yeah, Sue," Kathryn said, "why don't you go in too?" But Sue shook her head, so Kathryn spoke a little softer, in more of a conspiratorial tone, "Oh, is your cousin from Red Bank visiting?"

I screwed up my nose. Cousin? From where? Even though Kathryn had helped me understand menstruation, about those darkest female intimacies, she hadn't instructed me in the code, so I didn't have the foggiest idea what the two of them were talking about.

Sue shook her head. "Nah, not now. I'm just not a very good swimmer."

"Mom never liked us to go to pools because she was scared we'd get polio," I explained.

"Christy Bannister!" Sue gasped.

"Hey, Sue, Kathryn knows all that."

"Yeah, it's okay," Kathryn said. "Hell, my mother used to say the same thing to me. You know, before I got it."

Sue nodded. "Still, I think I'd just like to sit here and talk a while." She leaned forward in her chair.

"I'd like that, too." Kathryn twisted her head in my direction. "Just us girls, Christy. Go on, work on your breaststroke. Tomorrow we're gonna start on the breaststroke."

So I slunk over to the pool. In fact, it was so hot that I really wanted to go swimming, but I also was ticked off because I suddenly felt left out. I didn't *want* to hang out with two girls, but I did want the *option* to hang out with two girls. So I made a big production out of diving and backstroking with a vengeance. Occasionally, Kathryn would whistle and call out encouragement or instructions—"Think left!"—but I could tell she really wasn't devoting any serious interest to me. No, she was only gabbing away with my stupid sister who hadn't even wanted to come in the first place. So to hell with practicing; I started in on goofy stuff like doing cannonballs and diving for things I threw into the deep end.

It was when I came up to the surface with a pair of goggles I'd retrieved that I spotted Jake pushing his way through the little gate that opened from the garden. I was really surprised; I'd forgotten that a whole month had passed since he'd gone off to camp. Happily, I swam over to the side of the pool to say hello, and that was when I also saw Eddie, his brother, trailing Jake through the garden.

Eddie looked even more impressive than when I'd met him that time before—and dirtier, too, with work boots, jeans, and an old Oxford button-down white shirt that was open almost all the way down to his belly button, with the sleeves cut off to the shoulders. He was caked in dirt. "Hey, Kathryn," he called out.

She was turned the other way. "Who is that?" she asked, beckoning Sue to turn her around.

Even before she did, though, Eddie hollered again, "It's Eddie and Jake, *mademoiselle*. Two of the famous Brothers brothers."

He gave me a quick salute then, still striding toward Kathryn—and that was when he spied Sue standing up, turning Kathryn's gurney around. To himself, I heard Eddie make a little "grrrrr" noise as he kept moving forward, never taking his eyes off Sue.

As I got out of the pool and came over with Jake, I could see Sue's whole body blush nearly the same color as the pink panel bathing suit with print flowers on it that she was wearing. Poor Sue. She didn't know whether, as we would suavely say, to spit or wind her watch. She didn't want to act embarrassed, but in fact, she felt absolutely naked, actually meeting a boy in nothing but a bathing suit. Sue had taken off her shift and tossed it across a chair, so there was nothing she could do, nowhere she could retreat. So, as nearly as I could tell from my vantage, what Sue did was to stand there and pretend that she didn't have a body. And, of course, as I have already explained, she had a knockout body. In the vernacular of the time, Sue was built like a brick shithouse.

Notwithstanding, Eddie stayed cool. He was Johnny Rep, Eddie was. He was Joe Ivy League. He was shoe. Even guys who were Johnny Rep and Joe Ivy League still weren't necessarily shoe. That was the ultimate. And let me tell you: Eddie Brothers was shoe. He didn't leer at Sue. He acted as if she was just another old lady or something, merely acknowledging her presence as he took Kathryn's hand. "Hey, Kathryn, don't get mad at me. I know kids aren't supposed to come in the afternoons, but Jake just got back from camp so I thought I'd bring him over for a dip."

Jake stepped up and took Kathryn's hand, too, and said, "Hi, is it okay?"

Kathryn said, "All right, you can go in with Christy. But Eddie—you're absolutely filthy. You take a shower. And I mean a real shower, with soap. But first, mind your manners and say hello to Sue Bannister."

He turned to her, grinning. "I didn't know Christy was married."

Sue laughed at this clever joke.

I explained, "It's my sister, Eddie."

"Oh, I see," he said. And then formally, "How do you do?" He bowed his head a little to her, as we didn't shake hands with either girls or ladies in those days. Boy, was Eddie smooth. He was able to look right into her eyes and talk to her as easily as if she was a boy.

"Hi," Sue said. She was starting to stand up straight. I don't mean shoving her chest out like Dagmar or Marilyn Monroe, but the shrinking violet stuff was fading fast.

"Eddie'll be a sophomore at Yale this fall," Kathryn said.

"I'm doing construction work this summer," he explained.

"Oh," said Sue.

"Well, go clean up if you wanna go into my pool."

"Yes, boss." He yanked off his sleeveless shirt, waving it before him like a cape as he bowed low, and then, with a little skip, Eddie turned and jogged to the bathhouse.

Sue was left thunderstruck. Not only had her melancholia disappeared in a moment, but she had grown up about two years before my eyes. The coed!

She stayed close by Kathryn, but the intensity of their just-us-gals relationship was fading rapidly, especially after Eddie returned to our midst, golden clean, in boxer trunks, brushing the shower water from off his shining face. He was three-tone, his face and forearms tanned dark, then his biceps a slightly lighter shade showing he'd worn short sleeves some of the time, and then, finally, his torso and legs were an amber. It was very animalistic, suggesting some clever beast that nature had divined to blend into the jungle. Sue snuck glimpses by sitting back out of Eddie's purview then ducking forward for an instant to shoot him a furtive look.

Eddie played it perfectly. I found out later that he could dive off a high board as good as those guys in Acapulco, but Eddie didn't do that. Instead, he just dove casually in from the side of the pool, and instead of swimming around in perfect form, he only kind of dog-paddled over, messing around with Jake and me for a while.

"Eddie rowed for the Yale freshmen this spring," I heard Kathryn tell Sue, and Sue nodded gravely even though she didn't have a clue what that meant, inasmuch as we didn't have a great deal of familiarity with crew races in Terre Haute.

Soon, though, Eddie left Jake and me (enough is enough). Swimming to the far side of the pool, he lifted himself up out of the water and flipped himself nimbly around all in one strong, sleek motion so that he ended up sitting on the edge with his legs dangling into the pool in the direct view of the girls. After a while, in point of fact, after exactly the right amount of time, he called over to me, "Hey, Christy, what's your sister's name again?" Cool, as if he'd forgotten it. Sure. And as if she couldn't hear him asking me now. I reminded him that it was Sue. So, "Hey, Suzy Q, don't you swim?"

What could a girl do? *Don't you swim?* Not: wanna swim or like to swim? *Don't you*—somehow that seemed just so perfect. So shoe. Sue only glanced at Kathryn, who smiled a benediction, allowing Sue to say, "Well, all right," as she rose, as if this was mostly a matter of courtesy.

She took a seat at the side of the pool next to Eddie, and he started talking to her. Just like that. He never splashed her or jumped in and stayed underwater or anything like that. No, Eddie just talked to Sue in a calm, clear voice, except occasionally when he laughed naturally. I couldn't keep my eyes off them—off him. In fact, it struck me as a more impressive performance, him talking to a girl so easily, than doing a jacknife dive without making a splash or hitting a baseball or making a string of foul shouts. God, I wish I could've been close enough to have listened in and picked up some tips.

After a while, though, Eddie and Sue had talked for so long (with no signs of letting up) that I felt sorry for Kathryn, so I left Jake and went over to see her. "You know, Christy," she said to me right away, "I don't think you're going to hear a whole lot more about His Nibs in your house again."

# 14

Eddie didn't call that night. Or the next. (That was the one I was betting on.) It mortified Sue. She knew Eddie was working construction and wouldn't be at Kathryn's pool. But still, she was so beside herself that even though Pop got a ride to work with Mrs. Patterson that morning, left us the car, and Mom said Sue could use it, she said she didn't want to go over to Kathryn's pool.

So Mom dropped off Hughie and me, but almost as soon as I got there, I told Kathryn that I didn't feel well. Mrs. Slade drove me home. Right away, Mom got hysterical. The problem was, as far as my mother—any mother—was concerned, any child who felt the least bit sick in the summertime obviously had polio. At least until proved otherwise.

"Do you have a headache, too, darling?" she asked.

I said I thought maybe I did.

"Do you have a sore throat?"

I nodded, kind of. She put her head to my forehead. "Oh my God, you have a fever," she cried, and as she searched for the thermometer, she sent me to bed.

"But Mom, I have to deliver my newspapers."

And my mother screeched, "To hell with the goddamn newspapers, Christy."

It was rare enough that Mom ever uttered so much as a *h—l*, let alone took the Lord's name in vain, plus attached to a *d—n*. So now I was goddamn frightened. I could feel my head aching for sure now.

Mom phoned Pop at the plant and told him she was going to send Sue down with the car to bring him right home, but he told her to just sit tight and he'd get a cab. He told Mom to call the doctor—only then, of course, they both remembered that the doctors they knew were all back in Terre Haute. Pop said he would ask Mr. Gardner about a pediatrician.

Mom gave me some aspirin. I really didn't feel all that bad. It wasn't as if I was burning up with fever. My headache wasn't splitting; my throat wasn't raw. But, of course, everybody knew that polio didn't come on like gangbusters. Rather, it was...well, it was rather just like the way it was with me—a summer cold, a little fever.

"Just a hundred," Mom said, looking at the thermometer—a bit of a headache, and then, just like that, all of a sudden, you couldn't move. Your nerves were like fuses blown along your spinal switchboard, and you struggled to catch a breath, and so they zapped you into an iron lung. And there you stayed. Forever and a day. Everybody knew that. Every mother. Every mother's son.

Outside, I heard a car drive up. "Oh, thank God, here's the doctor," Mom screamed.

Only it was my father's voice, "Thanks so much, Trudy."

And then, "I'm praying for you, Bobby," is what I heard Mrs. Patterson say. To tell you the truth, that was when I really started to get scared.

Mom ran downstairs. The fan was on in my room, but the door was open, so I could hear. "Where the hell is that damn doctor of yours, Bobby?" Boy, she was almost yelling.

"Cecelia, please. He is on his way. Frank Gardner has gotten us—bar none—the best pediatrician in Baltimore. He will be here momentarily. Now, how is Christy?" But he didn't wait for Mom's answer. I could hear him starting up the stairs, then he was taking two steps at a time, and then he was standing right there in my door. "Hey, kiddo."

"Pop, will you call Mr. D'Ionfrio about my papers?"

"Look, don't worry about your papers. Soon as we get the doctor here, I'm gonna deliver them myself."

That was a load off my mind. "Thanks, Pop."

"And the doctor will give you something so tomorrow you'll be able to take care of your route again yourself. Okay?"

I nodded, smiling, and he put his hand on my forehead, sitting down next to me on the bed. I sighed. "Pop," I began.

"Yes?"

"Do I have polio?"

He brushed my wet hair back off my forehead, then kissed me there. "Christy, I am not a doctor. I know you have a fever and you have a headache. And a sore throat...?"

"Uh huh. A little."

"Okay, but I have no reason to think you have polio. All right?"

I smiled at that. Then, behind my father, I saw Sue come to the door. He obviously heard her, too. She expected him to turn around, but he kept looking at me, brushing my hair back. Finally, I said, "Sue's here."

"Yes," he said, but he still didn't turn back to her. Only, "What is it?"

"Pop, can I go out to a movie tonight?"

He kept his hand on my forehead, looking at me. "Sue, your brother is sick. Tell them to call back after the doctor comes."

"But, Pop, this is *very* important." I knew right away it was Eddie, the glorious inaugural telephonic contact with Eddie.

"I said," Pop declared, still not looking back at all. "I *thought* I said very clearly—your brother is sick, and we do not have the time to discuss movie plans until after the doctor leaves." Sue didn't answer; she just stood there. "Is that crystal clear, Miss Susan Bannister?"

"Yes, sir."

Over Pop's shoulder, I watched her slink away. The fact is, I felt a little sorry for Sue. Maybe just because it diverted me from my own situation. But I did say, "I think I know who it is. I think it's Jake's brother. Eddie. He's okay."

"I'm sure he is. But even if he is the king of France, we will discuss it later." He mopped my brow.

I thought a while. Finally, I said, "Pop?"

"Yes?"

"Pop, if I don't have polio?"

He swallowed before he answered. "I'm sure you don't, kiddo. I'm sure you don't."

"But if I really don't. If the doctor says I don't."

"Yes?"

"If I don't have polio, will you lend me seven dollars?" He looked at me quizzically. "I'll pay you back," I added quickly. "I'll make enough from the *News-Post* to pay you back by the end of the summer."

"Well, all right. But can you tell me why you want the seven dollars?"

"Do I have to?"

"Well..."

"I mean, it's nothing wrong, Pop. It's nothing illegal. It's not dirty pictures or anything."

My father smiled down on me. Then he reached into his pocket and extracted his bills. Pop always carried his money loose, while most of my father's friends kept their money neat in a wallet. (I liked that about him. It showed a certain panache, I thought.) He laid out two ones, then fished out a five, too. "There's the sawbuck," he said.

"I'll pay you back, I promise."

"Aw, it's on the house. If you promise me it's nothing to get arrested for—and if it is dirty pictures, I get to see 'em." He winked, and that made me smile, but then he jumped up because he could hear the doctor arriving downstairs.

I tucked the seven bucks under my radio. Just between us chickens, the reason I needed that was to make thirty dollars total, which is what it cost to send away for the Charles Atlas Dynamic Tension muscle-building course. It was advertised on the back cover of most funny books, with the bully kicking sand in Charles Atlas's face when he was an erstwhile bag o' bones like the incumbent me. Thirty dollars seemed to me to be a reasonable price to pay to strive to become as strong and as cool and as shoe as Eddie Brothers.

The doctor checked me out, felt me all over, took my temperature, and then he gestured to my parents to step outside my room. Right away, I piped up, "Please, doctor, I wanna know, too."

Mom and Pop glanced at each other, and my father shrugged, so the doctor put down his little black bag on the end of the bed and sat there. "Well, son," he began, "all I know right now is that you've got a summer cold."

My face brightened. "You mean I don't have polio after all?"

"I can't say that. I don't know. Yet. You've got the symptoms, but just getting the symptoms doesn't mean getting polio. It's also even possible that you've gotten a touch of polio."

My mother gasped. Pop took her hand. "What's that mean?" I asked.

"Now, don't worry, Mrs. Bannister. It's like when you get a vaccination." He turned back to address me. "You know, you'd actually be getting a small bit of smallpox so then you wouldn't come down with the whole disease. You understand that?"

"Yes, sir."

"We think that might be the way polio works. We think it's probably spread by unclean things—something as simple as dirty water, for example. Sewers. We think it's possible that once almost everyone actually got a little polio when they were children. Nobody even knew they had it. But as we've become so advanced with hygiene in our society, children aren't exposed to the same risks any longer. In a sense, our very advances have made us more vulnerable...at least to this one disease. Follow me?"

"Yes, sir."

"You see, it doesn't appear to be a coincidence that polio is most prevalent in the healthiest country in the world."

"We're a victim of our own success," Pop said, neatly turning polio into an American asset that any chamber of commerce would be proud of.

But I knew he didn't mean it that way. He was just trying the best he could.

The doctor picked up his bag and rose from my bed. "Christy, I'd like to tell you more now, but we just don't know enough, yet. Call me if there's any change. Call me immediately. Otherwise, I'll come by first thing tomorrow morning."

So, all I could do was wait. The thing was, too, that I didn't feel that sick. I could have gotten up, put a wrapper on, gone down, and watched TV. But we all knew the way polio came. And we knew that the chance for paralysis was even greater among older kids like me. There was a boy named Donnie Clarke two grades ahead of me in Terre Haute, and everybody knew the tale about how Donnie Clarke was riding his bike one morning. He didn't feel too good, and just like that, by the next morning, he was strapped into an iron lung. We all knew those kind of Donnie Clarke stories.

Hughie came in and stood at the foot of my bed. All this time, he'd been rooting around for his POLIO PIONEER button, which he'd been awarded this spring because his class in Terre Haute had been one of the ones where Dr. Salk's vaccine had been tried out. Hughie's class had been among the first ones, after Dr. Salk's own children, to be tested. Now he wore his POLIO PIONEER button as if somehow it were a talisman that could ward off the evil spirits of this disease from the subdivision. And maybe it did, too, because Hughie made me laugh some, even as I could hear Mom and Pop arguing in their room.

Mom: "You had no right letting him swim in that pool."

Pop: "Darling, shhh, he'll hear you."

Mom: "Letting him swim in a pool where a girl actually had polio."

Pop: "Cecelia, for Chrissake, we can't lock our children up, and—"

Mom: "I swear, Bobby, you seem to have lost full control of your senses since you moved to Baltimore. I swear, if Christy has polio, then..."

Pop (screaming): "Don't you dare ever use that word again."

Hughie ducked his head, embarrassed that he had to hear this, too. He stepped away, glanced out the window, and as soon as he did that, he did sort of a double-take. "Hey Christy," he called back to me. "Guess what? It's Kathryn."

"Whaddya mean?"

"I mean it's Kathryn. You know, from the pool."

"Where?"

"Right here." He pointed down below.

I couldn't believe it. I threw off my sheet and went over to the window. And sure enough, there she was. Herbert and Lavinia were rolling her out of the back of the station wagon. It was such a production to go anywhere that Kathryn seldom bothered. But here she was. I pushed past Hughie and leaned out. Then my head swam a little, so I rested it there on the sill before I called out, "Hey, Kathryn." I could see her head move. "Up here."

Lavinia turned the gurney around to where she could look up at me. "What're you doing up, Christy? Mr. Gardner told Mom the doctor had to come."

"Well, he did, but I heard you were out here."

"I didn't mean for you to get up. Are you feelin' okay?"

"I don't know. I guess." But, in fact, I was suddenly light-headed again, and so I had to lean back down on the sill.

"Look, you go back to bed," Kathryn said. Then, over to the side, I could see my father and mother coming out the front door to see what was going on. "I just wanted to call out a big 'hi' to you," Kathryn explained.

"Hey, thanks," I said. And then quickly, "Don't worry, Mom. I'm going right back to bed."

Mom nodded gravely, and Kathryn hollered, "Come back over as soon as you're well because we've got a lotta work to do."

Pop said, "Maybe the day after tomorrow, Kathryn."

That made me smile, so I pushed myself back up and waved. "See ya."

Softly, Kathryn called to Lavinia. When the old lady got over to her, she picked up Kathryn's right hand and drew it up by her mouth. Kathryn kissed her hand, so that Lavinia brought it out toward me as if Kathryn was throwing me a kiss. "Get well, Christy," she called up to me, and then as Pop helped Herbert slide Kathryn's gurney back into the station wagon, I could hear her singing, "Sh-boom, sh-boom, la-da-da-da-da-da-da-da, sh-boom, sh-boom." It came up loud and clear to my room.

And so Hughie helped me away from the window, and I fell back into my bed. I took some soup, and I could hear Sue thanking Pop for letting her go out with Eddie that night. But not long after that, full of codeine, I slipped off. When I woke up, it was the next morning, and the doctor was standing there with Mom and Pop. He shook me gently. "How do you feel now?" he asked, putting his hand on my brow. "Hmm, still a little temperature, I'm afraid."

Mom drew her hand up to her mouth and gasped a little.

"You still have a headache?" the doctor asked me.

I was so groggy and so weak that I had to shake my head to find out the answer. "Maybe, I guess," I whispered, and Mom gave out another sigh because she knew, as we all did, that that wasn't a good sign.

The doctor stroked his chin and passed me a cup of water to take some aspirin with. "All right, let's give a listen," he said, and he pulled up my pajama top and put his stethoscope to my chest. Suddenly, though, he stopped and peered curiously at my stomach. "My God, what's that?" he asked, and he drew closer. "Is that a black widow spider in Christy's belly button?"

"What?" I screamed, and instinctively my head shot up off my pillow so that I could see down just as my hands flew across my stomach to knock the black widow away before she poured her deadly venom into me.

Mom and Pop cried out, and Pop even took a step toward me. A black widow spider? In Christy's belly button?

But the doctor raised up his head and smiled gently. "I guess I was mistaken," he said. I saw the little twinkle on his face, and I understood. Even before Mom and Pop, I caught on. Immediately, I swiveled my head from right to left as if I were some kind of a puppet, and I waved my arms all around. Even though I was lightheaded and I really did have a little headache, I sprung up on my knees and started bouncing on the bed. Then I jumped clear out of the bed, swinging my arms all around and prancing up and down, yanking my head this way and that, and all the time yelling, "I'm not paralyzed. I'm not. I don't have polio!"

I saw Hughie materialize in the door with his POLIO PIONEER button on his pajamas. I hopped over to him, gave out a big Indian war whoop, and called out, "Ain't the beer cold!" which is what Chuck

Thompson said when the Orioles did something good. That threw Mom for a loop. "Go to war, Miss Agnes," I screamed. But Mom didn't care anymore what I was saying. She and Pop started crying and laughing, and they grabbed me and hugged me, which was a pretty good idea because by now, I was about to fall over, faint. The main trouble was I hadn't had enough to eat. Just soup.

"No, Christy," the doctor pronounced, "no, you don't have polio." And then everybody pumped the doctor's hand, and Hughie and I made so much noise that it woke up Sue about three hours early from her beauty sleep. There she was now, too, standing in the door in her wrapper, watching us all jump around until she figured out what was happening, too, whereupon she started crying for me and for happiness.

It was one good morning for the Bannister family. I wasn't paralyzed with polio, and Sue was waking up, madly in love with Eddie Brothers.

# 15

Soon, Eddie was very much a part of our family. Every day, as soon as his construction job was finished, he'd be by our house in his '49 Ford convertible. Mom let him take a shower in the bathroom that Hughie and I shared, and then, in his clean clothes, he and Sue would take off with the radio at 1230 on your dial, WITH, because that was the station most likely to play "Sh-Boom." Anyway, if it wasn't playing on the radio, Sue and Eddie would just sing *a capella.* "Life could be a dream, sweetheart...."

Sue wore her hair in a flip, and even in the summer, her skirt came down fashionably below the knees, almost all the way to her bobby socks and saddle shoes. Occasionally, she and Eddie would both go in Bermudas; plaid was the rage. Eddie came in a crew cut on top, white bucks at the bottom, and usually khaki pants and a short-sleeved shirt with an alligator on it that was rolled up high to bare his substantial muscles to best advantage. (Oh when, oh when, was my Charles Atlas course going to start arriving?) Sometimes Eddie wore his Yale '57 crew shirt and other times a boatneck. I'd never seen a boatneck before.

Moreover, unlike the Terre Haute high-school heroes who had preceded him—Danny Daugherty being the last in that line—Eddie acted like a mature gentleman. He even discussed business with my father, volunteered to do errands for my mother, and treated both Hughie and me with some dignity. Sue's erstwhile Indiana beaux had always blown off the kid brothers, but Eddie would tousle Hughie's hair and tell me mildly dirty jokes. If he got off early from the construction gang, he'd even invite me along with Sue in his snappy convertible so I could deliver my *News-Posts* in style. Definitely, there was a certain reflected glory being the brother of Eddie Brothers's chosen *inamorata*. Why, I figured that even Buddy would have to accept me better when he returned (especially with me all bulked up from my Charles Atlas course...whenever it came in the mail).

Sue had Mom and Pop over a barrel, too. They weren't all that keen about her devoting all her time to one boy—to a college boy!— but, as we all knew by heart by now, she had been the one who had sacrificed the most, leaving Terre Haute just before her guaranteed prom queen year. So they treated her romance with Eddie with kid gloves. Besides, whenever Mom would express even the tiniest of misgivings, Sue would say, "Don't you trust me, Mother?" Or, even better, invoking blood, "Don't you trust your own daughter?"

Sue knew, too, that even if Eddie were an older man, a collegian—a Yalie!—her parents valued him as a local aristocrat. Pop had learned enough about the society of his new city to understand that Eddie was pedigreed, that Brothers was among the very finest old Baltimore names. "Look, Cecelia," I overheard Pop say one night to Mom when they were having their usual calm, rational discussion on the subject, "this is not going to last. It's strictly a summer romance."

"Well, Sue certainly is not under that impression."

"Sue also believed that Danny Daugherty would never look at another girl for the rest of his natural born life, and she was dead right about that...for forty-eight hours."

"Oh, please."

"All right, what's so wrong with her having a little summer fling? And don't forget, thanks to Eddie Brothers, Sue's meeting all the right kids in Baltimore—and I would damn sight rather have Eddie pawing at her Maidenform than I would another Danny Daugherty."

"Oh, Bobby, that's perfectly awful."

"Well, I think Sue's traded up very nicely, thank you."

And, my mother's darkest fears aside, Eddie certainly was encroaching on that bountiful territory. Sometimes, in fact, I could see them necking. Well, I couldn't actually zero in on the action, but out my window I could see Eddie's Ford come slowly down Dogwood Circle late at night, there to park in the driveway of one of the new houses. Talk about convenient: a private make-out spot right next door to your girlfriend's house.

I retained all the confidence in the world, though, that my sister would remain a "good girl." After all, I knew that she hadn't given into Danny Daugherty's aggressive entreaties for a whole year after he gave Sue his ring, so she certainly wasn't going to let Eddie Brothers hit her for a home run in a couple of weeks when he hadn't even anted up the appropriate jewelry.

So one morning I even asked, "Hey, when's Eddie going to give you his ring?"

Sue shook her head and answered me in that insufferably patronizing way that people do only after they have just learned themselves what you just asked. "Oh, for Pete's sake, Christy, grow up. Eddie goes to college. They don't do that at college. Rings."

"They don't?"

"No, silly. In college, the boys have fraternity pins. If you're his girl, he pins you." And she tossed her head, sighed, and walked away, having suffered fools enough for this particular morning.

Unfortunately for Sue, though, she got stuck with me again soon enough because Eddie got off early when the special union crew that blacktops the roads came on his job this day. Despite Sue's grimaces, he offered me a ride over to Kathryn's, and in protest, Sue snuggled up that much closer to Eddie to make me feel even more out of it. It was amazing to me that he could even shift gears with her all packed up against him. Of course, would he complain if maybe he got a cheap feel every now and then when he jammed it into first or third?

Besides, what did I care? Today I was inviolate. Today my first installment of the Charles Atlas Dynamic Tension course had arrived in the mail. It came in a discreet plain envelope marked only, "C.A., 115 East Twenty-third Street, New York 10, N.Y." (On top of everything else, my first connection ever with the fabulous Gotham.) Already, too, I had taken it up to my room, shut the door, and torn into the envelope, yanking out the sky-blue cover inside, there to reveal the photograph of Charles Atlas himself. Just so there was no mistake, he was identified as, "Holder of the Title: 'World's Most Perfectly Developed Man,'" with his first signed letter to me beginning, "Dear Friend...."

Wow. I dove into the opening sentences. This wasn't going to be easy, my new friend cautioned me. If it was easy, anybody could look like him, anybody could be perfectly developed. It was going to be hard work, and he was counting on my devotion. Moreover, he wanted his students to perform his Dynamic Tension exercises naked before a mirror. This was more than I had bargained for. So I decided to meet Charles Atlas halfway.

I would use a mirror.

There, in my shorts, I began the first exercise, For Chest, Shoulders, and Back—making a fist of my right hand, pressing it down into the palm of my left. Push. Push back. Dynamically.

"Sh-boom, sh-boom. La-da-da-da-da-da-da-da, sh-boom, sh-boom...."

The whole way to Kathryn's I sang even more lustily than Sue or Eddie, for I thought I could already feel my muscles growing, sprouting like the first crocuses of spring, ready to burst out in all the right places.

# 16

Mrs. Slade ushered me up to Kathryn's room, where she was reading a book as Lavinia turned the pages. "Eddie drove me over," I reported.

"Yeah? How are the lovebirds?"

"Pretty hot and heavy," I replied, using an expression my mother employed (through teeth gritted).

Mrs. Slade said, "Eddie's older brother, Doug, was Kathryn's beau."

"Yes, ma'am, Kathryn told me that."

"My, there's no secrets between you two, are there?"

"Christy is my confidant, Mother. And now"—she smirked—"he fills me in on all the skinny about *l'affaire magnifique.*"

I didn't know exactly what that meant, but it sounded perfectly glamorous, so I laughed with her. Sometimes when Kathryn said something like that, something wonderfully sophisticated and alluring, I could picture her somewhere stylish looking so chic, probably in spike heels, with a cigarette holder and a cocktail glass. Sometimes I imagined her in jewels in a low-cut, gorgeous gown coming down a long, spiral staircase. You see, I never forgot how she'd looked in Mr. Brothers's home movies. I never forgot how she'd looked *moving.* Whenever I closed my eyes and saw Kathryn, I always saw her that way, flowing.

As much as I visualized Kathryn whole, though—saw her arms swinging and her legs striding, saw her rear end swishing, saw (even) her bazooms heaving under a sweater-girl sweater—I never once fantasized about her moving with me. I guess I was still too young to think about the two of us. Well, except this: sometimes I did visualize her and me diving into the pool and swimming—racing—together in her pool, side by side. But that was all. Kathryn Slade was only my friend, my good buddy, my best pal this one summer of my life.

Mrs. Slade and I rolled her out to the elevator, and after I got Kathryn out to the pool, I dived in and went through my usual paces—a little underwater swimming, freestyle, and backstroke. Then she whistled to me, and I swam over. "Okay, Bannister," she said in her coach's voice, "now for the last part of the medley: the breaststroke."

I scrunched up my nose. "I can't stand it. It looks so sissy."

"I agree. So, we're not gonna do the breaststroke."

That buffaloed me. "But how can I swim the Great Medley if I don't do the breaststroke?"

"Well, there's another kind of breaststroke," she told me.

"There is?"

"It's called the butterfly."

I wrinkled my nose again. I had heard the name, but it didn't mean anything to me. This was before the Olympics were on television. It was even before *Wide World of Sports*. So Kathryn filled me in. The butterfly had only been devised a few years ago, which had created quite a controversy because while the stroke technically was legal within the existing breaststroke rules, the butterfly was faster than the old breaststroke. That, Kathryn explained, drove the breaststroke purists bananas, and so to keep the breaststroke from becoming extinct, the butterfly was separated out as its own event. "It's not only faster," Kathryn told me, "it's not as genteel as the breaststroke. Maybe that's why I swam the butterfly."

"You did?"

"That's right, Bannister. It was my best event. Let's see if you can do it. Start off just standing in the shallow end."

So I jumped in, but right away I found out that she was going to work me harder than ever. "Imagine the reverse of the breaststroke," she began.

"Whaddya mean?"

"Well, we'll start with your arms. In the breaststroke, show me how your arms start."

I placed my hands in the middle of my Charles Atlas-less chest, then moved them out and away. "Exactly. You go forward and out with them, then pull them back. But with the butterfly, it's almost exactly the opposite. Bring your arms out wide." I did. "That's it. Now, you bring them out in a big circle and back to your chest. Go on, go on."

I tried, and I thought I did pretty well, but I didn't pass muster. "No, go around, Bannister, around. Think swoop. It's a big swoop." I thought swoop. I did swoop. "Better, better," she said. I tried again. "No, Bannister, you've got to bring your arms *way* out of the water. The butterfly sounds fragile, but it isn't. It's, uh, violent. Forget butterflies. Imagine you're reaching for something out there. And you're throwing yourself forward. You're thrusting, Bannister. Think thrust."

"I can't think thrust if I'm just standing here," I protested.

"Well, then, don't. Go on, throw yourself." And I did. I threw myself all around the shallow end, swooping and thrusting. Still, whenever I'd pause and look over at Kathryn, even if she said something like, "uh-huh," or, "you're getting it," I could still see the frustration on her face. It must have been so easy for her the first time she'd tried the butterfly. But now she just looked so pained watching me. "Oh, Christy," she finally said, "if only I could show you. Just once."

"Don't worry, Kathryn, I'll get it. For you. I promise."

"I know you will."

So I tried again. I threw my arms far, far out, grabbing for the air as I flung forward. And again and again. Then I looked back over at her.

"Almost. Almost. But don't reach with your arms—"

"But you told me—"

"I know, Bannister. But it isn't *quite* that way. It's different when you say it. You've got to make your body drive your arms. Okay?"

I tried again, not flailing so much now, pushing myself forward off the bottom of the pool. And once more. Then back. And two more. I caught my breath, afraid to look at her until I heard her assessment. Finally, "I think you almost had it right that time. Yeah. Try it again."

And I gave her one more. And another and another until I heard her say, "Okay, take a break." So I drifted over to her. "You're getting it, Christy. You are. You're a good listener. You'll make a good doctor."

"Why?"

"Because you'll listen to your teachers and then—even more important—you'll listen to your patients. Trust me. They can tell you more about themselves than all the medical books and all the stupid doctors can."

I fell out by the side of the pool, my arms stretched out. "Someday you'll be my patient."

"Yeah, I'd like that."

But then I turned my head up to her. "Naw," I went on, "you'll never be my patient."

She frowned, disappointed, even if we both knew this was all kidding around. "No?"

"No. Because they'll find a cure for polio, and then you won't need any doctor."

"Except the obstetrician for my baby," Kathryn said, beaming. But then, right away, she grew stern again. "Hey, Bannister, don't try to brownnose the coach. Bring me an RC, and we'll start working on your kick."

For that, Kathryn had me lean across an inner tube so that I wouldn't do any stroking and blur my concentration as I tried to learn to butterfly kick properly. But it was basically the same thing all over again, me trying to visualize her instructions, her getting frustrated that I couldn't pick up what had come so naturally to her. "Dammit, Bannister, how many times do I have to tell you to keep your legs together?"

"I'm trying," I screamed back, pausing for some breath. What I really wanted to tell her was that Charles Atlas was a whole lot tougher than she was, he was the toughest man in the world, but he didn't feel the need to scream at me to teach me Dynamic Tension.

But I kept mum. I sure didn't want anybody to know I was taking the Charles Atlas course.

"Come on, move your legs with your hips."

"Hips always move with legs," I snapped back.

"You know what I mean," she said, cross.

But I didn't know what she meant. We'd reached an impasse. There just weren't the words to describe what was so indescribably obvious to her. She pondered, sipping her RC. Suddenly, "You know. Like a dolphin. Just like a dolphin, Christy."

I tried to think of dolphins. I really did. Unfortunately, dolphins weren't famous then. They hadn't been discovered by Walt Disney, and we weren't yet on a first-name basis with any of them. "But I just don't know how dolphins move," I explained.

"Oh yeah, I'm sorry." She took another sip, thinking things through. "I got it," she cried out. "It's like, you know..." She paused again, mulling, then quickly, "Christy, it's like screwing."

I was shocked. As blunt as Kathryn could be with me, this was taking candor to a new plateau. "Kathryn?" I asked.

"I know. I know, but—"

"You know, I've never—"

"I know *that*. Me neither, Bannister. But I *think* kicking in the butterfly is sort of what it's supposed to be like."

"You think so?"

"Well, let's put it this way: that's the way I would do it," and we both blushed a little and laughed a lot. I started moving my lower body the way I imagined it was that you screwed (or maybe a dolphin screwed), and pretty soon I could hear Kathryn cheering. Then she whistled, and when I stopped, she called out, "Yeah, I think you got it. Yeah, yeah!"

I smirked, "The butterfly or..." I spit it out "screwing?"

"Both. Now get your mind outta the gutter."

"Why? So yours can float by?" Whatta riposte that was. In fact, I'd just heard it the other day from the cool lips of Eddie Brothers. But it stopped Kathryn dead in her verbal tracks. Grinning, I turned around on the inner tube again and started kicking and undulating, up and down, rhythmic, more spirited, more confident, until all of a sudden I heard Kathryn yell, "Throw away the inner tube!"

So right away I flipped it out from under me and instantly began my arm motion. There it was, all of it, my whole body, the whole stroke, arms and legs, together, one thrust, one swoop. I was rocketing the butterfly.

"Two kicks per stroke," Kathryn called out. "Two of 'em. Yeah, yeah."

At the far wall, I turned, and when I flipped back, I glimpsed Kathryn's face. I swear, there was such an expression of delight that it seemed to have lifted her whole body up. And then I was back in stroke. So wonderful, it felt so natural, so perfect—my arms coming out of the water in great loops, swinging out, curving back, starting again, my legs together, flipping, all of it propelling me, driving me on.

"Feet together," I heard her scream. "Keep your damn feet together." And I did. "Pull in your stomach muscles." I did that, too. "Don't take so many breaths. One every three strokes. You can do it." I did. I kept going, even faster, back and forth, until all I could hear was her whistling. I stopped at the wall.

She was smiling at me. "Just give me one more back-and-forth, Christy. Give it all."

I did. And then I did one more on my own.

I didn't need to hear Kathryn anymore. I knew I had put it all together. Oh, there were little things I was sure I had to perfect, but I had mastered the butterfly. I knew that. And when I pulled myself up out of the water and came to her, she just cooed to me. "Oh, Christy, you were wonderful," Kathryn said. "I felt like I was back doing it myself. I could feel it. I could feel you going through the water."

"Well, you know, you taught me," I replied, for even if I felt such a great swell of pride, I knew it was her that had steered me. "I didn't even know what a butterfly was. I didn't even know what it looked like. And you gave it to me."

"Thank you for that, Christy," she replied softly, and the way she looked at me, I knew she wanted me to touch her.

I did. I reached over and gently caressed her cheek, letting some drops of water from my hand stay there as I took it away before her eyes, tracing it down her arm to where I rested it upon her hand. She knew I was touching her. She knew that even if she couldn't see it or feel it. She understood these things, Kathryn did, because she was older than I and knew more about love.

This time, when she smiled so sweetly at me, it was different. It was soft and tender and full of far greater beauty than I had ever before seen her give to anyone. It was, in fact, a lover's smile, although I couldn't appreciate that then. Really, it was years later before I understood that Kathryn had made love to me in her pool that day—me doing what she told me to do, me moving my body the way she said to do, up and down, sensually, the water passing over and around me as if it were her in my arms and me in hers, so that even if I were still this scrawny pink virgin boy, Kathryn had somehow made me part of her this one summer's afternoon.

Of course, it was a long time before I appreciated this. But even back then, I did know enough to draw my fingers slowly across the top of her dead hand and then to grasp it in my own and hold it tenderly.

And I knew enough to tingle inside.

# 17

One afternoon I had to pass up my swimming practice with Kathryn because Mom made me go with her to buy me clothes for school. We were coming dangerously close to the end of summer. Should this ever skip our minds, there was an advertising jingle on all the radio stations which would bring us back to face facts. I heard it so much I can remember it better even than "Sh-Boom." It was from Robert Hall, which was the first discount store I ever heard of, and the jingle went like this:

> School bells ring and children sing:
> It's back to Robert Hall again.
> Mother knows for children's clothes
> It's back to Robert Hall again.

Of course, no mother of Christopher Bannister would take him to such a "cheap, tackpot place" as Robert Hall. So off Mom drove me to a more respectable haberdashery, there to buy the same khaki pants with a buckle in the back and the same button-down accessories for a more expensive price than we could have purchased them at Robert Hall. But buy me new school clothes we must. Why?

"Because you're growing like a weed," Mom said.

In fact, I wasn't quite yet growing like a weed. It is accurate to say, however, that I was threatening to do so. I was an incipient weed. Because of that, it made no good economic sense to buy something that would only fit me temporarily, so everything Mom bought me had to be a size or two too big so I could *grow into it*, which is another way of saying that when I went to school—to a new school—in a few weeks I would start off looking foolish. From day one.

"Please, Mom, I would rather wear my old clothes."

"I am not having any child of mine go off to school in old clothes," she replied.

"But the new ones won't fit me."

"You will grow into them very quickly, Christy." I couldn't win. I could only hope that my friend Charles Atlas would fill me out with his Dynamic Tension—although his most recent lessons had been about abdomens and necks—necks!—that were of little interest to me

Anyway, since I had gone along with Mom without throwing a tantrum in the store, she bought me a double lime sherbet cone at an ice cream parlor afterward. Mom had one of those things called rocky road or fudge ripple, whatever, that means simply vanilla and chocolate mixed. She had two scoops, too. Mom never had any weight problem. She ate everything and never gained a pound. Sue was that way, too; she had Mom's genes when it came to fat. This left me at a terrible disadvantage when I began to meet others of the female species because I had no home training whatsoever in how obsessive women could be about weight. As a matter of fact, thanks to Kathryn, I knew more about women and menstruation than I did about women and fat.

Mom and I had macaroons after the ice cream, too, but it was still fairly early in the afternoon when we got home. I went outside with Hughie to chuck a baseball around. I didn't even notice that Pop was out on the patio drinking a martini until Hughie made a bad toss and I chased the ball up that way. Pop was turned away from me, just standing there, holding his glass, staring vacantly out to where the house next door was being built.

That was when Mom came outside. "Bobby?" she said. "You're home."

He only shrugged. Myself, I just stood there wondering what the hell had gotten into Pop. Mom went closer. "Bobby, is that a drink?" she asked. "It's only four o'clock."

He turned to her and drained his glass. "I'm sorry, sweetheart," he said. He just tossed the glass away, over onto the lawn. "Dead soldier," he murmured. And then he turned to face Mom, and he moaned, "I'm sorry, but this is about the worst day I ever had. Well, since the war."

Mom ran toward him. "Oh, Bobby, what happened?"

"I had to do something I didn't want to do. Something...not nice."

He held out his arms then, and she fell into them, consoling him.

I picked up the ball and stood there watching them embrace. I was a little scared, all the more so that I could tell Mom was obviously worried. I'd never seen them like this before. Then Pop broke away from her and shook his head mournfully. "Oh, Cecelia, this wonderful old guy at the plant."

"Yes?"

"He's been there for years." He took a deep breath. "I had to send him packing."

I knew right away. I do not think the last word was out of my father's mouth before I screamed, "Sal Carlino!" It just came like that, reflexively. I wouldn't have even known that I'd said it, except, of course, that instantly my father whirled around toward me.

"Christy!" he shouted. "What the hell are you doing out here?"

I squeezed the baseball in my hand. He stepped toward me. I shook my head at him. Never in my life had I been so stunned. "Pop, you promised me. You promised. You said you'd never do that to Sal Carlino. *Ever*!"

Mom looked at her husband and son confronting each other, but she was more baffled than scared. She held out her hands. "Who is Sal Carlino?" she cried out.

Neither of us answered. Hughie came around the corner of the patio. He started to call for me to toss him the ball back, but then he saw this strange tableau and, like Mom, he just stood there, frozen and puzzled.

If Pop saw Hughie, he gave no sign. And he didn't look back over to Mom. Instead, he just kept walking toward me. "Christy, I didn't mean for you to hear—"

"But you told me, Pop." Instinctively, I began to back up. With each step Pop made intently toward me, I took one back, away from him. "You promised me. You would never let Mr. Gardner make you treat Mr. Carlino bad. You promised me that."

Mom said again, "Bobby, who *is* Sal Carlino?" But by now it was nearly a whisper, and all in anguish as she watched Pop come toward me and me glare at him.

I turned to Mom. "Sal Carlino saved me from the drapes. That's who Sal Carlino is, Mom. And Pop promised—"

That only confused Mom more. "Drapes?"

Pop held up his hand to Mom even as he kept looking at me. "Cecelia, please don't get involved."

"You promised me, Pop. You gave me your word of honor."

"Christy, let me explain, kiddo." He took another step toward me. I took another step back.

"This is gonna mean that Mr. Carlino's son won't go to college. Vinny will leave college now. How would you like it if I didn't go to college?"

"Come on, Christy, I can't control Vinny Carlino's life."

I was getting more and more worked up. In fact, no matter what I said, I really don't think I cared all that much about Mr. Carlino at this moment. Not now. It didn't even matter that he had freed me from the clutches of the drapes. Or that Vinny Carlino was going to leave Loyola and go back to Sparrows Point and never be a college man and an officer. All I knew was that my father had promised me something—emphatically, even—and he had reneged on that promise. And so, for the first time in my life, I was looking at a father who wasn't special, who was just someone who lied and betrayed like anyone else. Like other boys' stupid fathers.

And so that was when I reared back and threw the ball at Pop. It didn't hit him. Probably I didn't even mean to hit him. I don't remember for sure. I only do remember that I threw it as hard as I could, and it whizzed close by him. Mom could only gasp. I couldn't see how Hughie reacted right away, but his eyes were wide with fear then when I turned and ran away past him. Ran 'round the other side of the house, out our driveway, and down the street, down to where I got to one of the new houses.

Only then did I realize how tired I was, gasping for breath. I needed air for my lungs and for wherever else in your body the air goes out of you when you're scared and hurt. I wasn't crying, though. That was important to me. I was a teenager now, above the threshold for male tears. Still, I was working up to crying and I probably would have broken down soon enough, but that was when I saw Pop come out of the driveway and head down Dogwood Circle looking for me. He was jogging. "Please, Christy," he called when he spotted me.

I didn't move from off the curb.

He sat down there next to me and gently slapped my thigh. "I know you're upset, kiddo," he said.

"Don't call me 'kiddo,'" I snapped.

"You don't like 'kiddo'?"

"I *never* liked 'kiddo.'"

"All right, I'll never call you 'kiddo' again."

"Fine," I went on, more surly all the time. "Call Hughie 'kiddo.' See how much he likes it."

Pop nodded, happy to let me play out my venom on 'kiddo.' But I had shot my bolt and only looked away from him. Pop had taken his hand off my leg and laid it on the back of my neck. So now I not only scrunched my shoulders to signal for him to stop touching me, but for more dramatic effect, I shifted my seat on the curb a few more inches away from him. He got the point. Then while he was trying to figure out, anew, what to say, I snapped my head back toward him, and I snarled, "You know what?"

"No. What?"

"I'll bet you went to that whorehouse in Atlantic City, too. That's what."

That caught my father completely off balance. At first, he really couldn't understand what I was alluding to.

"I thought so," I sneered, taking advantage of his hesitation.

Finally, he sorted things out. "So," he began, "now you can't believe anything I ever told you. Right?"

I shrugged, suggesting that was the gist of it.

133

"Just because of this one mistake, you think your father is a total liar."

I crossed my arms. "Don't blame me."

"I'm not."

"Yeah, well, you told me this was the most important thing in the world to you. You were the one who made it such a big deal. And you told me not to mention Sal Carlino's name to Mom. And I didn't. I kept my word."

"Thank you, Christy."

"And you told me not to tell Mom how the drapes came over here, and I didn't do that, either. Because you told me not to. You told me Bannister men keep their word." He only nodded; he knew what was coming. "And then you do this."

"Yes," was all my father said.

"Well why, Pop?"

"Look, I can't do anything about Sal Carlino now, but I don't want you to hate me, k—." He had started to say 'kiddo,' but luckily, he had stopped himself in time. "I want you to trust me again."

"Why should I?"

"Fair question." He leaned back, lying out on the dirt. There wasn't any pavement yet. Just dirt. He stared up in the sky, trying to find the words. "Look," he finally began, "the best I can say is: things change. I know that's hard to accept, but you'll understand better when you get older. Things don't just stay the same. They change. They move."

He sat back up, picked up a stone, and chucked it over to a dirt pile by the new house. I thought maybe he was going to use the stone hitting the dirt as an illustration of things changing, the way science teachers always do, but thank God, at least Pop hadn't descended to that level. He only said, "Believe me, it broke my heart, but...something changed."

"Look, you told me this was a matter of principle, Pop. That's what you told me. And principles don't change. I may still be a kid, but I know that."

"Well, yes, but—"

"Isn't that what you told me? Always? Principles don't change."

Pop rooted around for another stone in the dirt. He hadn't expected me to confront him with that. The very worst thing in any argument is when somebody plays something back from you in exact contradiction to what you're currently arguing. Pop had to deal with that. He found a stone and turned it over in his hand. "Yes, I said that. And I don't dispute it. I am *not* going back on my word."

"Again." That was pretty snotty of me, but I couldn't resist.

He didn't take the bait. He only also said, "Again," and went on. "But sometimes—not often, but sometimes—principles collide."

"Like what?"

"Well, I'll give you a classic example," Pop said, and relieved to come up with a classic example, he launched into Oliver Wendell Holmes declaring that, notwithstanding freedom of speech, you couldn't yell "fire" in a crowded theater. It's a pretty impressive story the first time you hear it, too. And this was the first time around for me. It wears over time, though—every charlatan and phony enlisting poor old Mr. Justice Holmes in their defense in some far-fetched mis-representation. But, first time out of the box, the you-can't-yell-fire-in-a-crowded-theater argument plays awfully well. "So you see where principles can collide, Christy?" Pop concluded.

I nodded. "But, okay, then, what collided with Sal Carlino?"

Pop dared touch me for the first time in a while, holding his palm on my shoulder. And he had me gauged right; this time I accepted the gesture. "I'm sorry," he said. "I can't tell you that. Much as I'd like to, it's privileged information. It involves somebody else. Somebody who's a friend could've been hurt. That was what changed. That was what was facing me." He made a little grimace. "I just got my tit caught in a wringer."

I'd never heard that expression before, and mad as I was, it made me smile a little. A tit in a wringer was certainly every bit as vivid as what Mr. Justice Holmes had to offer. "Yes, sir," I said.

"And if I told you now, I'd be breaking my word to someone else."

"Yeah."

Pop looked directly at me. "So, if anything good can come outta this," he went on, "it's maybe someday you'll find yourself in a situation like this—"

"With my tit in a wringer?"

He laughed. "You like that, huh?" I admitted that I did. "Well, maybe having seen me go through it, you'll be better able to get yourself through—and do a better job than your old man did this time."

"Maybe," I said.

He slapped me on the back and stood up. "Okay, that's enough of me shooting my mouth off. I'll get outta your hair, Christy."

"All right." I think he hoped I was going to say it was all forgotten, all behind me, but it wasn't. I couldn't grant him clemency just like that. It wasn't that easy, even with principles colliding.

So when he understood that, he started to walk away, and for the first time I could see Mom standing way down by our house, anxiously watching the two of us. But Pop stopped after a few steps, and even walked back a step or two. "Whatever you might think of me," he said, "*I'm* very proud of you, Christy. I'm very proud that you could be so upset that I broke my word. I'm sure a lotta kids would've just shrugged and said: who cares?"

"Well, I guess I learned that from you, Pop."

He gave me a little salute. "Okay. So I learned something about me today, but I learned even more about you, and that's a silver lining to this whole mess."

After a while, I went back up to my room, and I started doing my Dynamic Tension exercises again. I did them with a vengeance, too—even the abdomen and neck stuff. Also, proudly, for the first time, I did them buck naked.

# 18

Almost everybody was back from vacation now, so Kathryn's pool was jammed mornings. I would've stopped going then, except Mom made me accompany Hughie when she didn't have to be one of the mothers in charge. What was even more infuriating, Sue would invariably show up with Eddie just as all the little kids had to leave, and they would greet Kathryn together, stroll to the pool together, dive in together, swim together—not to mention kissing underwater and exhibiting sundry other affectionate gestures of that nature.

Still, how could I complain? Eddie's summer job had ended, and so he spent almost all his time with Sue. That meant there was hardly an afternoon any longer when I couldn't deliver my *News-Posts* from the back seat of Eddie's convertible. Man, I was in clover.

Indeed, it was Sue who got sucker-punched. She was so sure that she had Eddie all to herself until he went back to Yale when, a bolt out of the blue, came competition. It wasn't another girl, though. That would have been simple. And a fair fight. There wasn't a girl on the face of the Earth that Sue Bannister feared head-to-head. But no, this was a new, invidious rival. Debutante parties. "The Little Season," Eddie explained. Eddie *had* to go to debutante parties every night.

There had not been debutante parties in Terre Haute, and so Mom's soothing observation that, had they existed there, Sue would have surely been a debutante was of no consolation. The only thing that mattered to her was that, all of a sudden, as Labor Day neared, Eddie was required nightly to attend debutante parties.

They were held at the grandest houses, at mansions, at great tents set up on lawns, or at the finest country clubs in be-chandeliered ballrooms where the Duchess of Windsor herself and all the other belles of Baltimore had danced down through the ages.

So there was Eddie, all morning with Sue. And all afternoon with Sue. But just as night shades started to fall, as boyfriends and girlfriends the world over started going out under the moon billing and cooing, Eddie would take Sue back to our house, then return home. There he put on his dancing pumps and his white dinner jacket with matching tartan bow tie and cummerbund, and off he'd hie to a wonderful party. There to drink with the other Ivy League boys and dance with the fancy college-girl debutantes—genuine, high-tone, honest-to-God *debs*—in expensive gowns with bare shoulders and crinolins that made their skirts flare out and whirl whenever Eddie took them in his powerful arms in time to the music.

While Sue sat at home in the subdivision with her mother and her father and her pain-in-the-ass brothers. The cheese stands alone.

God knows I had seen Sue in various Oscar-winning exhibitions of extreme emotional distress. But she had never seemed so helpless. Debutante parties were nowhere listed in the all-American book of life, teen division. The universal deal was: I'm your gal, you're my guy. But here was Eddie saying, sorry Sue, but the ground rules here in the Little Season are that I have to go out with other girls. I have to laugh with them and flirt with them and brush by their breasts and touch their bare shoulders as I take them into my arms and dance with them. I am obliged to spend my evenings at these deb parties. It is what the finest young gentlemen of Baltimore are required to do for their birthright. Going to debutante parties is my...

...duty.

In her abject frustration, lacking any other confidants (for she still had no girlfriends in Baltimore), Sue sank to such depths as to even discuss these matters with me. "You can talk to Eddie, Christy. Please."

"But I don't even know what these parties *are.*"

So in her despair, Sue could only visualize the scene, with

scores—yes, surely, hordes—of beautiful, charming, alluring, (not to mention) brazen women whirling in Eddie's magnificent arms to the usual dance fare, to Strauss waltzes and show tunes, to Mantovani, to, yes, even to "Sh-Boom." Tactlessly, Eddie had told Sue how all the best debutante bands—Lester Lanin, Meyer Davis, all of them—had broadened their repertoire for the Little Season to include "Sh-Boom." This particularly seared Sue's mind, this vision of Eddie dancing to "Sh-Boom" with other women in sequined ball gowns—and diamond tiaras, too, no doubt—and it kept her tossing and envisioning even long after Mom and Pop had made her turn off the light and go to bed.

Finally, Eddie came up with what he considered a solution. He would leave the dance early and go out with Sue then. "You mean...a late date?" she asked dubiously, for it was universally accepted that any girl who went out with a boy on a late date was a punchboard.

"I won't tell anybody," Eddie added quickly, protecting her reputation.

Sue was tempted. "But my parents would never let me go out late."

Eddie was ready for that. "Look, my parents are down at Rehoboth—"

"Where?"

"You know. The shore. They're down there with the Slades for a week. I'm babysitting Jake. So I could take you over to my house while I'm at a party and then meet you back there."

"Your house, Eddie?" Sue was incredulous. "I can't stay alone with you in a *house*."

"No, no. We'd go out, just like always, when I get back. You'd only be alone there with Jake. What's the difference whether you're sitting in a house with Christy or Jake?"

Sue thought that logic over. "Yeah, okay," she said.

But, unfortunately, she outsmarted herself. If she'd just stayed at Eddie's house and made out with him there instead of parked in his car next to our house, who would have known (well, except maybe for Jake, and he didn't count)? But Sue demanded that they have a proper date, so Eddie would change out of his tuxedo, and then he would take her over to the Toddle House for a hamburger. People would see Eddie and Sue there, and because everybody knew Eddie went to the deb parties, it was obvious to the world that he was having a late date. And there went Sue's reputation. She became known as "Eddie's chick from the subdivision," and it was sort of understood that subdivision girls were tarts. Even if there had never been a girl from our subdivision before. But it just seemed right— probably especially given Sue's big set of jugs. Soon, yet innocent and unawares, Sue was besmirched.

Even Kathryn heard. (It was amazing what Kathryn heard, given her inaccessibility.) When I was over at the pool alone with her one afternoon working on my butterfly, she began to hint, obliquely, at the gossip. I wasn't sharp enough to catch on, though, so finally I just spouted, "Kathryn, what *are* you getting at?"

"Scratch my nose, please. I got an itch there." I knew by now that when Kathryn had an itch—said she had an itch—it was her way of buying time. I scratched her nose.

"Well?" I said.

"Forget it, Christy. I really don't think we can talk about this."

"Why?"

"Because it's...well, it's about your family, and maybe that's none of my business." As you can see, Kathryn was getting off the ethical hook, making me beg to hear.

"Come on, Kathryn. Aren't we good friends?"

She smiled so sweetly. "Of course we are."

"Well, we agreed: friends shouldn't keep secrets, should they? Otherwise, it doesn't count, being friends."

"Uh-huh." She paused. "Well, okay, but it's about Sue."

"What about Sue?"

"Well, I keep hearing about her and Eddie."

"Yeah, she's crazy about him." I still wasn't catching the drift.

"I know. I hear she goes out with him on...late dates."

Now I got the point. "You mean like she's..." I took a long breath. "...putting out?"

Kathryn nodded very solemnly. "I'm sorry, that's what I hear."

I let that sink in. I could even feel myself reddening on Sue's behalf. I was so mad, in fact, that I actually stamped my bare foot. "Well that's BS, Kathryn. That's a crock."

"I hope so."

"Well, it is. She didn't go all the way with Danny Daugherty in Terre Haute, so she wouldn't do it with Eddie Brothers, either." I started to add some more in my sister's defense, but I stopped. I remembered my father. I'd believed him about Sal Carlino, hadn't I? "Well, I don't know, of course," I added. But when I heard myself say that, I got angry at myself. Here I was visiting the sins of my father upon his daughter. "No, I'm sure, Kathryn. I'm certain. Sue's a good girl. Like you." Kathryn's eyebrows arched. "You didn't do it with Doug Brothers, and Sue isn't doing it with Eddie Brothers." And then a bit belligerently, "How would you have liked it if they'd said that about you?"

Kathryn smiled, moving her head just so. By now I knew there were certain movements she made with her head that corresponded to how she would have moved her body if she still had a body that moved. It's hard to describe, but the way she moved her head would tell me that she would be shrugging or crossing her arms or jabbing me with a finger, whatever. This time, the way she moved her head, I knew she was clapping me on the back, throwing an arm around me in the manner of a comrade. "You're a good brother, Christy Bannister," she said, "but if you get a chance, tell your sister to be careful with Eddie. There's a lot of ways a boy can hurt a girl."

"A girl can hurt a boy, too."

"Yeah, she can break his heart. But that's all she can do. A boy can do lots of things to a girl."

"Okay," I said, but since the whole conversation was embarrassing me, I turned away then to go back into the pool.

Kathryn called to me, though, just as I stood there ready to dive in. "Hey, Christy." I turned back. "Have you gained weight?"

And there, for the first time in my life with a woman, the Earth moved. Or it stood still. Or both. For Kathryn had spoken the most wonderful words that had ever fallen upon my ears. Slowly, heading back over to her, holding my shoulders back even more than I usually did, I struck the most casual he-man pose that I had perfected before my mirror. "A little," I shrugged. "Three and a half pounds."

"God, I thought so," Kathryn said. "I knew you looked different." I beamed. "What're you eating? Lots of milkshakes?"

I sidled closer to Kathryn, trying to make my biceps bulge. "No, it's kind of a secret."

"I thought we were friends, and we didn't have any secrets."

There she was, putting me on the spot again. But I did want to tell her. I needed to share this with someone. Still...: "You won't tell? Promise?"

"Cross my heart."

"Well, okay. I'm taking the Charles Atlas course."

Kathryn cocked her head. "Really? The guy in the funny books who gets sand kicked in his face?"

"It cost me thirty dollars. I get a new lesson every week. I do 'em every day in front of the mirror."

"Lemme see you better. Turn around." I gave her a full three-sixty. "Well, it sure is working, Christy. I could tell. I could tell you put on weight."

I tried to contain my ecstasy at this unbiased assessment. "Yeah, I know. But don't tell anybody."

"I told you I wouldn't. But you gotta show me."

"Show you what?"

"The exercises."

"I can't show you the exercises."

"Why not?"

"Because they're private. You're supposed to do them in your own room. That's what Charles Atlas says." I drew a little closer. "You're even supposed to do them naked." Uh, oh. As soon as I'd revealed that little tidbit, I regretted it.

"Yeah, you do 'em naked?" Averting my eyes from her, I nodded. "Stark naked? Naked as a jaybird?"

"Hey, come on."

"Go on, Christy, show me one. I don't mean naked. But this is private enough."

Well, the cat was out of the bag, so the invitation was too tempting to decline. I set myself in a muscleman pose, bending low, then linked my two forefingers and pulled them hard against each other, lifting my arms over my forehead, then back down again.

"Wow," Kathryn cooed. "I could really see your muscles."

"Yeah, I know," I replied—although keeping my modesty to a fault. As so well I knew, us strong men are supposed to be the silent types.

"And you watch yourself while you're doing this stuff? *Naked?*"

"Well, you don't *have* to be naked," I assured her.

"Yeah, but I'll bet it's more fun, isn't it?" I blushed. She sighed. "I remember when I was about your age, Christy, and I would stand in my room in front of the mirror, and I'd throw out my chest and turn all around, studying my bazooms. If I looked long enough, I could just see them sprout, at least another inch or two." She laughed, letting me know it was okay to smile, that the joke was on her. So I made fun of myself, posing like my friend Charles Atlas did in the funny-book ads with my body twisted just so, one arm up, one down and back, muscles flaring everywhere in my new leonine body.

"Hooray," Kathryn cried out, and she winked, too, which was her way of applauding. So I started back to the pool, but once again she called to me. When I turned back to her, she'd changed her expression, and now when she spoke, her tone was very grave indeed. "Christy," she said, "I've got a favor to ask of you."

"Sure."

Kathryn said, "I want you to give up those Charles Atlas exercises."

"What?" I was incredulous.

"Listen to me. Just for a week. 'Til after Marines Day."

"But why?"

"Because I'm not sure that you're developing the *right* kind of muscles for swimming. I mean, you could bunch all up, Christy. You could get musclebound, and that would really hurt you in the race."

Talk about inner conflict. The idea that anyone would even suggest that I could be musclebound was more than I ever could have dreamed. Still, I had to protest. "But Charles Atlas says Dynamic Tension can't really work unless I do it every single day," I said.

"Christy, I promise you. A week off will not destroy your new muscles. I'm sure Charles Atlas would agree."

"But you really think I could actually get"—I savored the word—"musclebound?"

She nodded, solemnly. "There's the chance. And there goes everything we've done, dedicating ourselves to the Great Medley."

I pondered this dilemma before finally, reluctantly, agreeing to sacrifice my health and vanity for our greater cause. "Well, all right, but remember, I'm just quitting for one week."

"I promise I won't stand in your way beyond that," Kathryn declared. So, assured, I dove into the pool and began working strenuously on my backstroke.

Boy, these last couple of weeks, Kathryn had pushed me even harder. Our diligence was matched only by our deviousness. Why, in the mornings when I brought Hughie over, I made sure to flounder about in the pool as if I could barely stay afloat so that none of the mothers or children would be any the wiser to my progress. And I was sure no one suspected that Kathryn was turning the Hoosier landlubber into a fleet marine creature.

Unfortunately, on Wednesday, only five days before Marines Day, Buddy returned from camp, and all my hopes were dashed. His appearance absolutely devastated me. Buddy's baby fat had somehow, miraculously, melted off him in camp. Why, I wouldn't have believed that a person could be so transformed, except, of course, I was already seeing firsthand the wondrous makeover of the human body that Charles Atlas made possible.

But Buddy was not only suddenly sleek and powerful, but at just two weeks shy of his sixteenth birthday—the upper age limit to compete in the Great Medley—he was at the height of his powers. I noted ruefully how Linda fixed an admiring gaze on Buddy as his hard, lean new body arched off the diving board to slash into the deep blue waters.

My hope for victory was gone, all my work for naught. I mocked my stupid self: how easy, how foolish it had been for me to raise my expectations when it was only Kathryn and me working together alone on soft summer days. Oh, of course I was swimming faster. That was true; I knew I had improved a great deal. But once I set eyes on Buddy, on the new, improved Buddy, once I saw my competition for real, in the flesh, once I saw exactly what I was up against, my hopes faded to nothing.

Of course, Kathryn could tell. I didn't have to say a thing to her. Rather, as soon as I'd swum over to where she was by the side of the pool and collapsed there, she made this declaration, "Hey, Bannister, remember, we're not swimming for second place."

"I didn't say we were," I protested meekly.

"You didn't have to. I saw your face. One look at that fat fuck, and you quit on me."

My mouth flew open as, hastily, I glanced around making sure nobody had heard the ultimate indelicacy that had issued from Kathryn's fair lips. Apparently, no one had; life was proceeding normally around the pool, unviolated. Still, when I replied, I moved closer to her and whispered, "He's not fat anymore."

This did not slow Kathryn down. "Well, underneath, he's still a pussy. He'll fold up like a dollar suitcase if you put any pressure on him."

"Gee, Kathryn, I—"

"Look, Bannister, don't you crump out on me now."

I grimaced. "Don't worry. I'll do my best."

"That's not good enough. You and me—*we'll* do our best."

"Yes, Coach," I said. "We will."

# 19

That night Sue and Eddie planned another late date, but since the summer had grown warmer and muggier again, Eddie suggested they go swimming instead of heading off to the Toddle House. So underneath her blouse and skirt, Sue put on her favorite, her pink panel bathing suit with the flower pattern. And when Eddie came back from the evening's deb party, he changed into his blue trunks, she took off her outer clothes, and together, hand in hand, they left the Brothers's house and cut through the backyards to Kathryn's pool.

Eddie had assured Sue that Judge and Mrs. Slade were still away—after all, they were with his own parents down the shore—so no one would hear them swimming. No one would know. Only Kathryn and the servants were there, and Kathryn was long since asleep, her windows closed and the air conditioner roaring. In fact, Kathryn had no idea how long Eddie had Sue had already been there when she happened to wake up. All she knew, she told me, was that when she opened her eyes and glanced out into the bright moonlight, the two lovebirds were sitting at the edge of the pool, their legs dangling in the water and their teeth shining in their smiles.

Kathryn sometimes awoke in the night. Since she might need Lavinia to help her go to the bathroom, a string had been hung down so that Kathryn could turn her head and yank it with her teeth to call her nurse. On this occasion, though, Kathryn had no needs when she awoke. Probably, if the light from the moon hadn't been so bright this night, she would have fallen right back to sleep. But Kathryn always kept the shades open a bit, for even if it meant some light coming in on her, that was worth it, she told me, to be able to see out. She always felt so trapped, there in the iron lung; just to be able to look out her window gave her some sense of openness, of freedom. So when she turned to look out, she clearly saw Sue and Eddie laughing, their legs stirring the nice, cool water.

When Eddie tried to kiss her then, Sue laughed and pushed him away so he fell back on the lawn, arms flopped out, as if she'd K.O.'d him. So Sue leaned down and kissed him on her own terms, softly brushing his lips with hers before she sat back up again and sighed, "Oh, Eddie," to assure him there would be real kisses to come, in time.

Kathryn felt guilty watching, but neither could she help herself. It was not often that she got to see a real slice of life in action before her. Besides, she could not help remembering an evening with Doug Brothers that had taken place just a few weeks—or was it only a few days?—before she caught polio. It was almost in this exact spot, too.

Then, of course, there was no pool, and the garden was even more secluded. Doug would call her from his house, and she would sneak out there to meet him and make out. There had been a hammock in the garden right about there where Sue and Eddie were sitting now. It was in the hammock that Kathryn let Doug do something that she'd never allowed before, which was to unbutton her blouse, pull down her bra, and not only touch her breast, bare, but kiss her nipple. It frightened her so much, so wonderfully, because even if she stopped Doug at that—and she did—she knew in her heart that she loved what Doug was doing to her, and she feared it might not be much longer that summer before she would let him have her all.

All this in the hammock came back so vividly to Kathryn as she watched Sue and Eddie. It didn't even feel as if she was a voyeur so much as that Eddie and Sue were actors playing Doug and her. Kathryn could feel his tongue upon her. She smiled to herself and didn't even think to ring Lavinia to have her close the shade upon the pool and the night and her memories.

Sue let Eddie smooch some more, but when his hand drifted down to the top of her bathing suit, she grabbed it and yanked it away. Just because it was late, she wasn't going to act like a late-date girl. First, before making out, there had to be *some* respectable activity. Was not swimming the order of the evening? So, she pushed him away again, and Eddie, playing along, took another pratfall, only this time he fell forward, right off the edge into the water. Sue laughed at him. So did Kathryn.

Kathryn even turned away then, but she had to look back, and when she did, right away, even from the distance, she could see that Sue's expression had changed. She appeared worried. And then she was looking down into the water, searching for a sign of Eddie. And she couldn't find him.

Quickly then, Sue raised up on her knees so that she could lean over, the better to peer into the pool. But the shaft of moonlight only carried so far down. Sue called out softly, scared. Kathryn couldn't hear her—couldn't hear anything but the air conditioner—but she could see Sue open her mouth, form some words of fear. And she could see that Sue was growing frantic. She looked this way and that, even started scooping up the water as if somehow she could pull enough handfuls of it out of the pool so that the moon could pierce down deeper and show her where Eddie was.

Kathryn froze. She should have pulled the bell chord with her teeth right then. If only she had. Lavinia would have come running, and even if Lavinia and Maizie were the only ones in the house, they could do something. They could turn on all the pool lights, and Sue could find Eddie if the lights were on, and somehow she could haul him out. Lavinia and Maizie could help. They could call an ambulance. Eddie would be all right. If only Kathryn hadn't frozen. But she did. She waited; it just didn't seem like a tragedy soon enough.

Finally, though, she knew she had to turn her head to grab the string in her teeth and yank it, then to scream to Lavinia to hurry.

But just at that very moment, Kathryn saw it wasn't a tragedy after all.

Because that was when Kathryn saw Eddie emerge. The rascal. He had swum underwater way down deep, then across, catty-cornered to the far end. There, in that instant, the way he could with hardly a sound, like some movie-monster creature looming from out of a pond, Eddie had lifted himself in that one sleek move of his up from out of Kathryn's pool. Sue, pawing at the water, never heard him—not then, not next—as Eddie, on his tiptoes, dashed noiselessly around the pool, jumped over the diving board, snuck down the side toward Sue. Kathryn watched it all, relieved, even grinning now.

Poor Sue. She was in a panic. Unable to wait any longer, she rose up, ready to run to the house, to bang on the doors, to cry out, to scream for Kathryn, for anybody, for help.

But at the moment she got to her feet, Eddie caught up with her from behind, throwing his arms around her. He had pulled it off perfectly. Kathryn even had to laugh at Sue when she screamed with surprise. Then Sue got angry. "That wasn't funny," is what she surely said. Then she pouted. Kathryn saw Sue pound Eddie on the chest. But not really, of course. Not with any force. Because now the fury had begun to flow out of Sue, and soon there was nothing left but relief. Oh, Eddie.

So, when he wrapped his arms around her—tenderly now—and held her and kissed her, Sue kissed him back and snuggled up and let him squeeze her in his arms. Even the water on Eddie felt good on her body. It made her want to go into Kathryn's pool with him and kiss him there. That seemed the height of romance, to kiss a boy in the water under the moonlight.

So, when Eddie kissed her again standing on dry land, she let him, and then when he pulled at the strap on her bathing suit, she didn't stop him right away. She didn't want to stop him. Also, Sue was confused, strategically. Always before when Eddie advanced on her, the two were in his car. She knew instinctively, exactly what the territory was and how to align her defenses accordingly. But now it was different. They were standing up. And there were none of the usual barricades: buttons or zippers for Eddie to have to monkey with, a brassiere to confront. That was the step-by-step textbook Sue had studied. But this time, the strap came down, and then there was her breast: bared. Just like that. And Eddie was swarming over it with his hand while his mouth never left hers, pouring into hers. The other strap, the whole top, came down. How did he do that? Eddie was moving so quickly and over open terrain.

Kathryn couldn't take her eyes off the scene. It was mesmerizing in its passion. Kathryn could even see what would happen before Sue could react. She watched Sue moan some happily, watched her toss her head back and sigh as Eddie buried himself in her breasts, his hands and his mouth both consuming Sue in a way Kathryn had never known, never seen, never quite imagined.

God forgive me for watching this, Kathryn thought. But it was so enthralling. And it was moving so fast. Suddenly, Eddie fell to his knees on the grass there, and with one motion as he dropped down, so had he yanked at Sue's bathing suit, pulling it without a hitch down over her hips. Then, in one more nimble pull, he ripped it down further, past her knees.

And there, hardly before she knew it, stood Sue, naked, the whiteness of her bosom and her stomach and hips almost shining as the moon fell upon her and danced across the water. And now Kathryn gasped, for she had not expected this. Certainly not so fast. She had not expected Sue Bannister to be so easy, so hot, so lusty, so, so...raw. She had not expected her to be so giving to this boy.

But then in an instant more, Kathryn gasped again, for she saw Sue was not that. Not at all. Sue cried out, "No, Eddie! No!" She reached down, grabbing for her bathing suit, trying to drag it back up her legs. There was nothing else, nor any hiding. It wasn't like in the car. And she couldn't even reach her bathing suit way down at her ankles. Anyway, she needed to stop his hand now. It was *there*, his fingers. She cried again, "Eddie, please! Stop!"

Eddie was smiling—not at Sue's plight, but simply that he had done so well, played the game so nicely. It didn't matter that she was crying at him now and even starting to pound at his great, broad shoulders. It just didn't matter; he wasn't listening to her pleadings. Instead, Eddie pulled Sue to the ground, laying her down in the grass with one hand and the weight of his body, pulling his own bathing suit off with the other. Sue kept begging him to stop, and she kept trying to push him away, but she grew tired and helpless and very scared. So at last she lay silent, afraid to scream because surely no one could hear her, but just as afraid that if someone did come they would dismiss her as a fool or a slut for leading a poor boy on at a romantic place like this on a late date.

Kathryn watched it all. She was mortified. She had done nothing to help, and now it was too late. Even if she yanked the bell chord with her teeth, there was no way to stop Eddie. Yet still, Kathryn's eyes were drawn to the end of the moonlight, to Sue splayed there on the grass, her teeth gritted, her eyes full of tears, her head turned away from Eddie Brothers.

Finally then, Kathryn rolled her head away from the window and shut her eyes tight. She stayed like that, mad and disappointed at herself. When she did look back, Eddie was off Sue. It had not taken long for Sue to have her virginity plundered on the grass by the side of Kathryn's pool.

Eddie tried now to sweet-talk Sue, even to kiss her, but she only pushed him away. Since he'd had his, he didn't protest any longer, letting her scramble away. She grabbed for all she could, a towel and her pink panel bathing suit. "Hey, wait, come on, let's skinny-dip," Eddie called over to her, but when Sue didn't reply, he got up and stood alone by the pool.

Kathryn's eyes went from Sue to Eddie. Another reason to hate herself. Oh, she didn't tell me all that went through her mind, but enough so that I could gather how angry she had grown. She could not unlock her gaze from Eddie, poised there, naked, the moonlight shining off his amber chest and his milk-white thighs as sure as it had off Sue. Eddie's was a glorious body, lean and strapping, with the kind of muscles Kathryn loved—lithe swimmer's muscles, not the bunchy Charles Atlas kind.

And then, too, in the middle of his body, in the middle of his muscles, Eddie was still erect. He posed there a moment longer—for Sue, for himself—raised up on the balls of his feet. Sue refused to look up; Kathryn could not take her eyes off him. That much she admitted to me, flat out. I don't know if Kathryn had ever encountered a man's erection before. Oh, probably with Doug, groping in the garden hammock—but only to keep him in check, not to share him. But surely, whatever, she had never seen a man like this, naked before her in his wanton fullness, glowing white in the moonlight of a warm summer's night.

Then Eddie's body tensed as he prepared to dive, and with that, Kathryn was as revulsed for what she had watched as she was fascinated. *Who are these men?* she asked herself. She did tell me that. She told me those were exactly the words that formed in her mind. *Who are these men?* It upset her that she would never know any of them well enough to gain the answer.

Eddie dove then, head going first—what we called a "sailor's dive"—for he thoughtfully reached down and grasped his genitals to protect them when he hit the water. So Kathryn looked back to Sue. How utterly forlorn she was. She had managed to get her bathing suit back on, except that one strap was yet undone, and so her left breast hung out as if she had simply forgotten about it. She only shook her head and cried until she clasped her hands before her face, biting into her thumb.

Only when Eddie paddled back over toward her did she make the effort to pull the strap back up, to cover herself from him. Insouciantly, Eddie lay on his forearms, crossed before him on the side of the pool. As nearly as Kathryn could tell from her vantage, he had returned to chatting Sue up, trying to flirt with her. Evidently, it had occurred to Eddie that Sue just might not be altogether enchanted with him, that there might be some fences to mend.

Slowly, though, Sue turned away from him and started walking off into the shadows of Herbert's garden. Kathryn looked back toward Eddie. He seemed to give a little shrug after Sue, then flipped back, splashing some for effect. Kathryn watched for a moment, and then, out loud this time, this is what she said: "Take your dirty thing out of my pool. Take your prick and get out of here."

# 20

Mom had found a dentist and made appointments for us all the next morning. This had been discussed for days. Next Thursday morning, before we go back to school, all three of you children are going to the dentist for a check-up. *Do not dare plan anything else Thursday morning. Is that clear?* It most certainly was.

But here it was Thursday morning, and Sue wouldn't come out of her room.

In fact, she had even locked the door and would not allow Mom or Pop to enter her room. All we could make out, choked through tears, was that she had broken up with Eddie. "Judas Priest," Pop said, throwing up his arms, heading off to the plant, "there has got to be a limit on the number of these things one girl goes through a summer."

"That is heartless, Bob," Mom replied, momentarily coming to Sue's side even if Pop's spoken observation did pretty much match Mom's sentiments, unsaid. And so with no other option but to call the fire department and have them break the door down, Mom left Sue behind and bundled me and Hughie downtown to the Medical Arts Building. "Well, thank God it is only a few more days before she goes to her new school and meets a new boyfriend," Mom said as we headed away.

The good news was that neither Hughie nor I had any cavities. So, as Mom explained, to "celebrate," she would buy Hughie a new pair of school shoes. He sure didn't want 'em and I sure didn't want to go with him, but stuck at the store, I occupied myself, happily, staring down at my feet in the X-ray machine. It indicated in ghostly green light how far your toes went inside your shoes—knowledge gained at the mere price of radiating an entire generation of American children.

Still, after all that, the dentist and the shoes both, by the time we returned home, Sue was still ensconced in her room, moaning. Luckily, just then the phone rang, and Sue's death rattle stopped. "Who is it?" she called out.

"It's Kathryn," I shouted back.

Sue only sighed. Kathryn started right in on me. "Where the hell have you been, Christy?" she snapped.

"I told you. I hadda go to the dentist."

"Oh yeah."

"But don't worry. I'll be by as soon as I deliver my papers."

"Okay." There was a pause. "Listen, Christy, I know we don't want anybody to know we're practicing, but today I'd like you to get Sue to come by with you."

"I don't think so, Kathryn."

"I'm sure we can trust her with our secret."

"It's not that."

"Oh?" Kathryn asked, her voice much too curious.

"Look," I explained, "we can't even get her outta her room. She and Eddie broke up last night, and—"

"I know."

"You do?"

"Will you just tell her that, Christy? And then tell her I'd really like to talk with her."

"Well, if I can."

And, indeed, I even had to wait to pick my spot. But, as the day wore on, Sue at least began to make periodic forays of necessity to the bathroom and the refrigerator. At last she went outside, walking away, peering off vacantly into the fields beyond the house. I waited 'til she had been alone for a while before I finally dared approach. Even from a distance, though, she waved me off. "Leave me alone, Christy."

"Don't worry," I replied, "I don't wanna talk to you either."

"Good."

"But I have a message for you."

She tried to keep the same dull expression on her face, but curiosity broke the mask. Of course, she didn't want to hear from Eddie. From what I would learn had happened, I don't think there was any part of Sue that could ever tolerate him again. Worse, in its way, in the fashion of these times we were growing up in, Sue simply could not comprehend how Eddie could have done to her what he had. Her discombobulation was as great as her hurt. Our world then had rules, neat divisions, careful labels. Everything was *profiled*. And the fun, the game, our whole way of living was in stretching the rules, cannily taking all that there was to its limits. Only well-identified bad guys—communists, for best example—would actually dare flat-out *break* the rules. The price we paid for disciplining ourselves, maintaining the code, was a fair one; it purchased comfort, for we could be secure that (almost) everyone else had also agreed to abide by our rules. That was, I thought, what my father meant by honor. Eddie, though. He hadn't simply raped Sue; he'd violated the compact she been taught, the code that nice American people lived by. Although she surely couldn't have expressed it, the trust Sue had been robbed of was a greater loss than her virginity.

So, curiosity overcoming her incivility, she asked, "What message?"

"Kathryn wants you to come over with me."

She frowned. "Oh, Christy, grow up. Can't you tell I don't wanna go stupid swimming?"

"I didn't say swimming. Did I say 'swimming'? She just wants to talk to you."

That made Sue downright scornful. "Oh, please," she sighed, turning away.

I merely shrugged. "Hey, all right. But I think Kathryn wants to talk about Eddie." At that, I could see Sue's head jerk up. "She knew you'd broken up with him."

Despite herself, Sue turned back to me. "She does?" Even in her despair, it could not escape her that the desperate events of the evening past had taken place at the Slades,' and could that mean...?

Could it be possible that...? "How?" she asked sharply.

"I dunno. Why don't *you* ask her?"

Sue pondered that, but at the last, only shook her head. "Are you going over there?" I nodded. "Well, could you ask her...for me?"

"Okay," I replied, and because I didn't want to be with her any-more, anyway, I started to go away.

But then my sister shook her head again. Not at me. She only nodded it side to side in a way that appeared as if it might roll right off her shoulders. My, but she seemed so forlorn. She'd never looked this way when Danny Daugherty had done her dirt. "Oh, Christy," was all she said.

"I'm sorry, Sue. I'm really sorry."

"No."

"But I promise. I really am."

"No, you have no idea. You just have no idea how terrible it is," she said. I sensed that maybe this was some sort of an invitation to talk, for her to tell me precisely why this was so terrible, but I didn't know how to proceed. I didn't know whether I should say some-thing else soothing or walk up to her and put an arm around her or take her hand. Or what. But I was only fourteen years old, and worse, a boy, and so I just didn't know how to provide comfort.

"Sue didn't come," Kathryn said right away as soon as I showed up at the pool. It kind of annoyed me, too, for I was supposed to be the one who mattered—and here she was worrying about Sue.

"She's very upset," I said. "She asked me to find out what you wanted."

Kathryn took that in very seriously without answering. And Kathryn always answered. So I pushed on. "How come you knew she broke up with Eddie last night?"

Kathryn only looked me square in the eye and said, "Get into your suit, Bannister, and we'll practice."

So I followed orders, got dressed, then wheeled her over by the side of the pool.

"Okay," Kathryn said, "warm up."

I did a little of everything except maybe swimming under water

156

because that can really wear you out, all that holding your breath. After a while, though, I had to swim over to Kathryn because she wasn't saying anything to me. Usually she barked orders the whole time I practiced, egging me on, correcting me. But this time: barely a word. It was obvious she was distracted, and I assumed she was thinking about Sue. "Okay, Coach," I said, "whaddya want now?"

Her head snapped over to me. "All right, Bannister, you ready to go all out?"

"You mean practice the whole race?"

She nodded. "The whole shootin' match. After all these weeks, let's find out what Christy Bannister's made of."

So I scrambled out of the pool and took up my position, ready to dive in. The Great Medley was back and forth four times—first underwater, then freestyle, then backstroke, then finishing up with the breaststroke (or, in my case, the butterfly). "I'm ready," I said.

"Good. Then this is it. I want you to swim just like this was Sunday."

"Okay."

"Get this right then we'll taper off the next few days so you'll be fresh." Great. She was going to let me have some real action. I bent down, my arms out behind me in my best racing-dive pose. "On your mark," Kathryn barked, "get set..." I tensed. She stopped. "Wait a minute. Straighten up, Bannister." I did, happily, because her mind was back on business. "Okay, now keep this in your head. My father is the starter. He'll be standing up on the diving board. Now he's a judge, so he's the last guy to let anybody get away with a head start, but Daddy's also very rhythmic when he puts his judge's voice on, so as soon as he says 'get set,' you say 'one-Mississippi' and then go ahead and dive. Daddy will be saying 'go' at exactly that point. Trust me. Okay, Bannister?"

"Got it." And I shook my hands to get loose the way Kathryn had told me real swimmers did, and then I got back into the starting crouch again.

"On your mark...get set—"

"One-Mississippi," I whispered, and off I went, just an instant before she said "go." Perfect. In fact, I thought I even heard Kathryn say "perfect" just as I hit the water. And across the pool I went, underwater, not using any strokes, but only streaking with the momentum from the dive. The trick, she had taught me, was barely to skim under the surface, for the deeper you went down, the more wasted energy you expended pointlessly, vertically. Then, when I reached the far side of the pool, I poked my head up for air as I made the turn. You could do that easily if you stayed near the surface. But, of course, most guys would never dare come up for air in the Great Medley because it looked sissy, even if it meant that they would probably have to struggle a bit in the last few yards going back.

Kathryn knew all the tricks.

The freestyle followed. I made a good turn. The turns could make all the difference in the world. We'd worked on turns all August. Whatever stroke we practiced, we always finished up doing turns. And now I had turned into my backstroke. And I thought: *left.* Anyway, just in case I didn't think, Kathryn kept screaming out, "Think left, Bannister. Think left. I can't scream at you Sunday. Think left. Think left!" And glory be, I did, and I ended up straight, finishing at the spot almost exactly where I'd started. I had veered right hardly at all.

I came out of the turn into my butterfly, pulling myself forward, my arms thrusting out together in a swoop, my legs undulating like...well, you know. It felt wonderful. It was my best stroke, I could tell. And just for a moment as I rose up, I could visualize Jake and Timmy to one side falling behind me and Buddy to the other, just ahead. I pushed and I thrust, and there was the wall. I grabbed a hold of it and hung there right beneath Kathryn, huffing and puffing, grasping for air, waiting for her unstinting praise, for a rave review.

At last it came. Sort of. To wit, "Not bad, Bannister. Not bad. Improve on that Sunday, and you might even whip Buddy's fat heinie."

I tried not to show my disappointment in her appraisal, lifting myself out of the pool in that sleek Eddie fashion I'd worked on strictly by myself, sans even Kathryn's watchdog eye. "You think so?" was all I said.

She offered up her shrug-face motion. "Well, if you knock off the muscleman crap."

"Hey, I stopped doing my Charles Atlas exercises."

"All right. All right. Then maybe you have got a chance. You've learned what I taught you, Bannister, so it'll probably all come down to guts now." She let that sink in. "Of course, I don't know yet if you've got those."

I didn't give Kathryn the satisfaction of a protest. Instead, I flicked a couple droplets of water on her face. She blinked, but she also smiled; she liked it when I didn't treat her too deferentially. I wiped the water away, and she went on. "You know, Bannister, you have come a long ways. So don't screw it up. Some light practices in the next few days."

"Okay."

"And get some good rest." I nodded. "And when you come out here for Marines Day, take it easy. You're here to race. Don't do a lot of farting around with the other boys. Come over and sit quietly by me like you're being a mama's boy. Okay?"

"I gotcha, Coach." She grinned. It was the conspiracy Kathryn liked, I think, as much as the competition. I was leaning down on her gurney, stretching myself out, expanding my Dynamic Tension chest, filling my lungs back up. "So okay," I said. "Now tell me about Sue."

Kathryn's smile vanished right away. "That's between Sue and me."

"Well, she told me to find out what you wanted. She was the one who told me that."

Kathryn clicked her tongue. "All right. Just tell her I saw."

"Saw what?"

"Never mind. She'll know. And tell her I want to talk to her about it."

"Kathryn, I don't thinks she wants to talk. To anybody."

"I understand that. But you tell her..." She paused, rolling her head to look away from me. Then she turned back. "Can you keep a secret, Christy?"

"You know that."

"Well, you tell your sister that I say she can't let Eddie get away with that. You got it?" I nodded. "And if she'll just come see me, we'll decide what to do."

I nodded again, and solemnly, too, for even though I had no idea what Kathryn might be talking about, with each exchange her tone had grown more grave. And, to emphasize, she went on, "I mean it, Christy. You're not to talk about this to anybody else. This is strictly up to Sue."

# 21

Mom and Pop were going out that night.

It was the first time they'd been invited out since they came to Baltimore, and so, of course, Mom was in a dither. It was not just that they were going out, either. They were going to a party at the Gardners.'

What was Mom to wear?

Mrs. Gardner had called to invite them just the other day. *I know this is such terribly short notice, Mrs. Bannister, but Frank and I were only wondering if....* Maybe Pop made the connection that the invitation just happened to come the day after he did the dirty job on Sal Carlino. All Mom knew was that this was her grand entrance into the cream of Baltimore society. She was not only going to meet her husband's boss's wife, but all kinds of people who mattered, might matter, could/would matter. What to wear?

More to escape Mom's indecision than to look into his daughter's sustained distress, Pop went down and rapped on Sue's door. After her brief excursion outdoors, she had retreated back into her room. She moaned that she was okay but didn't wish to reveal herself to anyone. Pop shrugged. Mom screamed for him to come back and tell her how she looked. He returned, opened the door, and I heard him say, "That looks just great, sweetheart."

And then I heard Mom say: "Tell me the truth, Bobby."

And I heard Pop say: "That is the truth, Cecelia. I swear."

And I heard Mom say: "No. No. No, it just isn't right."

And I heard Pop say: "Jesus," and close the door and come back down the steps to where Hughie and I were watching TV. "I'll tell you guys a little secret," he said. "For when you get married."

"What's that?" I asked. I don't think Hughie looked up.

"When women ask you if they look fine in some outfit, they don't want to hear that they do."

"They want to hear they *don't* look fine?"

"Well, they don't want to hear that either."

"What do they want to hear?"

"I don't know, Christy. I don't know. All I know is that the main difference between men and women is that men just assume that what they own will look good on them—otherwise why did they buy it?—but women assume the exact opposite."

"Oh," I said.

"It's the main difference."

That was when we heard Mom come out of her room. Pop leaned in to us and whispered, "Now, when your mother comes down the stairs, you tell her how pretty she looks."

So Mom came down the stairs, and dutifully, Hughie said, "Gee, Mom, you look pretty."

Pop called out, "Hubba-hubba!" and wolf-whistled.

I said, "That dress sure is great on you, Mom."

But this chorus of praise was not enough. "Well, it'll just have to do," Mom groaned. "I don't have anything else." And she and Pop went out the door, he looking back to wink at me.

Right away, as soon as I heard the car start, I went up to Sue's room and knocked on the door. She told me to go away. I said, "Hey, Sue, I talked to Kathryn, and—"

"I really don't care, Christy." So I left and watched some more TV with Hughie.

When the program was over, though, I went back upstairs and called softly. But this time, when Sue told me to leave her alone, I didn't. In fact, I just went ahead and tried the door handle, and sure enough, the door wasn't locked anymore. As soon as I stepped in, too, I knew I'd done the right thing. Sue was glad I hadn't listened to her. Probably she'd been hoping all day somebody wouldn't listen to her. Poor Sue. There was so much pain and anger and shame jammed inside of her that had no place to get out to. She couldn't call up her old buddies from Terre Haute and explain. She didn't know quite how to tell her mother what had happened, and she certainly couldn't bring herself to talk to her father about that sort of thing.

She just perched on the window seat, all bunched up, staring into the dusk, the tears stained beneath scorched eyes. "Kathryn really, really wants to talk to you," I said, but she only shook her head without turning back to me. "She really does, Sue."

"I don't know her well enough, Christy."

"Well, listen up: she told me to tell you she saw it all."

Sue's head shot up from where she had it buried in her knees, which she had tucked up, her arms around her ankles. "She *saw?*"

"Uh-huh."

"She did?"

I nodded, and taking advantage of her curiosity, came closer. "What happened, Suze? What'd Kathryn see?"

"I can't tell you."

"Well, I know Eddie did something..." I searched for the right word. "Mean."

"Howdya know that? Did Kathryn tell you?"

"Not really. She just said I was supposed to tell you that you can't let Eddie off."

"She said that?"

"That's what she said. Sue can't let Eddie get away with it."

"Oh, I can't, Christy. I can't. But I just feel so awful." And that set her off again so that she started sobbing once more, gasping sobs so great that I actually feared she would tumble off the window seat. I rushed to her. She was so glad I did. Sue fell into my arms, still crying, but trying to talk at the same time, losing her breath, holding me tighter. I felt so useless and so strange, too. God, when was the last time my sister had deigned to hug her awful little bratty brother? Five years ago? Jeez, maybe even eight or ten. And still, even though I sort of knew that she had only accepted my solace in desperation, I also appreciated that all our years of trying each other's souls had brought us to this one moment together, shared, when

Susan Craig Bannister was so glad that she had a little brother to turn to.

And I was so glad to be there. "It's okay," I said. "It's okay, Suze. I love you."

Those words startled her. From her father or her mother she heard them all the time, never doubting them. From her rotten baby brother, the sentiment was something else again, and the beauty and the comfort somehow meant even more coming from me. Of all people. And for me, in that instant, I knew simply, at last, what it was that family meant.

Finally, there in my arms, Sue caught her breath. Although she really couldn't look me in the face, this is what she mumbled into my chest, hoping maybe the words really wouldn't escape, "Oh, Christy, I'm so bad." Then, though, she turned her head up toward me. "But he made me."

"He made you?"

"Uh-huh. I didn't want to." And this time she pulled her head back enough so that she could peer dead into my eyes. "I promise you. But I guess I got Eddie all excited, and I shouldn't have done that."

"Did you tell him to stop?"

"'Course I did. What kind of a girl do you think I am?"

"I know, I know."

"I said: 'Stop, Eddie, stop. No.' I promise you I did, Christy. But..."

"But...?"

"But he wouldn't. He just wouldn't. And...." She couldn't go on from there and fell back into my arms crying again. I started patting her gently on her back the way I remember my mother did to me whenever I felt scared or sick.

Only when I could feel Sue stop crying did I hold her away from me. "Look at me, Suze. Look at me." I raised her chin up. "Listen, if Eddie made you, it can't be your fault. It can't be. Then it's all his fault. Boys can't do things like that."

"That's what I thought."

"That's right. Pop told me there are rules for a gentleman." She nodded. "I thought Eddie was a gentleman."

"So did I. But he's not."

"No." Of course, it still didn't occur to me to say that Eddie had raped her because although certainly he must have, rape then was something that guys with fangs did in alleys to unsuspecting shop girls who strayed by unwittingly.

"And he's going to tell on me, Christy. He is. I know. He's going to tell people I'm a girl who—" She stopped abruptly, unable to speak the ugly words.

Still, that galvanized me. It was bad enough that Eddie had dishonored my sister, but that now he might compound that by slurring her in public made him even more heinous. Gently disengaging myself from Sue, I stood up and declared boldly, "No he isn't, Suze. No he isn't. I promise."

"What can you do?" she asked, trembling a little at such an unstinting declaration.

"Never mind what," I replied, which was a particularly honest answer inasmuch as I didn't know myself what I could do.

But now I had promised my sister, my damsel in distress, and my own father's broken promise about Sal Carlino resonated in my head as I left Sue's room. I could not let her down. At least one Bannister man was good for his word.

So what I did was, I went into my parents' bedroom, closed the door, and trembling, called up Eddie Brothers.

Luckily, Eddie didn't answer. Even better, Jake did. I asked for Eddie. "Christy, you want Eddie?" he asked.

"Yeah. It's personal."

"Well, he's out. He's over at Elkridge at a deb party."

"Okay. Thanks, Jake."

I don't know why I took off then. It was not—is not—my nature to be impulsive, let alone brave. Perhaps it was simply that, at that moment, I had crossed that threshold of becoming a man—and never mind that I still had the body of a boy and the voice of a girl. Maybe, in some way, I have never felt so much like a man—whatever that is supposed to be—as I did at this instant. All I know for sure is that somehow I had to act. So I rushed down the stairs and without a word, stormed past Hughie at the television set, ran outside, and jumped onto my bicycle.

Perhaps I would've felt more assured if I'd not given up my Charles Atlas Dynamic Tension exercises these past few days, but there was no sense crying over spilt milk. Since it was almost dark by now, I switched on my one dim headlight and pedaled out of the subdivision on my Schwinn.

# 22

Of course, while I had never been on the premises of the Elkridge Club, which was a very fancy place, very posh, it was near enough to the subdivision, and the golf course was visible all around. So I headed there directly, pumping up a big hill, pausing to catch my breath before negotiating the long driveway which led down to the clubhouse.

Even as I approached, coasting the last of the way, I could already hear the music playing at the party. The first song was "This Can't Be Love," followed by "Blue Moon." I left my bike in some bushes, pondering my next move. Even so far as I had come, I could still easily turn back. After all, Charles Atlas himself had finished his own full course before he bopped that bully on the beach. If only someone had challenged me. But, just my luck, there was no one outside, no one at the door to deter me and permit my discretion before my valor. The sign said: DINING ROOM CLOSED THURSDAY—DEBUTANTE PARTY. The path was, unfortunately, clear.

So, equal parts scared and determined, I followed the music up a staircase. As I came to the top of the stairs, the music grew louder—"A Fine Romance" it was now—and I could also begin to hear the other sounds of the party, the laughter and voices. I peeked around, then ducked across an anteroom that opened out onto the ballroom and hid behind a large curtain.

From that vantage, I could see the band in the alcove at the far end with tables arrayed to one side where everybody was seated now, having dinner. I was so immediately fascinated by the whole panorama before me that, at least momentarily, I forgot all about Eddie Brothers. The scene was just so completely foreign to me. The boys were not only dressed up in tuxedos, but they were stylish and fitted, looking as if they were altogether at home in them. Back in Terre Haute, we called such unlikely get-ups "monkey suits." But never mind them. The girls. Oh, the girls. How perfectly beautiful they looked to me, all tanned and done up, all be-crinolined in the most gorgeous gowns, all the more Technicolor for the boys being in their black and white.

On the bass drum, the band was identified as the Rivers Chambers Orchestra. When it broke into "Mountain Greenery," there were a lot of cheers, and one of the older men (probably the father of the debutante being honored) rose from his seat and began to dance with a girl with a corsage pinned to her breast. There was more applause, and somebody asked the mother to dance. Then, one by one, other couples left their seats and moved out onto the dance floor.

It must have been the end of the main course because the waiters began to remove the dishes. I could see there were more boys than girls—stags—and some of them were heading back to a bar that was set up in an adjoining room that was barely visible to me. That was when I spied Eddie carrying his glass over for a refill. He had never looked more shoe. He stood out, one of the few guys in a white dinner jacket—with matching tartan tie and cummerbund— even more handsome, more imposing than he had been in his more casual summer ensembles.

For just that moment, suddenly intimidated by the appearance of Eddie in the flesh, I prepared to dash away. Instead, though, I stepped all the way back behind the curtain and caught my breath and my courage. When I peeked out again, Eddie was returning to his seat with a new drink in his hand. But just then, the band launched into "Love Is a Many Splendored Thing," which was a slow, make-out number. Instantly, Eddie handed his drink to a buddy, whirled onto the dance floor, shot his cuffs, and headed directly toward one girl. There was no doubt. I'd already noticed her because she was clearly the most beautiful one there. Long legged, with dimples I could make out even from my distance, she was wearing a peach organdy gown that just about matched her glorious hair in tone; in style, it was strapless, cutting above her most glorious breasts.

I could draw the beeline Eddie made to her with a ruler. He tapped the shoulder of the smaller fellow she was dancing with and immediately, flamboyantly, swept her into his arms. His back was to me now, so I could see the girl clearly, see her smile and coo, see her teeth and those dimples. Quickly, though, Eddie drew her tightly to him, and she fell into him, pressing her body against his, her creamy cheek upon his, and they dipped and turned. I swear, the music dropped to a slower beat just to accommodate the glamorous two of them, cheek-to-cheek.

I wanted to scream out: Eddie Brothers fucked my sister last night, ladies and gentleman, and look, here he is tonight dancing cheek to cheek to "Love Is a Many Splendored Thing" with an altogether different girl. But, of course, I didn't. All I did, in my blue fury, was to edge full out from behind the curtain and stand there in the open, staring at Eddie dancing. I didn't care any longer if anybody saw me.

That was just when the slow dance ended, though, and everybody started screaming, "'Sh-Boom!' 'Sh-Boom!'" and the Rivers Chambers Orchestra lit into playing that the best they could manage. It was good enough, though: almost everybody still sitting at the tables left their desserts there, rose up, and started singing and dancing. When the part came to la-da-da-da-da-da-da-da, everybody sort of rolled their hands in the air, proud that they were so rash and inventive. God, if they only knew what wonders lay ahead: the twist, the mashed potatoes, and hand jive.

It was in the midst of all this excitement that the first of the partygoers noticed me, but I appeared as an innocent enough interloper, so it wasn't 'til one of the waiters saw me and pointed me out to the headwaiter that anybody paid any serious attention. Still, Eddie didn't see me—carrying on so, as he was, with the pretty thing in the peach organdy gown.

The headwaiter was an older black man, and when he approached me, he was polite, almost deferential. "Can I help you, young man?" he inquired. I imagine he assumed I was some member's son.

"Yes, please, sir, I have to see Eddie Brothers," I replied, pointing in his general direction.

"Are you Mr. Brothers's—?"

"Please, just tell him Christy Bannister is here."

This threw the old gentleman off, inasmuch as he'd anticipated me indisputably identifying myself as somebody's relative. Momentarily, though, my lack of credentials suddenly became moot because one of Eddie's buddies recognized me from all the time Eddie took me around delivering *News-Posts* in his convertible, and he called over to Eddie. He looked over his dancing partner's shoulder, and as soon as he confirmed that it was indeed me, he dropped her hands, brushed right by her, and headed directly toward me.

The buddy took great delight in this. Loud enough for everybody to hear, he shouted to the girl in the peach organdy gown, "Hey, Jeannette, better watch out! Eddie's chick from the subdivision sent her little brother over here to keep an eye on him." Hoots accompanied this comment, but Eddie never looked back as he zeroed in on me.

"Mr. Brothers, this young man—" the headwaiter began.

"It's all right, Ernest, I know him," he said, and as the old black man headed back to the dinner tables, Eddie greeted me, his voice jovial, but with the very direct question, "Hey, what th' hell you doin' here, Christy?"

"You know," I replied frostily.

"Did Suzy send you?"

I shook my head. "I gotta talk to you...on my own."

Even from our distance, I could hear Eddie's pals snickering at him, but he refused to give them any satisfaction, never looking back. Instead, he put on his friendliest just-us-guys smile and said, "Hey, Christy, come on, I'm in the middle of dinner. I can't just—"

"No, Eddie," I replied, staunchly (surprising myself), "I gotta talk to you right now."

"It's not the place, Christy. You're not invited here."

"I know that."

"Well?"

"Well, it's because"—and here I paused and poked Eddie right in the chest with a finger before I said it flat out—"it's because you fucked my sister."

Eddie blanched. Right away, he took me by the arm, hustling me off, glancing back only to make sure nobody had heard me. He steered me all the way over to the top of the stairs before he spoke in a half-whisper, "For Chrissakes, Christy, watch your mouth."

"Well, you did." I let the words lay there unembroidered by anger or vulgarity. Eddie stared at me, waiting for me to ease up, to cave in, to even...apologize. But I didn't budge. Finally, in fact, I said, "Just the facts, ma'am," which was pretty fast-thinking of me, actually, since it was the popular expression then from *Dragnet* on TV.

Only then did Eddie appreciate that I was going to be a tough nut to crack, so he threw his arm around me avuncularly and helped me down the stairs. "You're right, Christy," he said. Then quickly, in clarification, "I mean, you're right, we should talk now." He guided me out a side door around to where there was a practice putting green. It had eighteen holes placed about with little miniature steel flags set in them. The music was wafting out of the open ballroom windows just above us, but even though the tune stuck in my head—it was "Where or When"—it seemed then as if it wasn't real music, but background music as in a movie. It felt as if Eddie and I were all alone.

He lit a cigarette and offered me one even though he knew I didn't smoke yet. He blew smoke and pursed his lips then, appearing to think deeply. "Look, Christy," he finally said, "can we just forget who we are for a minute and talk man-to-man?"

I nodded dubiously. Eddie picked up one of the little steel flags from the holes and, with his cigarette in his mouth, swung it along the ground like it was a putter. "Good, because I know Sue is your sister, and I know you care a lot about her, and"—oops, hastily now—"so do I. So do I. But this is a man thing. You know?"

I just listened. I could tell that it unnerved him that I didn't so much as nod. So in another stab at camaraderie, he flicked his cigarette aside the way professional golfers did then and pretended to eye a putt and sink it, providing a little body English for even greater effect. Then he clicked his tongue, retrieved his cigarette, and took another drag before he turned back to me. "See, Christy, you'll find this out about girls. A lot of times they say no, but what do they mean?"

He looked at me for an answer. I just looked back. "They mean yes," he finally said. "They say no, they mean yes. I mean, hey, a girl can't just say yes or everybody'll call her hot, you know. So they say no, but they let you know, subtle-like, they don't really mean it."

"How?" I asked.

"You will know, Christy. You...will...know. Trust me. The first time it happens, you will say to yourself: now I see what Eddie Brothers was telling me that night at Elkridge." He said that with great authority, chuckled, tossed the cigarette aside again, and pretended to sink a long, twisting putt. "Birdie!" he shouted.

I didn't let my expression reveal any attitude. Only when he reached down to pick up his cigarette did I speak up, saying, "That's not what Sue says. She's crying, and—"

He stood back up, holding his hands up and out to reassure me. "Christy, Christy. Slow down, pal. Sue is one great gal—Jesus, what a great gal—but of course she's upset. She wakes up today feeling guilty she let a guy have her cherry last night. I mean, of course she's having second thoughts. I wouldn't respect her so much if she didn't. Any nice girl *would* have second thoughts, and just 'cause your sister's lost her cherry, it doesn't mean she's not a nice girl."

Silently, I stared back at him. There was just enough light coming out of the ballroom windows that we could see each other clearly, and I could tell that it rattled him when I didn't say anything. Glib guys like Eddie preyed on responses, whether in agreement or otherwise. Finally, he had to say, "You see what I mean?"

"What difference does it make?"

"Whaddya mean by that?"

"Well, you just told me that when Sue said no it meant yes. So I say yes, I say no, it all means yes to you. Right?"

Eddie chuckled. "Okay, okay. Touché on me, huh?" He stepped closer, and this time he tried to whisper his way into my confidence.

172

"But seriously, Christy, you're going to find this out. I mean, I can tell—I...can...tell—you got the looks of a real ass man about you. You're a *potential* real ass man. And you will find out what I'm saying is true because it's the guy—you—and the girl, and it's like a game." He pantomimed a putt again. "And sure, I know Sue's your sister, and you want to believe her, but I'm telling you the honest truth straight out because between us guys, between you and me, she really wanted it, Christy. She really wanted it bad."

I paused only briefly before I said, "You know, Eddie, you are really full of shit."

He didn't show anger at that, only shook his head in studied disappointment at me. "Hey, Christy, what is this? I agree to come out here with you to have a polite conversation man to man, and all you do is come back with more garbage mouth."

"Well, you are, Eddie. You are so full of...it."

In frustration, he waved the little putting green flag at me. "Okay, Christie, that's enough. I tried. You tell your sister that if she wants to discuss this subject with me to call me herself. And you can tell her, too, that it's pretty childish of her to get you involved." Then he turned around to stick the flag back in the hole.

"She didn't ask me, Eddie," I said, holding my voice steady. "Sue doesn't even know I'm here." He shrugged. "And guess what? I didn't even learn about last night from Sue."

That stopped him dead. He froze, leaning down, keeping his grip on the flag. "What the hell does that mean?"

"It means somebody else saw you." Eddie cocked his head, confused. "Somebody else watched what you did to my sister."

"Whaddya mean?"

"I mean Kathryn saw. She saw what you did out her window."

For the first time, I could see that Eddie was really discombobulated. There was no snappy comeback this time. The best he could do was turn to me and try to be shoe. Only you can't try and be shoe. "Hey, come on, Christy," he said. "Christy, Christy. You're gonna believe the gimp? She's probably just jealous it wasn't her getting some of this." He gestured with his thumb, jerking it toward his crotch.

So that was where I hauled off and kicked him. Right square in the balls. The nuts. Ye olde family jewels.

Somehow, at the time, it seemed even worse to me, what he'd said about Kathryn because I knew Kathryn couldn't ever do anything about it. I knew Sue was going to be all right again. Someday. Maybe even someday soon. I had enough perspective to know that. No matter how much she was crying now, no matter what a horrible thing had been done to her, and how horribly upset she was, she was going to be okay. It wasn't all that big a deal, lifetime. Eventually, she was going to *let* somebody else screw her, and from what I understood about screwing, she was going to love it. I knew that's the way these things came out in the wash. But Kathryn. I couldn't stand the way Eddie put her down—forever.

So that's why I was inspired to kick Eddie Brothers square in the balls as hard as I possibly could with my good white-buck shoe.

God, but it must have hurt him. He doubled over with a sound as if the air was oozing out of him. The little putting flag fell involuntarily from his hand. He reached down at the pain, so that he had nothing to break his fall, and slowly tumbled over, right shoulder first. Then he lay there on the green, whimpering.

I snatched the putting flag up. It was about three feet long, heavier than I imagined, with an iron saucer on the bottom that permitted the golfer to flip the ball up out of the hole. I was so damn mad that, as soon as I had that stick in my hand, I started to swing it down at Eddie. That could have really done some damage, too. There's no telling how much. But he saw the blow coming and threw an arm up before his face, screaming out, "Jesus Christ, Christy," and that was enough to bring me to my senses, sort of. I stopped the force of my swing, except I did carry the effort all the way through in slow motion just enough to tap him with the saucer-end. It was sort of a symbolic hit. Then I flung the stick aside, and it made a big, ugly gash where it landed.

Eddie doubled back up, still moaning. Boy, I had really got him. I even started to wonder if maybe I'd somehow permanently wounded him.

Or, even worse, maybe I hadn't wounded him enough, and he was going to recover momentarily and beat me to a bloody pulp.

So, cowardly or not, I made my exit. I didn't look back either. I just found my bike in the bushes and started pedaling like crazy to get away. It's funny, though. Out on the main road, at the bottom of the big hill, there was an old gas station, a Betholine-Sinclair with a green dinosaur on the sign. I rode in there to the phone booth and called Kathryn. I couldn't tell Sue what I'd done. Not for months; I didn't tell her until Christmas vacation, as a matter of fact. But I had to tell Kathryn right away.

Mrs. Slade answered the phone and went up to Kathryn's room. They had one of those gizmos that fits over the head like operators wear for Kathryn. "Christy?" she asked, when Mrs. Slade got it in place.

"Yeah."

"What's up?"

"I just wanted you to know what I did."

"What's that?"

"Well, I went to see Eddie Brothers."

"You did?"

"At a debutante party."

"Really?"

"Yeah, and we went outside, and, uh—"

"Wait a minute, Christy. Mother, could you please leave the room so Christy and I can talk, privately?" There was silence for a few moments as Mrs. Slade departed, and then Kathryn spoke up again. "Okay, Christy, you can go on."

"Well, I—" I stopped again. I didn't know quite how to phrase this for Kathryn. "This is hard to say."

"Say what?"

"What I did."

"You did something?"

"Yeah. To Eddie."

"To Eddie?"

"Yeah, what I did was, I..."

"Come on, Christy, you can tell me."

"Okay. Kathryn, I kicked Eddie in the…" But when I paused there, even if only for a second, Kathryn jumped right in.

"The balls?" she screeched. "You kicked Eddie Brothers in the balls?"

"Yeah, I did." I could hear her laughing. "Is that okay?"

"Well, Christy," Kathryn replied, "it's a good start."

# 23

Sue was no better when I got home, or the next morning, either. She just stayed in her room. I was even glad that Mom made me go out with Hughie and get our back-to-school haircuts. It was kind of a dreary day, too, so when I rode over to Kathryn's afterward, I found her all alone with Lavinia, leafing through the new *Life* magazine. Lavinia took her cue right away and went inside. Kathryn asked me for all the delicious skinny on my brave encounter with Eddie and then for an update on Sue.

"She still won't even leave her room."

Right away, Kathryn said, "She's gotta get away."

"Yeah, I know. But she won't come over here."

"No, I don't just mean outta her room, Christy. She's gotta get away from Baltimore." My head yanked up at that. "Gimme one of those coffin nails."

I picked up the pack of Old Golds, put one in her lips, and lit it. "Whaddya mean get away?" Kathryn let the cigarette hang there, looking rather like one of those gun molls in the *Crime Does Not Pay* funny books; I took the cigarette out of her mouth so she could speak more easily, if not so dramatically.

"Look, Sue has nothing but bad thoughts about Baltimore because something very, very terrible happened to her just after she arrived here, and she hasn't got any good memories of Baltimore stored away to cancel that out."

"Yeah."

"See, if I'd gotten polio in a new place, I never could've stayed there. Sue's gotta get away."

"Yeah." All that made perfect sense to me intellectually. Only then I had to consider the next step, namely where exactly could Sue get away to. Idly, to enhance my wisdom and maturity, I took an actual puff on the cigarette, managing without coughing. But:

"Stop that, Bannister!" Kathryn yelled. "I told you: no smoking before Marines Day."

"Oh yeah," I said, properly chastised by my coach. I gave her another drag. "Kathryn, if Sue goes away, where does she go away to?"

"Boarding school," she replied straightaway.

"Oh," I said. However, we'd never applied a great deal of thought to boarding school in Terre Haute. "Where is a boarding school?"

"There's lots," Kathryn said, mentioning a couple specifically that she thought would be right for Sue. One was in Rhode Island and the other in Massachusetts. It all sounded terribly exotic to me.

"But I don't think Pop would go for it, though."

"Why not?"

"I don't know. It just sounds so...different. It's expensive too, isn't it?"

"So what? Hey, Christy, your father's gonna make lots of money."

"He is?"

"He's the president of a company, isn't he? And that's exactly the kind of men who send their children off to boarding school."

"Well, we never had any money before." I put the cigarette back in her mouth. "My father's setting aside some money for my college."

"Hey, you know what I say to that?" I shook my head and took the cigarette back out so she could speak more clearly. "I say to hell with your college. Nothing personal, but that's four years down the road. Right now, we gotta worry about Sue. Anyway, four years, you watch, your old man is going to have plenty of money."

"You think?"

"He started off great. Mr. Gardner tells everybody he's a whiz, your father, and then after he fired the Italian guy—" I didn't interrupt Kathryn. She just stopped dead because she realized she'd said something she shouldn't have said. So for diversion, "Gimme one more puff."

"Sal Carlino?" I asked. "How did *you* know about Sal Carlino?" But she only blew some smoke and gave me one of her face shrugs. "Come on, Kathryn, how did you hear about that?"

"You know," she said, clearly uneasy with the whole business. "Mom and Dad are real close to the Gardners, and so they were talking about it." And then, quickly, cleverly, she put the onus on me. "How come you knew about it, Christy? Does your father tell you everything about his work?"

"Well, some things, yeah. Pop told me about how he had to fire Sal Carlino even if he didn't really want to because sometimes principles collide. You know how principles collide."

Kathryn said, "Oh sure." At her most snide.

"What does that mean?"

"Never mind."

But I smelled a rat. "What do you know, Kathryn?" I said that in a louder voice, so she turned away from me. So, louder still, "Come on, what do you know about Sal Carlino?"

"Go change into your bathing suit. It's time to practice."

"Not 'til you tell me."

"Oh, come on. Don't be an adolescent, Christy. It's very unbecoming of you."

"Well, don't you start keeping secrets from me. That's very *unbecoming* of you."

"You wouldn't like it if I did tell you," she snapped back.

"So try me."

"No."

"Why?"

"Because."

"Because why?"

"Because you're too young to understand."

"I am not."

I was getting hot, and Kathryn could tell, so she backed off some. "Just about this one thing, Christy. Really." She spoke that softly, even with care, but it sounded patronizing to me. I was so frustrated. It just didn't make any sense that Kathryn knew about

Sal Carlino.

"Tell me, Kathryn. Please. I wanna know."

"Christy, I'm not supposed to say anything."

"Well, you already have."

"I know. And I'm sorry. But I'm not saying any more. Now, you gotta do some laps. Go change into your bathing suit."

"I'm not going to."

"All right, fine, if you don't care about Marines Day, lemme have my cigarette again."

"You tell me first." She shook her head. It infuriated me. So I took the cigarette and inhaled, and then I held it right in front of her face. Oh God, how awful I was to do that. So mad, so mean, so childish. So unbecoming. "Tell me, Kathryn. Then you can have your cigarette." I moved it even closer to her face so that the smoke curled up and made her blink.

She waited, silent. I wouldn't move the cigarette away. Her eyes locked on me. Then, ice cold and measured, this is what she said: "Even you, Christy Bannister. Even you."

And I knew she was right. Yes, *even me*. But I didn't know how to get out of this mess I'd made. I wouldn't back down. I kept the cigarette there, before her.

Kathryn did about the only thing she could, which was to rear her head back the best she was capable of and bring it forward, spitting on my hand. In fact, it was hardly any spit at all. But it made me madder still. So I took my hand and rubbed it across her forehead, sticking her own spit back on her. Kathryn did not flinch, not even at that. So I took another drag on her cigarette and then flicked it away, thumb and forefinger, the way tough guys did.

"Oh, Mr. Cool," Kathryn sneered. "Real easy greasy."

And that cracked me. God forgive me, but I turned back to Kathryn, and I put my thumb under my forefinger, just like I'd flipped that cigarette, and I did the same thing to her cheek, zinging her. This time, she really flinched.

But just as quickly, the instant I zapped Kathryn, I hated myself. I could not believe what I'd done to her. I wanted to call out: *I'm sorry! I'm sorry, Kathryn!* But the words could not get past the shame.

Softly, she shook her head. But her lips curled. "Aw, now you're a real he-man, Bannister. Just like Eddie. Just like your father."

That set me off again. I waggled a finger in front of her face. "Hey, listen," I shouted, "I don't care what you call me. But don't you ever talk that way about my father."

"Listen, you wanted to know, Christy. You wanted to know about Sal Carlino. But that's only part of it. It's your father. Your wonderful father has a girlfriend down at the plant." My mouth flew open, my eyes bugged. "So, are you old enough for that?"

"I don't think that's funny."

"No, it isn't funny."

"So how can you say something like that?"

"Because it's true. Because Mr. Gardner found out, that's how."

I held my head with my hands and screamed out, "No!"

"So are you happy now? You gonna hit me again, Christy? Hit the gimp?"

I reached down, fumbling for her hand, then grabbed it, holding it tight. "Oh, I'm so sorry, Kathryn. Please, please." Suddenly, I remembered, too, how I'd rubbed the spit from my hand on her forehead, and I started wiping that off with a towel.

"It's okay, Christy," she said, gently. "I don't care about that." She closed her eyes, and when she opened them, she said, "Oh God, I'm so sorry I told you. You're too young, Christy. I didn't mean to."

But I wasn't listening. "It's Mrs. Patterson, isn't it?" I asked. "The divorced lady."

Kathryn only nodded.

But now that my father's sin had a face to it, I collapsed altogether. I hated for a girl to see me cry, but I didn't care anymore. I slumped down onto the ground, falling to my knees, my head flopping over next to Kathryn's. Oliver Cromwell came over and sniffed around, curious, but I hardly patted him when he snuggled up to me. Kathryn did the best she could. She said my name and soothing things, and she stretched her neck as far as she could so that her head could touch mine. It was only like her hair touching mine, but I could feel her there and she could feel me, too, and that helped.

And so I cried myself out. When I was finished, I raised my head up, and I said, "Why? Why, Kathryn? Doesn't Pop love Mom anymore?"

"Oh, I'm sure he does. It's just...men. But then, I don't know men, Christy."

"I don't think I wanna be one," I said, forcing a tiny little smile.

She winked at me. "Yeah. But if I don't know men, I do know loneliness. I'm an authority on that. I guess your father was just very lonely."

I twisted around so I was sitting on the ground with my back up against the sides of Kathryn's gurney, Cromwell to my side. But I also reached up then, and took hold of her hand again. "Now I know why he told me about the whorehouse," I said.

"The what?"

"Yeah. Because he wanted me to think how good he really was. Sure."

"What whorehouse, Christy?"

"Never mind." I just sat there then, staring out into Herbert's garden, thinking about my disgusting father, thinking about him kissing Mrs. Patterson, French kissing her, probably, slobbering all over her, touching her...

Kathryn could guess what was on my mind. "Don't think about that, Christy."

"My father disgusts me. Him and his honor."

"I'm sure he's a good man. He just made a mistake. A lonely mistake."

But I was barely listening anymore. Instead, suddenly, I knew what I had to do. I let go of Kathryn's hand and jumped up and started running toward the house.

"Christy, you can't leave me alone," she called after me.

"I'll tell your mother," I hollered, but I kept on running all the way into the house.

Mrs. Slade was in the living room reading the *New Yorker*. "Mrs. Slade, can you go get Kathryn?"

"Why certainly, Christy." She could tell I'd been crying, so she was nice enough not to inquire further.

"I need to call a cab," I blurted out.

"All right."

But although I'd always heard people saying they were going to call a cab, I really didn't know how you went about that. "Do you just call them on the phone?"

"Yes," Mrs. Slade said, "but don't you have your bike outside?"

"Yes, ma'am, but I have to go see my father down at the plant. It's very important."

"I see. Well then, let's just look in the *Yellow Pages* under 'taxi cabs,' and I'm sure we can get one in a jiffy." Mrs. Slade took me into the kitchen where the *Yellow Pages* were and called a taxi for me. I was too embarrassed to face Kathryn anymore, so I went out the front door without saying good-bye and waited by the gate on Old Florist Avenue until the cab came. Unfortunately, I started crying again, too.

# 24

The receptionist recognized me right away from the other couple times I'd been at the plant, and because I was the president's son, she immediately got out from behind the desk, leaving a phone ringing, and led me through the door that said, OFFICES.

Occasionally in life, things happen before you, laid out, as if a mural had been painted at that very moment, illustrating the panorama of your whole present existence. Here is what greeted me as I started down the hallway of offices.

At the far end, at the door to his office, my father was greeting Mr. Gardner, who clapped Pop on the back while smiling in what struck me, in my dark mood, as a conspiratorial manner; neither of the men saw me as both entered Pop's office

A workman with a dolly was in the process of removing the last of Sal Carlino's effects from his office to the hall when Mrs. Patterson, who was checking on the move, suddenly appeared, stepping out of her office so that I almost bowled her over as I outdistanced the receptionist in my headlong rush to confront Pop

I swerved not to crash into her. "Why Christy, what a pleasant surprise," she said.

The unexpected sight of Mrs. Patterson left me speechless.

The receptionist said, "I was taking him to see his father."

"Then I'll be his escort now, Shirl." She turned back to the workman. "Leave the boxes in the lobby, Ralph. Mr. Carlino's boy will be by to pick them up."

"Yes, ma'am."

She turned back to me. "Your father's in with Mr. Gardner right now."

"It's important," I said.

"Well, let's go into my office until their meeting's over. You can tell me all about your summer. And you must be excited about your new school. I want to hear all about it."

She gave me a big smile. I looked around. The receptionist was disappearing back down the hall, and the workman had returned to Sal Carlino's office, retrieving the last of his belongings. Still, I lowered my voice to make sure no one else could hear. "I don't want to talk to you, Mrs. Patterson," I told her.

"Oh, I see," she replied, momentarily taken aback, but her smile only changing into an earnest, understanding gaze.

"You know," I felt obliged to add.

"I do?"

"You should."

"Well then, Christy, I think that's all the more reason why we should have a little talk." I just stared at her. "Or are you afraid of me?" she asked.

"'Course I'm not."

She had bluffed me perfectly and pointed now toward her open office door. As I passed in front of her, Mrs. Patterson took her hand and, ever so casually, laid it cupped at the base of my neck. It was very natural, a way of ushering me in. Of course, I took that gesture in the most dramatic way, instantly imagining that very hand, clasping my father around his neck, drawing his eager lips to hers, then doing whatever else it is loose women do with their hands while they seduce pliant, married men. Vigorously, I ducked and shook my neck, and immediately, she removed the offending hand.

Mrs. Patterson shut the door behind us, beckoning me to take the seat in front of her desk. "I'll stand, thanks," I said for no good reason except that I was still enough of a child to think that anger could best be expressed by perversity.

"Well, if you don't mind, I'm going to sit down," she said.

"Fine with me."

I watched her go around her desk and could not help thinking that, at least for an older lady, she really was some dish. I don't think I'd ever paid much attention before, but now that I knew Mrs. Patterson was a vixen, her appearance struck me. She had wiles, is what Mrs. Patterson clearly had. Her long skirt swished in a way that my mother's never seemed to, and I also noticed that she had much larger earrings than I was used to in women. There was something about that, bigger earrings. She sat and lit a Chesterfield. "So, you're mad at me." I nodded, keeping the meanest possible expression that I could summon up on my face. "I understand."

"You do?"

"There's only one possible reason why you could be mad at me, Christy, so yes, I can understand."

She was being much too sympathetic, so I went on the offensive. "You screwed my father, didn't you, Mrs. Patterson?"

She blew smoke and nodded. "You know that's not a very nice word to use in mixed company, but since you did, let me say: we screwed each other, your father and I."

I didn't know how to respond to that, so I only shifted on my feet—although maintaining the most menacing expression I could.

"Grown-ups do that sometimes when they shouldn't, Christy, but it isn't the end of the world. I'm only sorry you found out."

"You thought you could get away with it, didn't you?"

She let that go. Instead, "Can I ask you who told you?"

"Wouldn't you like to know?"

"But you just now found out?"

"Suppose I did?"

"So you're going to run into your father's office and tell him?"

"Yeah."

"I wish you wouldn't do that, Christy."

"You can't tell me what to do."

"I know I can't. I wouldn't try to. I only said 'I *wish* you wouldn't.'"

"Yeah, I'll bet you wish I wouldn't."

Mrs. Patterson stubbed out her cigarette even though it was only halfway done. "Christy, even if you hate me, can I ask again: will you please sit down? It's so much easier to talk. Sit down and listen to me, and then if you still want to go see your father...." She shrugged.

Reluctantly, I took the chair. "All right, for a minute," I snarled.

"Thank you."

"So, what're ya gonna tell me?"

"Whatever happened with Bobby—with your father—and me is over."

"That doesn't make it right."

"No. I'm just telling you it's over, Christy. Kaput. It ended not long after you got here. Your father came to me, and he said, 'Trudy, that's it. Never again.' And that was it. So yes, it happened, and yes, it was wrong, but no, I really don't know how it'll help anything just for you to tell him you know."

I shifted in my seat. "The trouble with my father is, he's changed since he came to Baltimore."

"What do you mean...changed?"

"It's not just..." I paused, looking for the right word. After all, "screw" was certainly out. Finally, I chose 'carrying on.' "It's not just carrying on with you. He fired Sal Carlino when he promised me he wouldn't."

"Oh," Mrs. Patterson said.

"He always made such a big deal about being honorable, but ever since he got to Baltimore—"

Mrs. Patterson held up her hand. "If I tell you about that, Christy, if I tell you, will you go home and not go see your father and—"

"I'm not making any deals with *you*," I snapped.

"Okay, okay. I'll just tell you then. But you have to promise me on *your* word of honor never to repeat this."

"All right."

She took a breath then pulled off her big earrings and shook her head a little. "Your father swore to me, Christy, that he would quit Gardco before he would fire Sal Carlino."

"He told me that, too."

"And he meant it. But then, when he went in to tell Mr. Gardner that, Mr. Gardner told him that he was going to fire me."

"Why you?"

"Well, for having an affair with your father. For being a bad girl."

"Oh."

"And your father said, 'Frank, you can't do that to Trudy.'" For the first time, Mrs. Patterson lost a little of her composure. She looked down, picked up one of her earrings, and began to fiddle with it.

"What'd Pop say?"

"Your father said: 'Frank, it takes two to tango. I had the affair, too. It's not right just to fire Trudy.'"

"No," I said, involuntarily.

"But, your father told me that Mr. Gardner said, 'Well, Bob, that's the way the cookie crumbles. If you defy me and refuse to fire the dago, then the dame goes.' That's the way it was, Christy. The dago or the dame. If your father refused to fire Sal, I got fired. If he quit, whoever replaced your father would fire both Sal and me."

"I get it."

"Lemme tell you. Most men would have said to hell with the dame. Matter of fact, most fellows would probably *like* to see the dame cleared out so she wouldn't be around to maybe embarrass them. Your father felt obligated to me because he was the one who'd gotten me in that mess." She lit another cigarette and stared out the window that looked over the plant, with the smoke pouring out of the huge chimneys.

"So," Mrs. Patterson went on, "your father sacrificed poor Sal for me. If he'd told me, Christy—I swear, if he'd told me I'd've said, 'Don't do that, Bobby. Don't do that for me.' But he never asked me. Frank asked him what he was going to do, and your father said, okay, he'd fire Sal. He begged Frank. He said, give him just two more years 'til his boy can graduate from Loyola, but Frank wouldn't bend an inch." She leaned forward on the desk, looking at me. "How old are you, Christy?"

"I'm fourteen, ma'am."

"Well, if you live to a hundred, I hope you never have to make a decision like that."

"Yes, ma'am."

"It killed him, Christy. You see? Your father doesn't have to be punished anymore."

"It was his fault, though, wasn't it? It was Pop's fault."

"He doesn't deny that. He said, 'Frank, it takes two to tango,' didn't he? He said exactly that. Okay?" And she rose up, holding herself with her hands on her desk, leaning forward just enough so I could see down her front some, see the edge of her bra. "Okay, Christy, your father slept with me. He broke the commandments. He committed adultery. Okay. And he regrets it, Christy. He's sorry. He felt he had to fire a man who did no wrong because *he* did wrong. Your father feels like hell."

She gave a little push then, raising all the way up. "Let me tell you something, Christopher Bannister. Your father is about the most wonderful man I ever met in my life, and your mother is the luckiest woman in the world to have him for a husband, and you are the luckiest boy to have him for a father. And I just ask you: please forgive him his...his sin with me."

She reached into her pocketbook on the desk there and pulled out a little lacey pink handkerchief and dabbed at her eyes. Then she said, "I'm sorry. I have to go to the little girls' room to fix myself up."

"Yes, ma'am."

She came around the desk, but paused in front of my chair. "You can stay here as long as you want, Christy. I'll be in the lobby. Please come down there and let me drive you home. Please don't go tell your father."

For just an instant, as she passed me by, she held her hand on my shoulder. This time, I didn't mind. By now, in fact, I almost liked Mrs. Patterson, which scared me, because it made me realize how my father could like her so himself—maybe even like her more than my mother.

I never left the chair, but I don't know how long I sat there, whether it was only a minute or two or a much longer time. I thought about my father, and I thought about what he had done to my mother and what he had done to me and our family. I also thought about how much I thought maybe I still loved him nevertheless. I thought about all these things again and again in a swirl until finally I knew what I had to do.

I got up and opened the door. For just a second, I looked down toward the lobby where Mrs. Patterson was waiting to take me home. It made me consider one more time. But then I sighed and turned and started walking the rest of the way down the hall to my father's office.

I could see the door was open. Mr. Gardner had left. Over to the right, I saw Miss Mulroney, the old lady who was my father's secretary. I had met her a couple times before, too. She was completely surprised to see me. "Christy?" she said.

I kind of nodded, but just kept right on going into my father's office. He had heard Miss Mulroney, so he looked up as I stepped through the open door. "Christy?" he asked. "Is anything wrong?"

"Pop. I'm sorry, but I have to talk to you. It's very important. I have to talk to you."

"Of course, of course." He jumped up from his chair and shut the door. "How did you get here?"

"Oh, I got a cab," I replied, as if that were my normal mode of transportation.

"Sit down, sit down," he said, gesturing to one of the two big leather chairs in front of his desk. "This must be very important if you took a taxi to come see me." He sat down in the other big chair and leaned toward me.

"Yes, sir. It is important. It's the most important thing, I guess, in my whole life."

He reached over and touched me. "You're all right?"

"Oh, I'm fine, Pop. This really isn't about me."

He stared at me curiously. Maybe it even crossed his mind that I had found out about Mrs. Patterson. I looked him directly into his eyes as he had always advised me to do when addressing someone. "Well, sir," I began, just to make sure I could talk and breathe at the same time.

"Yes?"

"Well, sir, I want you and Mom to send Sue off to boarding school."

# 25

All Pop did was wrinkle up his nose and say, "What?"

"I said, *sir,* I think it would be best if you sent Sue off to boarding school."

"When?" he asked, although I could tell that was only the best *other* question he could ask because he couldn't just ask 'what?' all over again.

"Well, the Narragansett School for Girls opens on September 24th, and I'm pretty sure we could get her in then."

"You are?" Pop would have had no preparation for this conversation under the best of circumstances, but that I, of all people, had sprung it on him, left him as confused as what it was all about in the first place. So I took advantage of his utter disorientation and barreled on.

"Yes, sir. See, we'd drop Sue back a year so she'd repeat eleventh grade. They call that fifth form at the Narragansett School for Girls, but it's really just eleventh grade. And we'd have her repeat that."

"Why would *we* do that?" my father asked, starting to get back into the game.

"Well, you know, Pop, it just wouldn't be good for her to go to a new school for only one year. And she wouldn't be too old or anything because you know when Sue's birthday falls."

"Yes, of course."

"It's been a pretty rocky summer for Sue, what with Danny first and then Eddie—you know, breaking up—and I think this would be the best thing for her."

Pop leaned toward me. "Well, what does Sue say?"

"I haven't talked to her yet."

"Oh?"

"No, sir. This was Kathryn's idea."

"It occurred to me that you wouldn't have had any great familiarity with the, uh, Narragansett School for Girls on your own hook."

I could see the humor in that, and so for the first time, we both chuckled. "Yeah, Kathryn had a good friend who went there, and the girl's father gave them lots of money. So we're sure we can get Sue in even if the school's all filled up or something."

"I see," Pop said. "I'm glad you and Kathryn have taken care of that contingency, too." He was being facetious, but I didn't quite catch on. So I plowed ahead.

"You or Mom—probably Mom—could take her up on the train. You get off in Providence, Rhode Island," I explained, and since Pop kind of nodded then, I assumed that this took care of just about everything. Except, of course—except I was pretty sure this would be coming:

"Christy, in your detailed conversations with Kathryn, did you two ever stop to talk about how expensive boarding school is?"

"Oh, yes, sir. In fact, I brought that up myself."

"Well, that was white of you. So how much, exactly, is the Narragansett School for Girls?"

I shifted in my seat. "Well, we don't know *quite,* but Kathryn is going to look into it."

"Well, Christy, it was very thoughtful of you to worry about your sister's emotional well-being, and I also appreciate Kathryn's concern, but you can save her the time of finding out how expensive that school is."

"Sir?"

"Because however expensive, it is too expensive. I'm sorry Sue has a broken heart, but mending that with boarding school is out of the question."

He reached back and grabbed his cigarettes off the desk. That gave me time to consider my thoughts. Because I'd had a pretty good idea that this subject was going to come up, I'd prepared myself, but I wanted to make sure that I said my piece just so. Pop lit his cigarette. I looked out the window, which was wide open. Gardco hadn't put in air conditioning yet, so what with the floor fan and the industrial noise from outside, I spoke up to make sure he heard me clearly. Turning back to Pop, looking him straight in the eyes, I declared flat out, "No, sir, it isn't."

"Isn't what?"

"You said boarding school was out of the question. It isn't."

Pop pretended to genuflect toward me. "Oh, it isn't? Well, thank you, Mr. Financial Expert."

"No, sir, it wouldn't be too expensive because you have that money set aside for my college education, and I want you to take that and give it to Sue. Then she can go to boarding school."

Pop leaned back, inhaling. "Listen, Christy, I do appreciate your caring so for your sister, but that money—that's for you."

"Why?"

"Whaddya mean why?"

"Why is that money for me?"

"For God's sake, Christy, because you're a boy. A boy needs a college education. Already, I got to get started saving up for Hughie."

"That's not fair, Pop."

"Judas Priest, Christy, we're not talking about fair. We're talking about reality. We're talking about girls and boys. Your job is to get a job. Sue's job is to get married."

"Maybe not," I said. "Maybe Sue'll want to be like, you know, Mrs. Patterson." Pop turned away, looking out the window. "That's possible, isn't it?"

"I don't see what that has to do with the price of eggs," he declared.

Apt as my example was, I knew enough not to press the Mrs. Patterson analogy. Instead, I just announced, "Well, I won't take it."

"The money for college?"

"No, sir."

"So you won't go to college?"

"Not if it isn't fair to Sue. I'll just go into the service and save up and go to college when I come out." I was being a little melodramatic, but it did take Pop aback that I had thought out these alternatives.

"I see," was all he said.

"But then, I probably won't have to do that—"

"No?"

"No, sir. Because you're the president of a company, and everybody says you're doing a really good job. Even Mr. Gardner tells people that. So I'm sure there'll be money enough to send me to college in a few years even if we spend my college money now to send Sue to boarding school."

My father smiled at that because, after all, everything else aside, I had just complimented him pretty handsomely. "Well," he said, "you certainly have an answer for everything."

"Kathryn helped me," I explained modestly.

"I can see." But then, for the first time, he couched his question in another sort of tense, indicating that he might actually accept the *premise* of boarding school, if not the actuality. "So," he began, "what in the world might make you think that your sister would go for this cockamamie idea?"

I leaned forward. "She's been very upset, Pop. I know grown-ups usually think kids only think they're upset. But Sue really is. Really and truly."

Pop pondered that. "Is there something you're not telling me, Christy? I mean something besides Sue just getting her heart broken by these boys?"

I crossed my legs and folded my arms, considering. Bannister men were honorable and didn't traffic in lies, but it was also true that Bannister men didn't sometimes volunteer the truth, either. So after I collected my thoughts, I avoided his specific question and answered in the vague abstract. "It's been one tough summer, Pop. A lot of things have happened to all of us." He drew on his cigarette, which gave him the chance to avert my eyes. "You know, us moving and all."

"Yes," he said softly, "the moving."

"Look, Pop, you told me when, you know, when you did what

you did to Sal Carlino"—he winced—"you told me that sometimes there're difficult situations, and you said I just had to take your word for that. Well, okay, you asked me to take your word about Sal Carlino—"

"I really don't think we have to bring Sal Carlino into this, Christy."

"No, sir. I just mean you told me how hard that all was for you. And"—I swallowed—"I believe you, Pop. I was mad at you at first, but I thought about it and thought about it, and finally I decided that if you told me you had caught your tit in a wringer, then you really had."

"Thank you, Christy."

"Well now, I mean, I don't wanna say Sue has her tit in a wringer."

"No, I don't think that would be such an appropriate figure of speech with your sister."

"But she has been very upset. And I just want you to take my word about that."

Barely, he nodded, but only indicating that he'd heard me, not that he necessarily agreed with me. Just then the four o'clock whistle blew, ending the day shift. There was a lot of chatter as the night men milled about outside, ready to take up their posts in the plant. A lot of them were carrying the day's *News-Posts*. Pop went to the window and glanced out at the scene, then beckoned me over. "I always like this part of the day," he said, putting his arm around my shoulder. "The men coming, the men going—the plant just rolling on. It gives me a good feeling like maybe I really am accomplishing something with this"—a pause—"funny old life of mine."

And then, just like that, his thoughts came back to me, and the soft smile on his face grew wide and deep. "But I'm not sure anything in my life can ever match what you just said, Christy. Imagine a boy willing to give up his college money for his sister."

I blushed.

"What a fine, young gentleman you've become, Christy. I only hope you can be as much of a gentleman for the rest of your life as you've shown me today."

"I think being around Kathryn this summer has taught me a lot. You know, about caring."

"Well maybe I could use some of the same lessons from her," Pop said. "Maybe I could use a little refresher course in being a gentleman."

"I'm sure you don't need that, Pop. I'm sure you're always a gentleman."

"Well," my father said wistfully, "I hope so, Christy. I do hope so. I've found out that being a gentleman is something you have to keep on working at." And he slapped me on the back three times. I could tell he wanted desperately to tell me why he thought he needed a refresher course, because he'd been screwing Mrs. Patterson, and I knew he wanted to apologize to us all for letting the family down, but I understood that he was doing the best he could under the circumstances.

# 26

By now, over the years, the mothers had their preparations for Marines Day down pat. Mom had been assigned brownies; they were starting her off easy. Others of the mothers were delegated salads and cold cuts, cakes and cookies. The fathers cooked the hamburgers and hot dogs on the barbecue. There was sweet corn from the Eastern Shore and plenty of watermelons. The one thing the Slades provided was, as always, their cherry tomatoes from Herbert's garden, but the *piece de resistance* was Mrs. Brothers's special Maryland crab cakes. Of course, there was also lots of good Maryland beer—National Bohemian, Gunther, and Arrow—plus sodas and ice tea. It was a gala. It was a fête. Marines Day was a spectacular.

Mom was terribly upset that Sue said she wouldn't come because Eddie probably would be there. Mom said her absence would be a mortal insult to Judge and Mrs. Slade, not to mention Kathryn. I said I knew for a fact that Kathryn would understand, and Pop allowed as how that was good enough for him. So Mom reluctantly acquiesced as long as Sue promised to use the afternoon getting all her clothes out so they could inventory what else she needed to shop for and take to the Narragansett School for Girls.

The argument did make us fashionably late, though, so Marines Day was already in full swing by the time we four Bannisters arrived. Presiding over it all was Judge Slade, who was resplendent in his traditional Marines Day outfit, which consisted of red bathing trunks worn under his old blue parade tunic. He waved his dress saber.

Buddy had just returned the sword to him, for whichever boy won the Great Medley got to keep the saber for that whole year.

Periodically, the judge would stand up on the diving board, wave the saber for attention, and then make announcements about the refreshments available or the afternoon's schedule or the introductions of guests. Because we were new to Baltimore and this was our first Marines Day, he made a big to-do about the Bannisters.

I picked up a Royal Crown from the wash tub and went over to see Kathryn. "What's that, Bannister?" she snarled.

"What's what?" I didn't have a clue.

"What's in your hand, Bannister? In...your...hand."

I stared dumbly at the bottle. I still didn't get it. "You know. An RC."

"Oh, you drink carbonated beverages right before the Great Medley, do you? Hey, I got an even better idea, Bannister. Why don't you just tie an anchor around your leg?"

I still didn't quite understand why an RC would be bad for me, but I certainly wasn't going to argue with Kathryn. I laid the bottle down pronto.

"A little water," she told me. "Nothing else." She saw me looking around then. "Don't worry, Eddie won't come."

"I wasn't looking for him," I lied.

"Yes, you were." But she laughed a little at that, and it relaxed me some.

"So how do you know he won't come?"

"Because he assumes Sue is coming, and he doesn't want to see her any more than she wants to see him."

"Oh, yeah."

"And besides, Eddie's scared to death of you."

"That's not funny."

Just then, Judge Slade hopped back up on the diving board and called for the first event of every Marines Day, the inner tube race. It was for fathers and small children (even Hughie was too big), and the competitors started assembling. "Now listen up," Kathryn told me.

"To what?"

"I told you: listen to my father's cadence. Remember? On your mark, get set...."

"Oh, yeah," I said, and then I pushed Kathryn over to the side of the pool where she could be right on top of the action.

The fathers and children jumped into the water, each pair jamming into an inner tube. The judge raised his saber high. I listened carefully for the cadence. And I never heard a word.

That was because just as Judge Slade prepared to start the race, I saw Eddie Brothers pushing open the garden gate. The race went off, fathers paddling, children shrieking, everybody laughing. But my eyes only followed Eddie as he went over and shook hands with all the right grown-ups, stopping last to charm Mrs. Slade.

The race ended. The judge called it a three-way dead heat and started handing out little ribbons and trophies. Kathryn was diverted, happily, because one of the winners was one of her older brothers and his little son. But as soon as her nephew got his award, she returned to business. "Did you get the cadence?"

I shook my head. "There's Eddie."

She assessed that turn of events for a moment. "Tell him to get over here," she ordered me.

"Me?"

"You heard me."

Delicately, I slunk in his direction. By now, Eddie was talking to Judge Slade. I hung back. Eddie was saying how terrific it was to be here at another Marines Day and how magnificent the place looked, and the judge was saying how great Eddie looked and how wonderful it was that he was here. As soon as the judge walked away, Eddie turned and glared at me. "Get the fuck away from me," he growled.

"Kathryn wants to see you," was all I said back.

"I've been saying hello to her parents. Do you mind?"

That was when Kathryn whistled. Even for her it was the loudest whistle ever, and the whole party came to a dead halt. "Eddie!" she called out then, and sheepishly, as everyone else laughed, he walked past me toward her. I wanted to hide, but I didn't manage that quickly enough because, almost as soon as Eddie reached Kathryn, he turned back to me, waved his arm, and hollered, "She wants you, too."

At the diving board, the judge climbed back up, the saber in one hand, a beer in the other. "All right, time for the three-legged race," he called out. "Mothers and daughters. Let's go, ladies, let's go." All the girls giggled, but one by one, they started to line up, each mother and daughter sticking a leg apiece into the burlap sacks.

I walked over to Kathryn. "All right," she said to Eddie, "I want Christy here so he can tell Sue exactly what I'm going to tell you."

Eddie held up his hands. "Okay, fine, Kathryn, but just let me say something first because the reason I came is, I understand, uh, Christy told me you thought maybe I was a little outta order over here the other night."

"Out of order?"

"On your mark," the judge called out, "get set..." Damn it—I missed it again, listening to Eddie.

"Yeah, you know, Kathryn. I guess Sue and me kinda got carried away. Hey, you know how it is. You were a—" He stopped himself. Too late.

"I was a girl once. Is that what you were going to say?"

"Come on, Kathryn. I came over here to explain."

"Explain?"

All this time, there was whooping and hollering for the three-legged race. Out of the corner of my eye, I saw Aggie and her mother tumble right over.

Eddie was taken aback. It didn't seem as if Kathryn was being quite as understanding as he had assumed she would be. After all, he was making an effort, and if you were shoe, making an effort was invariably good enough. So, quickly, his contrition turned to peevishness. "Yeah, yeah. And I don't mind explaining. But how 'bout him, Kathryn?" Eddie jabbed a forefinger toward me. "How 'bout a little explaining from him? You know what he did? He comes over to a deb party. At the club, Kathryn. At the Elkridge Club. In the middle of the party. Uninvited. He crashes. And he asks to see me, and I'm polite enough to go outside with him, and when I'm not looking, you know what he does?"

Playing dumb, suppressing a smile, Kathryn shook her head.

The judge cried out, "And the winnah of the 1954 Marines

Day three-legged race is Sybil and Sally Mundy!" Cheers and shouts.

"This kid here, when I'm not lookin,' he hauls off and kicks me right...right where it hurts. If you get my drift, Kathryn. Right where it hurts. Let him explain that."

Kathryn's expression was almost beatic. Ever so sweetly, she said, "I'd explain that by saying I think you're very lucky, Eddie."

"Lucky?" He shrieked that so high he reminded me of me.

"That's right. Because if you were some colored boy down on Pennsylvania Avenue who did what you did to a girl at my pool, they'd throw you in jail."

Eddie was absolutely speechless. He looked around as if help must be coming from somewhere. But nobody was even paying attention. The judge was back up on the diving board, ripping off his dress blues, calling for all the men to prepare themselves for the cannonball competition. Finally, almost sputtering, Eddie said, "You're not being fair, Kathryn. It was just one of those things."

"Okay," she said, "here's another one of those things. Get outta here, Eddie Brothers. Get your little red ass off my property. And if you ever dare step foot here again, I'll call the police. And Christy, if he ever comes near your sister, I'll expect you to do the same thing."

Eddie looked at Kathryn, unbelieving.

The judge started things off with a magnificent cannonball. The whole crowd—especially the part doused by his monstrous splash—erupted in cheers and laughter.

"Did you hear me, Christy?"

Eddie glanced over at me.

"I heard what you said, Kathryn."

"Good. Okay, Eddie, that's all. Go on, get outta here." He shook his head then, mechanically, took one step away. "Oh, Eddie," Kathryn called softly to him then, and he stopped and turned back, sure there would now be some kind of a reprieve. "I am sorry Christy kicked you in the balls."

Eddie smiled and looked over at me.

But Kathryn kept on. "Because I would've liked to have done that myself."

Eddie's mouth dropped again, but since he had no inkling of how to respond, let alone protest, he screwed his face up into a scowl and stalked off past the pool and through the garden gate, never once looking back, even as his mother called after him. Kathryn said, "I think I'll have a beer, Christy," so I fetched her a National Boh.

We watched my father cannonball as she sipped beer through a straw. Pop made a pretty good splash. "Not bad," Kathryn allowed. "No prize winner, but not bad for a rookie."

Hugh was very proud. He ran to Pop and shook his hand as he climbed out of the pool. Mom smiled in reflected glory. Kathryn spoke up again, but with a different tone in her voice. "I'm sorry I told you about your father the other day."

I gave her another sip of beer. "And I'm sorry I acted the way I did with you. That wasn't very nice of me."

"All right, it's over Bannister. Good, you can get your mind back on the business at hand."

"Okay," I said. I put the beer bottle down and pushed my fist into my other palm—just a touch of Dynamic Tension to get my body into a warm-up mode.

"Concentrate," Kathryn told me. "Put everything else out of your mind and visualize the race."

So all during the egg toss, which the judge called for now, Kathryn and I didn't speak as I concentrated on being intense. A couple times, when I was sure everybody was watching the egg toss, I leaned down and tried to touch my toes. "Good, good," she whispered. "Stretch those muscles. Stretch 'em out."

I was getting nervous. I had to pee, too, all of a sudden, but it was too late. As soon as Judge Slade handed out the egg-toss trophies, he ascended the diving board again, waved his saber in great swooping circles over his head, and began trilling like Johnny Addie, the famous boxing ring announcer who everybody knew from the Gillette Friday night fights. "Ladeez and gennulman, your attention, puh-leeze. Your promoter, Miss Kathryn Slade, is proud to present the afternoon's main event. For the champeenship of Marines Day, the one and onleee, the Great Medley!"

The guests joined into the spirit, cheering and yelling. Kathryn let out one of her finest whistles. "And may the best man win!" the judge went on, thrusting his dress sword high in the air so that it caught the sun and glinted. "The champeen wins possession of this great saber 'til next Marines Day!"

The crowd roared again, but Kathryn didn't whistle this time. Instead, under her breath, out of the corner of her mouth, she whispered to me, "Get loose, Bannister. Shake it out."

Judge Slade brought his saber down, holding it by his side, taking up a position of attention. From his pocket then, with his free hand, he pulled out a ten-cent kazoo and began playing *The Marine Hymn*. After a few bars, he laid up the kazoo, and as soon as he opened his mouth to sing, the whole assemblage instantly joined in the chorus:

From the halls of Montezuma, to the shores of Tripoli...

The moment I chimed in, though, Kathryn whispered, "Can it, Bannister. We'll sing, you swim."

So for the rest of the song, I hung my arms limp and shook my hands, and then I picked up my feet, one by one, and shook them too. I even shook my head. Until:

We are proud to wear the emblem of
the United States Marines.

Instantly, the judge saluted, and all around the pool, here and there, other men brought their right hands smartly to their temples. These were the veterans. I saw my own father come perfectly to attention, and he and all the others held there, standing rigid in their bathing suits as if the United States Chief of Staff himself had just come down Old Florist Avenue to inspect them. Finally, the judge roared, "At ease, men!" and everybody relaxed and cheered.

"All right, now," Judge Slade cried out, "in this corner, in the, uh, green plaid trunks, the defending champion, Buddy Casper!"

Buddy stepped forward up to the edge of the pool, and veteran that he was, he raised his hands above his head, clasping them high. The party roared, the smaller children edging closer. This was no nickel-dime egg toss. This was no rinky-dink inner tube race. This was the Great Medley. The real McCoy. And Buddy Casper was a hero in these parts on Labor Day weekend, a legend in his own time.

"Matter of fact, ladeez and gennulmen, Buddy is the *two*-time defending champion," the judge went on, "and this is his chance to be the first boy ever to win the Great Medley three years in a row. And you know, folks, if he does, I'm proud to say that he retires the trophy." The judge raised the sword high again. "Yes, three in a row, it's yours for good, Buddy."

The champ held up his right thumb and looked as cocky as all get-out.

"How old are you, Buddy?" the judge called down to him.

"Fifteen, your honor. Be sixteen next month."

"Well, that means it's Buddy's swan song in the Great Medley, so it's your last glimpse of greatness here today."

Buddy nodded humbly, taking the words at face value. Others chuckled and cried out, "Yeh, champ!" and things of that nature.

"Okay," the judge went on. "Now, the challengers. I hope we've got some this year. Come on, boys. Anybody gonna take Buddy on?"

"Yeh, Jake Brothers!" his mother called out, and ducking his head in mortification that his mother could make such a scene, Jake stepped forward.

I glanced down at Kathryn. She winked at me, and I moved out next to Jake. A few people cheered, notably my parents, Hughie, and Mrs. Slade. Then Timmy came up, and a kid I barely knew named Karl Something, and a little boy named Scooter, who obviously didn't have a prayer. More secure in numbers, we all started advancing toward the side of the pool where the champ awaited us.

Just then, out of the corner of her mouth, I heard Kathryn hiss at me, "On the left, goddammit, Bannister. On the left." So I stopped and leaned down, pretending to brush something off my foot. That allowed Jake to pass in front of me so I could cross behind him and take up the starting spot at the extreme left. That was Kathryn's plan because, as she advised me, when all the others swimmers started veering right during the backstroke, as they surely would in this company, no one would knock into me. Kathryn thought of everything.

When all the challengers were lined up, the judge held up his saber again and bellowed out, "And now, will you all please rise for the presentation of the colors and our national anthem?"

I didn't know anything about this, but everybody who did immediately looked over to the pool house and watched as two little boys emerged out of it. They were the Slades' grandsons, one of them carrying an American flag, the other the Maryland colors. Red, white and blue; black and yellow. Escorted by Mrs. Slade, who held a papier mâché torch—Lady Liberty herself!—they marched along the far side of the pool, heading toward the judge.

At the same time, Kathryn's two brothers moved over to her gurney and began to push it along toward the deep end, too.

The judge and Mrs. Slade helped their little grandchildren up onto the diving board, where, as they had been instructed, they stood to attention, holding up their flags. Next to the diving board, Kathryn's brothers wheeled her to a halt, swinging the gurney around so that her feet pointed toward the pool. Then Judge Slade came down off the diving board, and assisting his sons, the three of them tilted the chaise up, holding it there, so that Kathryn was at a forty-five degree angle, peering out over the top of her respirator.

There was not a sound from the crowd. All afternoon, no matter what was going on, even when the judge was up there making important announcements, invariably, at least one or two of the little children would be crying or whining. But now, as if jaybirds had swooped down and plucked out their tongues, there was not a word, not a whimper, not a rustle. Oliver Cromwell sat up on his hind legs beside Kathryn, as if even he were at a respectful attention, too.

Softly then, when she decided that she was ready, Kathryn opened her mouth and began:

Oh say, can you see, by the dawn's early light, what so proudly...

Frank Deford

All of us put our right hands where our chests held our hearts.

Her voice spilled out, the words drifting over her pool and onto the garden all around, so that Kathryn's soft sounds lay there upon the flowers no less than the starlight seemed to cling to them when she looked out her window at night.

> Whose broad stripes and bright stars,
> through the perilous fight. O'er, the ramparts we...

Never did she hesitate, never did she falter. I didn't even know Kathryn could sing, except maybe something silly like "Sh-Boom," and how she managed to now with no breath of her own except what that respirator squeezed into her lungs, I will never know. I guess she just believed maybe she could, so she did.

Sometimes yet, I hear again where some idiot congressman with nothing better to do will rise in the Capitol and claim we need a new anthem because the "Star-Spangled Banner" is too warlike and too difficult to sing, and I will say to myself: you damn fool, if Kathryn Slade could sing the "Star-Spangled Banner" the way I heard it on September the fifth, 1954, when it made the sky more blue and the grass more green and the whole blessed land more dear, then don't tell me it can't be sung or tell me any other song can sound more precious.

> ...gave proof through the night that our flag was still there...

I would have cried, surely, but I knew Kathryn would be terribly disappointed in me to allow myself to become so distracted before the big race. We'll cry, you swim, Bannister. So I kept a straight face and only let my soul wander.

> O'er the land of the free and the home of the brave.

"Racers ready!" Judge Slade called out.

# 27

I was lined up closest to the shallow end, Jake to my immediate right, Buddy to his, then Timmy, Karl, and Scooter. The crowd buzzed. "All right," the judge cried out from the diving board, "everybody know the drill? It's eight laps, over and back four times. First two laps underwater, then freestyle the next two, then backstroke, then finish up breaststroke." We all nodded.

The judge glanced down to Kathryn where her brothers had rolled the gurney back to the side of the pool, near to where we were lined up. "Right, Kathryn?"

"That's it, Dad."

"Kathryn's the umpire." She acknowledged the honor. The crowd pressed closer. "Okay, then," the judge called out. "You boys: on your marks." We all stepped up, our toes curling over the edge of the pool. "Get set." I crouched and leaned forward, saying, "One-Mississippi," to myself. I had his cadence. I thought I did. Okay, I pushed off. And yes, exactly then as my arms flew out and my feet pushed off, Judge Slade bellowed, "Go!" and already I was safely away, a split second ahead of the other five boys.

I skimmed just below the surface, making sure not to go down too deep, but even before I reached the wall on the first lap, I could tell that my brief lead had vanished. Jake was square on my flank, and I could see another dim form ahead of him. Buddy was already on top. That discouraged me, so that, just for an instant, I thought about staying underwater—not coming up for a quick breath.

But at the last, I remembered what Kathryn had drilled into me: take the breath, Bannister; give up a moment here to have more energy later. So I stuck up my head and gulped a mouthful of air. I was the only one, the lone sissy in the lot. Even little Scooter was determined to make it back and forth without taking a breath.

After the second lap underwater, when I came up to go freestyle, I could hear the crowd screaming and hollering. As I made the turn—nice turn—I saw that Jake had moved a bit ahead of me, and worse, Buddy was a whole body length in front. He stretched that out even more as we went back and forth freestyle, but when I made the turn again, rolling over into my backstroke, I could hear Kathryn. I don't mean I could hear her voice, but clear in my mind, she was shouting, *Think left, Bannister! Think left!* And I did.

I arched my back and pulled my arms up and around, beyond me and down, and I swear, I wasn't but halfway across when I saw that I'd actually caught up again with Jake. By the time I touched the far wall, I'd even edged ahead of him for the first time since I'd gotten my head start.

Jake kept sliding away from me, angling right, just as all the others did, too—Buddy worst of all. He would have cut right in front of Timmy except Timmy had himself sliced in front of Karl, and in turn, he'd almost swamped poor Scooter. Only I was heading straight as an arrow, and when I came to the end of my backstroke leg, reaching over my head, touching the wall, I could see that I had cut well into Buddy's lead.

Just then, as I flipped over to start my butterfly, I caught sight of my father standing right at the edge of the pool, screaming encouragement down at me. It was strange. I'd always wanted so much to do things to make my father proud of me, but since I wasn't that good an athlete, I usually didn't shine much when he came to watch me play games in school or at Little League. But when I happened to see him in this fleeting instant, I really didn't think about Pop. It wasn't because I'd been disappointed in him, either; it wasn't because I was mad. I mean, I was glad he was there, and I really appreciated him cheering for me. But the only person I really wished I'd seen was Kathryn. I wished I could have been able to look in her eyes and been able to hear her scream for me. I wanted to wink back at her and promise her that I believed maybe.

I pushed off then, rolling over to swoop into my first butterfly stroke. With Jake safely behind me now, I could make out Buddy clearly, two lanes over. He was slightly ahead, but moving straight once again with a nice, smooth breaststroke, his arms moving out and around from his chest, his frog legs kicking.

And here I was, butterflying, making much more of a white-water mess, bringing my arms up and out of the pool, flopping back down, my legs undulating obscenely. With each violent stroke, I felt surer and stronger, especially since I could tell that I was inching up on Buddy. Even better, just as we reached the far wall, with only the final lap to turn into, I could see Buddy sneak a glance over, and his eyes latched onto mine so that Buddy could tell how close I was behind him. For the first time, I think it occurred to him that he actually might not win Judge Slade's dress saber.

So off the turn I came in a burst of confidence, cutting his advantage some more, spurring me so that now I brought my arms way up until I felt as if I was some kind of great water beast rising above the waves, almost flying out. Now, too, each time I pitched forward my head was up so that I could see the people watching dead ahead. I not only spotted Pop again, but Mom and Hughie alongside him, and even Oliver Cromwell barking at all the fuss.

And here came the wall—the finish line—growing closer and closer with each stroke. I swooped again, and I could see, out of the corner of my eye, that I had just about caught Buddy. So then, with one huge last lunge, I brought my arms out of the water, and I threw my body forward with all my might. Reaching out, I could feel my fingers touch the wall right there beneath where my family was screaming for me.

I knew I'd out-touched Buddy. In fact, I really didn't even care what Judge Slade decreed. He had come down off the diving board to sight the finish along the side of the pool, and I was sure that he must have seen that I'd beaten Buddy. Still, Judge Slade usually just called out "dead heat" when a race was close. I was ready to accept that and never mind, because I had believed maybe that I could win and now I believed that I really had, and that was good enough for me.

Everybody turned to the judge to see how he would call it. He froze, but I could see that he was looking at me, and suddenly I was sure he was going to call my name. Just at that moment, though, Buddy's mother pushed through the crowd, shouting to the judge. Mrs. Casper was a formidable presence, too—heavyset, altogether freckled, and now, as always at Kathryn's pool, she had a flowered bathing cap on her head. "Judge, Judge," she hollered, "that boy wasn't doing a proper breaststroke." She pointed down at me in the water. "The rules say the last part of the medley is a breaststroke, not some kind of a whirlwind." And for emphasis, Mrs. Casper swung her arms in a loop, in a broad imitation of my butterfly.

There were some laughs at that and other dark murmurs confirming my nefarious actions. The judge appeared completely baffled; he even scratched his head. Then he pointed his sword toward Kathryn. "Well," he declared, "I may be a good judge of some things, but by God, I sure don't know the swimming law. My daughter's the umpire here."

Mrs. Casper turned to her. "You know the boys are supposed to do a breaststroke, Kathryn. You know that."

Kathryn spoke up loud and clear. "Christy was doing what's called a butterfly."

"I thought so," Mrs. Casper interrupted.

Undeterred, Kathryn continued, "The butterfly is an alternative to the breaststroke."

"But sweetheart, is it legal?" Judge Slade asked.

"It's so legal it's been allowed in the Olympics," Kathryn replied. "They used it in Helsinki."

"Well then," the judge declared, "if it's legal for the Olympics, it's certainly legal in the jurisdiction of Kathryn's pool! And so for 1954, I am proud to announce that the winner of the Great Medley is..." He paused one more time, suffering the glare of Mrs. Casper. It would have been so easy for him to rule a dead heat. But instead, Judge Slade raised his sword then and brought it down like King Arthur upon my head while he shouted out, "Christy Bannister! In the closest and best-est Great Medley ever. Buddy Casper second, Jake Brothers third. Let's hear it for all the boys!"

Jake reached across Buddy to shake my hand, and as soon as Buddy saw that, he shook my hand too, if perhaps not quite as earnestly. Then all of a sudden, I felt two other hands under my armpits, and my father was yanking me out of the pool and hugging me to him even if I got him wet all over again. "I had no idea you could swim so well, Christy," he said.

"Thank you, Pop," I replied, and I let him kiss me on the cheek even though that embarrassed me terribly. Mom kissed me, too, so Hughie dashed off, horrified at this gross exhibition of public familial affection. All sorts of other people crowded round to congratulate me, and Linda actually said, "That was real neat, Christy," so I swelled my chest and tensed my biceps in the manner that Charles Atlas did it at the beach just before he bopped the bully.

Judge Slade parted the well-wishers so that he could step back up before me again, only this time Mrs. Slade had broken her way through the crowd to join him. "Well, Christy," the judge said, "you saved my sword for me, and so I'm proud to present it to you for your safekeeping for the year." He handed it over to me with both hands, broadside, one under the hilt, the other under the blade. I took it that way from him just as Mrs. Slade reached out and kissed me on the cheek. "Congratulations, Christy," she said loudly—but then she leaned closer, and into my ear, she whispered, "I'm not supposed to root for anyone, but I was for you."

"Thank you, ma'am," I said. I probably blushed some, too.

At last, then, I could turn to where Kathryn lay. I pushed past Scooter and some other little boys who were admiring me, the new champeen, and came to her. For the longest time, we just stared at one another, smiling. Finally, Kathryn said, "Nice race, Bannister."

And I replied, "Good coaching, Slade."

She liked that. She broke into an even greater smile, and I knew then that Kathryn wanted very much to kiss me. The reason I knew that was because I wanted very much to kiss her, too. And the way we had grown together this summer, Kathryn and I usually thought the same way and wanted to do the same things at the same time.

But I understood that kissing her wouldn't be a good idea—not because she was a girl and I was a boy, but because it wouldn't appear to be presentable inasmuch as she had been the umpire for the race, and I had won on account of how she had ruled. Even if she had ruled absolutely, perfectly correctly. But since I couldn't kiss her, I just reached down and gently brushed away a tear that had slipped from one of her eyes, and when I did that, Kathryn smiled all the more. Softly then, so no one else could hear, she said, "I love you, Christy."

Immediately, I replied, "I love you, too, Kathryn." It was easy to say, too, because it was the truth. Kathryn smiled broader yet, and another tear came to her eye. I was amazed how wonderful I felt because I really hadn't understood, until that moment, how I had it in my power to make happy another person on the face of this Earth.

# 28 *Autumn, 1954*

"Mom called last night from Rhode Island," I told Kathryn. "She— and Sue, too—they both think the school is great. And Sue's already met some friends."

"I told you it'd work out fine," she said. I was wheeling her out by the pool, Oliver Cromwell leading the way with that choppy little authoritarian walk of his. I'd been at my own new school for a couple weeks now, and I'd been busy, so it'd been a while since I'd last seen Kathryn. In fact, it was officially the fall now, Saturday, September 25th, but it was still summer warm, and Kathryn's pool still looked inviting. No one else was here, though. Once Marines Day was over, it was as if a curtain fell before Kathryn's pool. Before Kathryn. Until next Memorial Day when the pool was opened again. "They're going to come and drain it for the winter next week," she said.

"Oh yeah."

"I'll miss it, Christy. I'll miss all the people," Kathryn told me. But the words were without pity or bitterness. They only consti- tuted a simple statement.

I placed her gurney right next to the pool, just about where she'd watched me in the Great Medley. Then I sat down beside her, took off my shoes and socks, rolled up my khakis, and dipped my feet into the water. "It's still pretty warm." I said.

"The nights bring the temperature down, but Daddy says it's still nice enough to go in when the sun's out. Why don't—" She stopped herself. "Bannister, what in God's name is that on your shoes?"

I picked one up and innocently studied it. "You mean this?" I asked, pointing to the sole.

Kathryn peered at it. "Those aren't—noooo." She wrinkled her nose as if she'd smelled something very bad. "Don't tell me those are...taps."

"Sure. See?" I held a shoe right up before her face.

She grimaced even more. "Don't you think they're tacky?"

"Hey, everybody's wearing 'em."

"That wasn't the question, Mr. Tackpot. Will you be wearing pegged pants and a duck's tail next?"

I laughed, secretly more proud than chastised that Kathryn might think I could be that rebellious. "Hey, come on, I'm not a drape or anything. They're just taps."

"Okay, okay. I guess it happens in the best of families." Kathryn laughed again, but even then, I think I understood something of what was, more seriously, going through her mind. The taps, foolish little accessories that they were, also were symbolic, indicating how quickly I had already been inculcated into another culture. I was at school now, and there were new friends I'd met, boys and girls—girls my own age, girls to make me cringe and posture, not older, crippled girls like Kathryn, whom I could joke with and talk to like a normal person. I think both of us knew this represented the end of what had been, that even come the next summer, it could never be quite the same again.

She noticed me staring away, being pensive, and called to me. "Hey, dreamboat," she said. My head jerked up. "No, not you, shipwreck." I frowned. She stuck out her tongue at me. "Oh, don't take a little ribbing so seriously," she told me. "I'm glad you're fitting in so well at school."

"It's okay," I acknowledged begrudgingly.

"Got a girlfriend yet?"

"Hey, Kathryn, knock it off."

"Oh, you're such a silly goose, Christy. You can tell me."

"All right—if," I said.

"Well, if you do, don't get a Catholic girl. They can't French kiss."

"Kathryn, come off it." You'd think by now I wouldn't let her get my goat so easily, but in matters of love and lust and body parts, she always did me in.

"Don't be so embarrassed," she said, purposely embarrassing me more. "It's probably easier to cop a feel off a Catholic. I mean, a girl's got to do *something*."

Okay, that did it. I'd give her some of her own medicine. I got up from the pool and faced her. "All right, what did you do when you were my age?"

That caught her off guard, too. "Hmmm," was all she said, but smiling salaciously as if she'd been one real hot ticket. And then, even more devilishly, "Well, lemme just say this, Christy; whatever, I'd've done it with you if you'd been my age."

And that really made me blush. But Kathryn was a wonderful flirt, and besides, she didn't get that many opportunities anymore.

"I guess in a way you're catching up with me, too, Christy," she went on. "You're almost fifteen, right?"

"In February."

"Yeah, I was seventeen the summer it happened. Not much older than you. Still a girl."

"I know," I said.

"I'm sorry," she said.

"Why?"

"Because I probably talk about it too much."

"No you don't."

"Promise me?"

"You don't."

"I try not to. But I can talk to you. And it was like everything stopped then. Ever since, I can't tell whether I'm still a girl or not. Sometimes I think I'll always be seventeen as long as I live. Other times, I don't think I'm any age at all. It's like I'm not really a body anymore, either. I'm not a body and I'm not an age."

I didn't know how to answer that, so I pushed a lock of her hair back in place even though it really wasn't out of place. "Thanks," she said. "Now, why don't you go for a swim? Last chance this year. Last chance to swim in 1954."

215

The water had felt good on my legs, too. But, "I didn't bring a bathing suit."

"Ah, so what? Go skinny-dipping."

"What?" I screeched. If Kathryn had suggested that I become a communist or partake of cannibalism, I could not have been more appalled at that suggestion. I responded properly hysterically, all the more so that my voice had just started to change so that it carried through a range of octaves that Rosa Ponselle would've killed for. Even Oliver Cromwell shrank back from the painful sounds I emitted.

"Judas priest, take it easy, greasy," Kathryn replied. "There's no one else here, and you can just turn me around so that my prying eyes will never be privy to the secrets of your body. Hey, that's one of the advantages of hanging out with a quadriplegic."

"Well, you know," I said, a little embarrassed at my extreme reaction. The truth is, I would've been mortified at just about any prior stage of my life for anybody human, male or female, to see me in the altogether, but now I was even more sensitive. That was because at this particular phase of my, uh, development, it was not only my voice that was finally changing. There was some new foliage now, and even some structural improvements in that nether neighborhood that I wanted to be kept under wraps until all modifications were complete.

"Look," Kathryn went on, still teasing me, "Maizie is in the kitchen; Lavinia is taking a nap in her room; Herbert is off; Mom and Dad are playing best-ball or some damn thing over at Elkridge; and if any stranger should come along, I promise you I'll have their eyes put out with a hot poker."

"That's really, really funny."

"Hey, Christy, if it's such a big deal to be naked, then just forget it."

That, of course, is exactly how you back a teenager into a corner. "Who said I wanted to forget it? Did I say I wanted to forget it? Did I, Kathryn? I never said I wanted to forget it. In fact, you should know, Miss Smarty Pants, that I'm naked all the time. I always do my Charles Atlas exercises naked now. Always. Naked has nothing to do with it. At all. Okay?"

"What does?"

Uh-oh. Had to think fast. "Well, it just so happens that I don't have a towel with me."

"Why didn't you say? There's still towels in the bathhouse."

"Well, why didn't you tell me before?" I asked. At my most indignant.

Kathryn moaned, but now I had to live down the challenge. I went into the bathhouse, officially, completely disrobed, then wrapped myself in the largest towel I could find. Back at the pool, I painstakingly turned Kathryn's chaise around (with one hand, holding my towel firmly in place with the other) so that she could not possibly see so much as an inch of the pool. Satisfied, I checked carefully to make certain that no peeping Tom's were hiding in the garden and that Lavinia had not snuck up to peer out Kathryn's window. All right. Only then did I go to the side of the pool and, faster than the speed of light, drop the towel and jump in. "I'm in," I announced proudly when I surfaced.

"I know," Kathryn replied. "I heard the splash. But don't worry. I can't hear you naked."

"Real funny."

"So how's it feel?"

"Great. I'll do the butterfly." And I did, up to the deep end and back, all out. When I was finished, I leaned on my arms at the side of the pool behind where she was located. "That really felt terrific," I informed her.

"Hey, Christy," Kathryn said, "tell me something."

"Yeah?"

"Doesn't that kind of—you know, the water—when you go fast like that, doesn't it put a little stress on, you know, your whatzit hanging down?"

I couldn't believe that. Even though she couldn't even see my mortification, I turned red anyhow. "Hey, come on, what kinda stupid question is that?"

"It's not a stupid question. It's a pertinent question. Just because I can't look doesn't mean I can't ask pertinent questions."

Actually, of course, it wasn't a stupid question. Now, I don't know if it was a pertinent question. But anyway, it certainly was an embarrassing question. "Well, I think it's a stupid question."

"Isn't that why they make jockstraps?" Kathryn asked. "You know, Christy, to kind of tie up the loose ends."

I was so totally discombobulated with all this, particularly the latter terminology, that the only response left to me was to duck under—there where I couldn't be further embarrassed, but where I could better formulate thoughtful, clever rejoinders. So as soon as I popped back up and heard her say, "Well?" I suavely put the ball back in her court.

"Look, Kathryn, I wouldn't ask you about, uh, bosoms. I certainly wouldn't ask you what it's like to go swimming naked with bosoms sticking out."

"Bosoms are altogether different," she replied. "They're round and smooth. They're aerodynamic. They're not all jagged and flippety-floppity, like—"

That was just too much intersexual interrogation. "Okay, let's not talk about this anymore."

"All right, Christy, let's talk about heinies."

"I said let's not talk about this anymore."

"But heinies are different. We've both got heinies."

"Okay, so what about 'em?"

"Well, I was just thinking. What I remember, the last time I went skinny-dipping—it was with my brother's wife up in Squam Lake one night—and what I remember is how funny it was swimming along with your rear end stuck up outta the water and the air blowing over it."

"Yeah, heinies are sorta aerodynamic like bosoms," I said, finally getting into the swing of things.

"Yeah. I remember how weird that was. But maybe that's just because it was at night, and it was cool. Is it the same way now, in the sunshine?"

"Lemme test it out." I threw myself into a freestyle, swimming lickety-split down to the other end and back.

"Well?" Kathryn asked.

"You're right. It felt like the wind was just blowing all over it, like my rear end was sticking *wayyy* up...like one of those things on the submarines."

"Periscopes."

"Yeah. That's the way it feels. Funny." I hoisted myself out of the pool, quickly snatching up the towel and wrapping it round me—just in case the word had gotten out all over Baltimore that Christopher Bannister was swimming naked, and therefore hundreds of curious perverts and girls had shown up for a look-see.

"It's good to know we've got heinies in common," Kathryn declared when I came around where she could see me. She asked me to get her a cigarette then, and after I lit it for her and put it in her lips, she asked me if I wanted one, too. She was talking again with the cigarette hanging from her lips like a gangster girl, but this time, all of a sudden, she acted like she was playing poker in some prairie saloon. "Give me two, cowboy," she said, through the smoke. "I raise you the ranch." I laughed. "It's okay now," she assured me, returning to her regular voice, but with the smoke still curling up over her eyes. "You wanna be grown-up and have a cigarette—it's okay. The Great Medley's over."

"No thanks," I replied. "I promised Pop I wouldn't smoke. At least 'til I'm sixteen."

"You promised him?"

"Yeah. I gave Pop my word." I took the cigarette from her mouth.

"So you're not mad at him anymore?"

I sat back down again, my back up against the gurney, looking out to the garden. "I didn't say I wasn't still mad at him."

"Well, don't be."

"That's easy for you to say. Your father didn't screw some other lady."

"Christy..."

"Yeah?"

"Gimme the smoke again." So I twisted around—always making sure that my towel absolutely protected my modesty—and put the cigarette back in her lips. Actually, I don't think she cared all that much about the smoke. I think Kathryn just wanted to be able to look at me as she talked. "Look, you should be upset," she said. "Your father did a bad thing, but then Eddie did a really terrible thing."

219

"I know." I took the cigarette out, but I kept looking at her.

"But listen to me. Everybody's bad some. Everybody's cruel. Not just men. I'm an expert on this, you know. They all left me, my friends. I became terribly inconvenient to them, so they left. And now the kids and their mothers, they come here when the summer starts and leave when it ends. They just leave me and forget me. But I don't dwell on that, Christy. What good would it do me to get angry just because people only come to see me because of my pool? What good? I would have died already without my pool."

"Aw, no," I said reflexively.

"No, no, that's the truth, Christy. I don't think it's gonna be some stupid infection that kills me." She signalled with her eyes for another drag, and I gave it to her. "I'll never die in the summer. I just wouldn't let myself."

"Come on, Kathryn."

"No, I'm sure. I've only stayed alive this long because I have the pool, and I know, well, anyway, there'll be people for me to see again in the summer. I'm like a butterfly in a cocoon the rest of the year. But at least I get to be a butterfly some. Most people like me are always in a cocoon. So I don't get mad. And don't you stay mad either. Okay?"

"Okay," I said, and maybe I even meant it. I sat back down again, and when I did, Oliver Cromwell came over and plopped himself down on my lap, and I stroked him with one hand. Then I put out the cigarette and turned around some so I could hold Kathryn's with the other.

"Good," she said, and I squeezed her hand even if I knew she couldn't feel it. After a while, though, when she broke the silence, she said, "Don't you have somewhere to go, Christy?"

"Well, sorta. I'm supposed to meet some guys from school at a record store over on the York Road. But it's not like a big deal or anything."

"Hey, that's great you've got friends at school already. So now go on with 'em. You've done your duty here."

I shook my head vigorously. "Kathryn, hey, that's not fair. You're not my duty. Ever."

"You're right. I'm sorry, Christy. I didn't mean it like that. Not you. What I meant was, you don't ever have to give me anything else."

"Whaddya mean? I never even gave you anything before."

She shook her head slowly. "Listen to me, Christy. You will grow up, and you will give people you love things. You will give some pretty girl a locket or a bracelet." I blushed. "No, you will—soon. And when you marry, you will give your wife a beautiful ring and then your children presents and money and all sorts of wonderful things. But Christy, whatever you do, for as long as you live, you'll never give anybody anything as much as what you've given me."

I swallowed and squeezed her hand again, touched, even though I still didn't know what it was she thought I had given her.

"You see, you gave me a summer, Christy. What a wonderful present. A whole summer. Thank you, honey."

That was the only time she ever called me "honey," but it didn't embarrass me, and I let it go because I was thinking more about the rest of what she'd said.

"Well, you gave me much more," I told her, but I wasn't old enough or wise enough to know quite what that was. So I couldn't thank Kathryn precisely, the way I was taught, like with a thank-you note. Instead, we just sat there a while longer, silent, the soft September sun on my back, the little dog resting on my lap, and my best girl before my eyes, all three of us full of love for one another.

# 29 *May, 1955*

I would drop over and see Kathryn a few times as the winter passed. She had Maizie make a cake for me for my fifteenth birthday in February, and there was much to-do on that occasion about how my voice had changed completely. Kathryn spent the first five minutes talking real deeeep like Basil Rathbone or Tennessee Ernie Ford until I told her, hey, okay, come on, it's not that funny, knock it off. Which she did, although she gave me a raspberry.

The subdivision really took off that winter. Suddenly, there were houses flying up and people moving in all around Dogwood Circle. Why, it was getting so crowded that Mom screamed a lot at Hughie to look out for the traffic. It was hard to believe that only a year ago, when my father first arrived in Baltimore, ours was the only house in Nottingham Valley Estates. The drapes had long since lost interest in harassing us, and even the fanciest sorts of our neighbors seemed resigned to our existence as certified Baltimore residents.

On Wednesday, the 25th of May, we received a long letter from Sue. Her exams started in a few days, but what she was writing to tell us was that she had fallen madly in love with an "adorable" freshman from Brown. She wanted to know if, after school finished and she made a cursory trip home to touch base with her dear family, she could promptly return to New England and spend the summer on "the Cape" with her best friend, Lila, whose family had a house in a place none of us had ever heard of then called Hyannisport. (Actually, only Pop amongst us knew what "the Cape" was.)

We never did see much of Sue anymore, either, except possibly over Christmases.

That same day, coincidentally, I found out about my vacation. Mr. Gardner, who was on the board of the Home for Incurables, called to say that he had been able to get me a job there for the summer filling in as the lowest of the low orderlies. "Christy thinks he wants to be a doctor," Pop had told Mr. Gardner proudly. At first, Mom wouldn't even hear anything about the idea—her son working at the Home for Incurables amidst people who had polio—but then, after Dr. Salk had come up with the cure in April and Hughie and I got our shots, she acquiesced. We were safe now, safe to go to movie theaters and use water fountains and swim; all God's children would grow up healthy.

Gardco had just completed its first year under my father's aegis by showing an increase in sales of 12.7 percent, the largest in the entire P.E. industry. It began to look pretty certain that there would be plenty of money to send me to college. Mr. Gardner proposed my father for membership in both the Maryland Club downtown and the Elkridge. The latter was contingent on Pop taking up golf—which he did, thereby becoming a *bona fide* businessman.

Mom had found a church for us, she'd become active in the PTA, and joined both a bridge club and a Great Books club. Hughie and I made lots of good friends at our schools, and I made the honor roll and the JV basketball team (second-string). In fact, the reason I was a little late getting home from school this Wednesday was because I had to stay over to participate in elections for the Civic Association for the next school year. I could hardly wait to tell Mom and Pop proudly that I had been chosen as the tenth grade representative to the Club council.

And, of course, on top of all these goings-on, Wednesday, May the 25th, 1955 was also the day that Kathryn died.

I sensed it the instant I saw the Chrysler Imperial parked outside our house. I knew Kathryn was dead. Mrs. Slade was inside, waiting for me, talking to Mom, but she didn't have to say a word for me to know. "We cannot mourn," Mrs. Slade told me. "Kathryn made so much of her short life. She brought great joy to this world."

"Yes, ma'am, she sure did."

"And we had her longer than we could have ever imagined. None of the doctors thought she could live this long."

"It was the pool, Mrs. Slade. It was Kathryn's pool," I said. I knew I had that on the best authority.

"Yes, I believe it was, Christy," Mrs. Slade said. "But it was always such a trial. We came so close to losing her last spring."

"I didn't know that."

"Yes, I don't suppose Kathryn would have burdened you with that sort of bad news. You brought such pleasure into her life. You gave her such a spark last summer." And with that, Mrs. Slade rose off the sofa, came over, threw her arms around me, and told me how much I had meant to Kathryn. And that finally made me cry, so I hugged Mrs. Slade back and told her how much Kathryn would mean to me for as long as I lived.

She took a step back then, but held onto my arms, my Dynamic Tension biceps, so that she could steady herself and look straight into my eyes. "Do remember her, Christy. You're so young, so you can keep her memory alive longer than anyone."

"Mrs. Slade, don't worry. Kathryn won't ever *let* me forget her."

She kissed me for that. "Now Christy," she said, "the judge and I would like you to be one of the pallbearers."

"Gee, I—" I stopped there because I really wasn't sure what being a pallbearer entailed.

"Oh, that is so touching, Aurelia," Mom said.

"I would be honored, Mrs. Slade," I said.

"I know how much it would mean to Kathryn. After all, you were her favorite." She picked up her purse. "Doug Brothers will call you."

"Jake and Eddie's brother?"

She nodded. "The judge and I thought to ourselves that there were really only two boys Kathryn ever loved, and that was Doug and you."

"Yeah, I guess."

"Doug was Kathryn's beau when she got polio, Cecelia. They were sweethearts," Mrs. Slade explained. Then she turned back to me. "I don't know quite what you and Kathryn were, Christy, but it doesn't matter what exactly."

"No, ma'am."

"Now, there is one other thing, Christy. It was a request Kathryn made yesterday when she understood she really was at the end. She could barely talk at all, but with the only energy left in her, she managed to say that she wanted you to have Oliver Cromwell." She turned back to Mom. "Is that all right, Cecelia, taking in a dog?"

"It will be just fine, Aurelia."

I just started to cry all over again, really babbling.

Mrs. Slade hugged me once more and said, "Cromwell was her child, Christy. She didn't have much to leave behind, but she wanted you to be the one to have her baby."

My father suggested that it would probably be best not to pick up Oliver Cromwell 'til after Kathryn was buried, which was on Saturday. The church was packed. A lot of the crowd was Kathryn's friends who'd slowly stopped coming to see her while she'd been alive, but who showed up now when it was convenient to say good-bye.

Kathryn had made one request for her funeral. Both her parents disagreed with her, but they had promised her they would honor her wish. It was that her casket would be left open. Mrs. Slade told me this is what Kathryn had said to her, "Mom, I don't care how I look. I don't care what you dress me in. I don't even care if you lay me out without a single stitch of clothes on. But when I die and I finally get this respirator taken off me, I want everybody to see my body without that thing all wrapped around me. Just once, I want everyone to see Kathryn Slade by herself."

Mrs. Slade dressed Kathryn in a beautiful, long, sky-blue gown, but when I went up to look at Kathryn before the service began, it was amazing how little attention I paid to that, to the gown, to her body. I mean, I always knew Kathryn had a body, and I had seen in the home movies how well she'd used it before the polio, so really, I didn't have to *see* it. I did like the gown, though. I really did. But I was especially glad that the lipstick she wore was the perfect shade of red, just right for her hair. Of course, Kathryn's hair didn't have to look so outstanding now that we could see all of her.

I also thought that she would have liked seeing me all tricked up in my blue blazer with white ducks, a button-down shirt, and a rep tie. So then I said to her, "Hey, don't worry now. I'll take care real good care of Cromwell."

That's when I realized someone else had come up to the casket and was standing right behind me. I turned around and recognized Doug Brothers immediately, even if he was older now and much better looking than in the one picture of him at the debutante party that Kathryn kept in her room. He laid a hand on my shoulder. "Christy?" I nodded. "My brother told me how well you two got along."

"Jake?"

"Well, yeah, him too, but I talked to Eddie at Yale. He's in the middle of exams, but Eddie told me you and Kathryn were just amazing together."

"I guess we were, yeah."

"Eddie also told me to tell you something, and maybe it's appropriate to tell you this here," he paused, "right before Kat."

Instinctively, I glanced down at her lying there. "What's that?"

"Well, what Eddie said was to be sure and tell you that—let me make sure I got this right—that you and Kathryn were absolutely right, and he was very sorry. He told me that he'd made up his mind to come by and see Kathryn when he got home next week and tell her himself. And I was to tell you that. Do you understand the message?"

I looked back at Kathryn. "Yeah, tell Eddie we understand," I said. "And tell him to write Sue and tell her that too."

"Sue?" Doug asked.

"Yeah, write Sue. He'll know."

Doug nodded, then stepped forward to stand beside me, right up by where Kathryn's head lay. I could see the tears welling up in his eyes. He put an arm around my shoulder. "Oh, I'm sorry you never saw her before the polio," he said. "Kat was something to see, Christy. She was so beautiful. This great, long graceful body. She could run and dance—oh, you shoulda seen her shag—play tennis, ride horses, swim. God, could Kat swim. And dive. Even jackknives.

Nobody ever moved so pretty as Kathryn did. I just wish you coulda seen her."

"Well," I said, "since I never got to see her do any of that stuff, I guess maybe it was easier for me to see her heart."

Two days later, Monday afternoon, Pop drove me over to the Slades' to pick up Oliver Cromwell. He had another errand and would come back for me. "You're all right now, aren't you, Christy?" he asked.

"I'm fine, Pop. I promise. I'll just get all Cromwell's toys and stuff."

I started to get out of the car, the family's new Buick. "Well, let me tell you," he said, "the way you've conducted yourself, you've brought honor to the Bannister name. How people talk, it seems like now I'm just Christy Bannister's dad."

I closed the door, but leaned back in through the window. "No, sir, I'll always be proud to be Bob Bannister's son." I meant that, too.

"Thank you for that, Christy. Thank you."

Pop drove off, and I headed up to the house. The judge and Mrs. Slade weren't there, so Lavinia found Cromwell, and then together we rounded up his food dish and leash and all his other dog belongings. Pop still hadn't returned when we got everything ready, so I called to Cromwell and he followed me out to the pool.

The spring flowers had almost all bloomed and faded by now, and what was left before the summer heat would wilt everything was the most extraordinary array of green—the grass, the leaves, the shrubs, all so perfectly green, if each a slightly different shade, so that it seemed there could be only one color for all the world. Except, of course, there in the midst of all the green was the shimmering blue of Kathryn's pool—God's tear.

Today was Memorial Day. It would have been the Grand Opening for the summer of '55 if only Kathryn had still been alive. Kathryn had told me about the Grand Opening. No, it wasn't up to the spectacular standards of Marines Day, but it was still a good show. The judge himself would always christen the pool for the new summer by diving in first, but then whoever had won the Great Medley would follow with a reprise of his victory, all eight laps.

After that, it was Katie bar the door, all the little kids jumping in, everybody splashing and hollering. But, of course, here it was Memorial Day, time for the Grand Opening, and this year there wasn't a soul here but Cromwell and me.

The two of us went over to the edge of the pool, and I reached down and felt the water. It was cold as hell. But I didn't care. I don't even know what got into me. "I'm going in, Cromwell," was all I said, and just like that, I took off my shirt and socks and my shoes with the taps on them. I didn't hesitate a second more, either. Off came my khakis, and then my underpants, and it didn't even cross my mind that the Slades might be back or Lavinia could be coming out to get me or that all of the neighborhood could be pouring through Herbert's green garden to look me over.

I didn't care. I stood there naked as a jaybird, and I cried out joyously, "On your mark...get set...go!" And I dove into that frigid water and started swimming the whole Great Medley just the way Kathryn had taught me. Underwater first, but stay shallow—and come up for a breath after one lap. Then the freestyle with my rear end sticking up, white in the wind, so Kathryn could spot it from heaven. The backstroke next. *Think left, Bannister! Think left!* And then finally, of course, the butterfly. Our butterfly. How quickly it all came back to me. My arms in great loops, my body thrusting high out of the water, my legs kicking like a dolphin—all of me, now coming to the finish, faster, faster, faster.

I would have to defend my title this year at Marines Day, 1955, when another summer was past, and I had to believe maybe that I could win again for Kathryn and keep the judge's saber in the subdivision.

# About the Narrator

Dr. Christopher R. Bannister has enjoyed a long and distinguished career as a physician and medical researcher. A graduate of Williams College and the Johns Hopkins Medical School, he practiced at Johns Hopkins and later at the Kennedy-Krieger Institute, where he served as director. Subsequently, he became director of the Institute of Child Health at the National Institutes of Health in Washington. Upon his retirement, he was honored with the lifetime achievement award from the American Academy of Pediatrics.

Dr. Bannister and his wife of thirty-two years, the former Fredricka Simpson, reside in Annapolis, Maryland. They are the parents of two grown children, Todd Fairly Bannister and Kathryn Slade Bannister-White, and three grandchildren. Dr. Bannister is the author of numerous medical articles. This is his first book.

# About the Author

Frank Deford's work can be found across a broad range of genres. He has written fourteen books on many subjects. Two of them, *Everybody's All-American* and *Alex: The Life of a Child*, were made into movies. Mr. Deford has also won many honors as a magazine writer and is a member of the National Sportscasters and Sportswriters Hall of Fame. He has been a commentator on National Public Radio for twenty years. On television, where he is now a correspondent for *RealSports with Bryant Gumbel* on HBO, he has won both an Emmy and a Peabody Award. This is his eighth novel. Mr. Deford resides in Connecticut with his wife, Carol.

## DATE DUE